W9-BLU-834

THE SALT IN OUR BLOOD

THE SALT IN OUR BLOOD

AVA MORGYN

ALBERT WHITMAN & COMPANY • CHICAGO, ILLINOIS

Library of Congress Cataloging-in-Publication data
is on file with the publisher.

First published in the United States of America
in 2021 by Albert Whitman & Company
ISBN 978-0-8075-7227-6 (hardcover)
ISBN 978-0-8075-7229-0 (ebook)

Printed in the United States of America
10 9 8 7 6 5 4 3 2 1 LB 24 23 22 21 20

Photography sourced from Unsplash (@domediocre, @nikhilmitra, and @yonkoz)
Cover artwork and book design by Aphelandra

For more information about Albert Whitman & Company,
visit our website at www.albertwhitman.com.

For my mother, Ruth, and her mother, Mary,
whose own story of estrangement inspired this book,
and all the women who challenged me to be a better,
more compassionate version of myself.

I.

I HAVE NEVER SEEN A DEAD PERSON BEFORE.

As I stand in the doorway of my grandma Moony's room, this thought floats across my mind. But her lifelessness is unmistakable. Something fluid has left her limbs, and they lay rigid at her sides. I can't say exactly how I know that without touching them. I am simply aware of an unyielding quality that wasn't there before. Her mouth is open, but her jaw is set at an odd angle. She must have been snoring again. Her lips are white, like bleached cotton. I look for the telltale signs of breathing, using my own pounding heartbeat as a measure, but there is no rise or fall of her chest beneath the sheet. Her eyes are closed as if in sleep, but even without the gruesome stare, I know she's no longer here.

And of course, there is the fact that Moony is always up before the sun. Her alarm clock on the nightstand reads 8:30 in harsh, red, block numerals. I stare at the numbers until my eyes glaze over and my vision blurs. They remind me of something I've misplaced since standing here—a flash of scarlet in my dream. The dream that woke me up. A dream of skeletal men riding skeletal horses through a forgotten battlefield, their red sashes blazing under a merciless sun, their black flags waving in a hot wind. Death on parade.

I blink and rub at my eyes. I fold my arms over my chest, willing the night terrors away. I don't like to entertain fantasies, good or bad, give them room to breathe and grow, to spread like mold across the wrinkles of my mind. Moony always said an overactive imagination is just another gateway to sin.

She is as still and blank as paper. I cannot bring myself to step into the room.

I cannot go to her.

It occurs to me that I should be sad. That I should scream or cry or express some deep and troubled emotion. After all, Moony has practically been a mother to me for the last ten years. She won't be here now to watch me graduate from college with a "sensible" degree, or remind me that art should have a point, or ground my wilder tendencies. But all I feel is a vacancy where the sadness should be and a brutal clarity that makes everything around me look sharper and brighter than normal. Like the faded, yellow-floral curtains pulled across her picture window that seem as though they've been drawn on with a highlighter. Or the edge of her cotton lampshade, where every speck of lint is rising like the hairs along my arm. As though this moment when my grandmother has died is more real than any other moment in my short life. Being just this side of seventeen, I would assume that there will be more moments like this one, more violently alive moments. And yet, I don't believe it standing here.

I think this is the first time I've ever really seen Moony. Really noticed her sagging breasts like paperweights rolling off her ribs and the patches of white-pink scalp that show through her short hair when she doesn't have it combed just right. I think this is the biggest impression Moony has ever left on me—the biggest impression life will ever leave on me. But I suppose this impression doesn't belong to life at all.

The carpet is like burlap against the soles of my feet, but the seam at her doorway won't permit me to pass. There are things one should do in a moment like this. Words to be spoken. Authorities to be alerted. Affairs to put in order. I know nothing about Moony's affairs, except the scattered bits she told me—social security every month, an account somewhere with money saved for my college, paper bills that come in the mail every week and get sorted into stacks on her desk in the hall. I'm not sure anyone knows more. But as I am the only one here, I realize it falls to me to take the proper steps.

My stomach rumbles beneath the oversized SeaWorld T-shirt I slept in. Is it wrong to think of food when you just found someone you love dead? There is a definite not-rightness about it. But I can't say it's completely wrong. I'm not sure my stomach has gotten the message that Moony has died. Clearly my heart hasn't, so how could my stomach? Only my brain is online right now, and it's not telling anyone else. Not yet.

I contemplate having a bowl of cereal while I figure out what to do. I should make a list. Moony was always making lists—grocery lists, to-do lists, lists of weekly sins she needed to share in confession. She was big on lists. Lists provided structure, and she was big on structure. She would like it if I made a list about her. I register a small sting of emotion at this thought, but it doesn't sink deeper than my clavicles, like a piece of ice lodged in the throat. Uncomfortable, sure, but you can still swallow around it.

I walk to the kitchen and take the magnetic pad of paper off the fridge. I decide cereal can wait. It would look wrong if I ate first. Moony always believed someone was watching. Mostly God. And not in a kindly, mother hen sort of way. More in a devious, *gotcha* sort of way. God was watching Moony, and Moony was watching me. I'm not watching anyone.

I sit at the table, the vinyl seat sticking to my naked thighs, and begin. I write *#1*.

With any plan of action, something always comes first, but it's not obvious to me what that would be. It's here that I realize I'm not thinking clearly. My brain may be online, but it's not running on all cylinders. Even my metaphors are confused. I try to imagine myself as someone else, a total stranger. What would that person do if they found their grandmother dead? My stomach rumbles again, and all I can think about is cereal, but I refuse to eat.

It takes a good seven minutes, but I finally realize the first step. I am not cut out to handle this alone. So, I think there must be only one step for me. I write, *Tell someone* on the magnetic pad.

I could go next door. Eric and Damien would help me. But Moony hated them. In part because they're gay—a grave indecency at best and an unpardonable sin at worst, according to her very non-PC, pre-Vatican II-era Catholic logic—and in part because their cockapoo always shit in our front yard. She would not appreciate them seeing her this way.

Moony didn't have any real friends. Acquaintances, maybe, like the lady at the drugstore who always put extra peppermints in the bag when she got her medications refilled. But no one close. Moony didn't let anyone close. Except me.

I don't have many friends of my own, and the ones I do have are useless here. I've tried a couple of sleepovers with Julie Perkins, and I always eat lunch with Jaq and Gracie. But I can't imagine us discussing this over chicken tenders in the cafeteria. Besides, it's summer.

And I am woefully short in the relative department. Only child of an only child. Absentee father. Dead grandfather. My family tree has one branch and two names. Scratch that—*one* name now.

The sting returns. It sits a little lower this time, like a pill working its way down my esophagus.

I don't want to face the last remaining name on my family tree, but I can't see that I have a choice. Frankly, Moony would probably prefer Eric and Damien. But now that the thought has registered, even a magic eraser wouldn't scrub it out. It's the right thing. I know that. The same way I know that eating cereal is wrong and that Moony's arms no longer bend.

I sigh deeply, resigned.

I should know her number by heart, but I don't.

I have to get up and go to the little writing desk in the hall. That's where Moony keeps her address book. We got her a cell phone three years ago, and I put all her contacts in it, but she could never figure out how to look anyone up. With Moony, you learn pretty quickly not to push things. She is old-fashioned and prefers it that way. *Was* old-fashioned, I mean.

It won't be under *G* for *Gage* because she changed it years ago, though I'm still listed as Catia Gage on my birth certificate.

And Moony was always Edna C. Gage. But that wasn't good enough for her.

I flip to the *R*s for *Rush*. Which is perfect for her because she rushes into everything—sex, relationships, jobs, parenting... *not* parenting.

I find it quickly, since Moony seems to know very few people with *R* names. She knows very few people period. I pick up the phone receiver and stare at the little glowing buttons. *I don't have to do this*, I think. I could *not* call instead. I could pack a bag and walk out the front door and not tell anyone. I could get in Moony's car and drive to Connecticut or Portland or anywhere. I could never speak to *her* again. I could pretend none of this happened.

But in my heart, I know I cannot abandon Moony like that. I can't let strangers find her. I stare at the phone. I could call someone else. Really. *Anyone* else. I could call the police. But even that seems wrong. She should know. *I* should tell her. I don't have to do this, but I will.

I dial the number and press the phone to my ear until I hear it ringing. I am agonizingly aware that the open door to Moony's room is just behind me and to the right. And then I become aware of other things. Or rather, other *not* things. The absence of the smell of coffee and chicory. The quiet where the sounds of the television—the clipped and hurried speech of newscasters—would be.

There's a click and muffled laughter. I can picture her finger over the speaker of her phone, but to the side a bit so that it doesn't completely drown out the sound. And then a breathless, "Hello? Edna?"

"No. It's me."

"Cat?"

The laughter stops and her breathing changes automatically. As though she's holding it in, letting it out slowly through her pinched lips with control.

I am unfazed. "Yes."

"H-hi, sweetie. This is a surprise."

Her tone is higher now, laced with sugar. I am aware that she is trying to impress me, to sound maternal and together. I feel guilty for my unaffectedness. Doubly so now that Moony is dead, and I can only react like some kind of teenage android. "I know."

I hear my own voice come out shaky and faint. This is not how my thoughts sound. They are solid before they leave my mouth, like they've been carved out of ironwood. I don't understand what I'm hearing.

"Is everything okay?" Her tone changes again. Her voice deepens as she drops the act and flattens to a practical, no-nonsense edge.

This change softens something within me. It catches in my throat, a noise that is wholly unhuman. "No," I manage.

"Catia, what's wrong, baby? What's happened?" There is a desperate ring under her words, the panic that precludes bad news when it could be anything, which is always so much worse than when it actually becomes something.

"It's Moony. I...I think, I mean I *know* she's died."

There is silence. No breathing. No background noise. I imagine even her heart has stopped beating, the world around her frozen like the scene inside a snow globe. "I see," she says at last, the words as short as she can make them.

The chill creeps through the receiver and wraps itself around me like a shroud. I see the flash of scarlet from my dream again, the line of sashes sagging over rib bones. *Please don't make me ask*, I think. What kind of mother would make me ask?

I hold my breath.

"I'm coming," she says after a moment. "Give me a few hours to make the drive."

"Okay." My body sags in relief. More so because she didn't make me ask than because she is actually coming.

"And, Cat?"

"Yes?"

"Don't stay there, honey. It's bad luck to be alone with the dead."

I hang up without responding. The only thing she and Moony shared were their superstitions.

I glance over my shoulder toward the open door to her bedroom. I imagine a draft emanating from it. My arms go prickly. I decide Eric and Damien's is a good choice after all. I rush to the kitchen and grab the box of cereal to take with me, pulling some dirty shorts out of the hamper in the garage before starting for the front door.

I am nearly out of the house, one hand on the knob, when the latch inside me breaks. My grandmother is dead, and my mother is coming to get me. The flood of feeling that my brain was so focused on holding back rushes into every cell like blood after your leg has gone numb. The pain is incomprehensible, and the sound of my sorrow penetrates my consciousness like a thousand angry spears.

I sink to the floor, my back against the door, and pull my knees inside the SeaWorld T-shirt as I sob. I would like to believe that every tear was for Moony, for her tight laugh and clockwork schedule. For the biscuits she would make on Saturday mornings and the cans of hairspray she used to set her hair just so. For the countless nights playing Uno at the breakfast table and the smell of Murphy's Oil Soap as it would fill the living room every Friday morning after mass—the very same they used in the parish hall. But I know it was hearing my mother's voice that weakened the hinges of my resolve, and even if this teary-eyed unwinding is considered a "normal" reaction to grief, I hate the feeling of my control puddling on the floor with my emotions—and I hate her all the more for being the one to release it.

II.

SMALL TOWNS ARE ALL THE SAME. BY THE TIME I'VE made it to the last bite of cereal in the bowl, Eric has already managed to set off a cascade of texts and phone calls that mean nearly two-thirds of our town knows that Moony is lying stiff and untouched in her bedroom next door.

I settle into one corner of the couch and pretend to watch some high school drama, but Deena whines at me continuously, and I can't make my brain stick to anything for more than a few seconds. It took me a good half hour to peel myself from the polished wood floor in our entry and make my way across the lawn. I haven't cried again, but the purge of emotion has left me feeling hollowed out, like one of those gourd birdhouses they sell at the Charity Guild craft fair.

And my heart beats like the second hand of Moony's vintage watch. *Tick...tick...tick...*

Counting down the moments until my mother arrives.

It is the wolf I notice first.

I am standing at Moony's bedroom door; it opens onto a field of yellow flowers like her curtains. The sun is setting and the sea of blooms pales to a diaphanous white. In the distance, the dying flowers begin to dance with a wind I can't feel. I watch as they finally part like the pages of a book falling away from each other. The wolf emerges, bristly and arctic, yellow eyes gleaming as it leaps through the meadow toward a barrier of trees.

I follow, reaching the trees moments after the wolf, and squeeze between them. That's when I see the boy. He stands under a low-hanging limb wearing a yellow waistcoat. He is taller than the wolf, but not by much. His face is odd, with eyes too large and cheeks too sharp and a chin that tapers to a point. A pack slung over one shoulder drips a menacing red at his heels. He grins, as if he has been waiting for me. He spins and takes off, the wolf sprinting beside him.

I press on, catching only flashes of golden waistcoat or moonbeam fur in the gloom ahead. Even though I run at full tilt, I can barely manage to keep their trail until I break into a clearing and see the boy standing, bright against a blackening sky. I open my mouth to call out, but he turns, his eyes dancing with mischief. I feel the hot tickle of deceit snaking through my bones. The wolf releases a low, mournful howl. The boy's lips curl with the same wicked grin he wore earlier. And then he flings his body forward.

I watch, dumbfounded, as the wolf leaps wildly behind him and they both disappear.

I take off through the deep grass after them, skidding to a stop at its edge just before the earth drops out beneath my feet, my toes curling over the cliff's face. Staring into a void of swiftly ascending night, it's as if the world has been turned upside down, and the sky is beneath me instead of above. Laughter bubbles up through a tangle of clouds parting below. I hear the panting of a large animal behind me. I turn to see the boy with the yellow waistcoat standing there, his wolf sitting on dazzlingly white haunches beside him. His grin twists into something maniacal, and his arms spring out, propelling me over the edge into the yawning night.

I am out of time. I am out of earth. Everything washes black.

I open my eyes to find Deena licking my hand as though it were coated with honey. My mother is just inside the doorway speaking with Eric. I recognize the part of her hair first—a little to the right and fringed with coppery flyaways at her temples. I wonder what I will remember about Moony when ten years have come and gone. There are the obvious things, like the color of someone's eyes or how tall they are. But the real nuggets are the weird, little things you don't even realize you're noticing, like someone's crooked incisor or the pattern of freckles on the back of their hand. With my mother, it has always been the part of her hair, the way it flops to the left in a heavy wave of auburn that used to smell like passionfruit from her shampoo. That, and the deep, throaty laugh she would give when something really tickled her—a gift courtesy of her decades-long cigarette habit.

I decide then to remember the soft pads of Moony's fingers, which were always wrinkled as though she had spent too much time in the tub. I couldn't choose what would stay when my mom left me at seven years old, but I can choose now. I will remember Moony's fingers. And I will remember the wicked names she called Deena the cockapoo under her breath when she'd catch her squatting in the yard. And her lists. And the scent of Murphy's Oil Soap, like old wood and orange peels.

I sit up, and my mother shifts her hazel eyes from Eric to me. "You're awake," she announces. She gives me a smile, but the skin puckers between her eyes.

"You're observant."

Eric calls Deena to him, tucking her up under one armpit like a clutch purse. My mother always liked Eric and Damien. They are her kind of people, colorful and unique. She would "pop over" to "catch up" with them after her visits with me. These are things my mother does; she pops and catches, as though life is one big series of dance moves. Moony would never pop. Moony would never dance.

"I should probably let you two chat," Eric puts in. "I'll make some coffee."

"Don't trouble yourself, Eric. We're going to get out of your hair," my mother tells him.

"Are you sure?" He makes a questioning glance in the direction of Moony's house—*our* house. There are a lot of funny beliefs and superstitions floating around this state, especially where the dead are concerned.

"They've already taken her," my mother reassures him. "And I stripped the bed. We only need to pack Catia's things, and then we can hit the road. We should make New Orleans by nightfall."

"Yeah, sure," he chirps, happy to have his role in our family saga—however helpful—draw to a close.

I wipe at my eyes and stand up. "What do you mean? What about her funeral?"

If there's one thing I know, it's that Moony would want a full Catholic send-off, with a mass and everything.

My mother clears her throat. "I've made arrangements. She's being cremated, and they'll call us when her ashes are ready. We'll pick her up then and find somewhere nice to spread them, okay?"

"So we're not going to have a memorial or anything?" I am aware my voice is shrill. But I feel a mounting panic at the wrongness of this and even more at the idea of leaving my home.

My mother gives Eric an apologetic glance. "Can we talk about this on the drive?" she asks, cutting her eyes at Eric to indicate how uncomfortable we're making him.

I purse my lips and start for the door, eyes cast down.

"Thank you again," she tells him as we exit. "I'll let you know what happens."

Eric nods sympathetically, and I realize that in my mother's version of events, Moony and I are the difficult ones. But that's Mary for you; she's never wrong in her own mind.

Outside, I freeze. I won't take another step until she tells me why we're not giving Moony a funeral. I tell her as much.

She sighs. "There's no money, Catia. Not until the house sells. What would you have me do, keep her on ice until then? I've spit bigger than this town. It's not exactly a thriving market. Who knows how long it could take to sell this place?

"The realtor is arranging to have the furniture hauled to the Salvation Army. I called her on the way down. We'll leave her a key under the back step; I already made a copy. When we make the trip to get the ashes, I'll meet with her to see where we are at that point, but the house should be listed within the next ten business days."

"What about the account?"

She sniffs in air and lets it out in a huff. "What account?"

"I don't know. An IRA or something. It had money for my college."

My mother's eyes are flat. Her lips twitch on one side. "Maybe it did once."

"What are you saying?"

"I went through her desk, Catia. I have her paperwork. There is very little money left in that account, and that will be taxed once I finally get through the paperwork to inherit it. We can't exactly wait."

She turns for the car, flipping her hair over a shoulder.

"What about my college?" I call.

My mother's shoulders slump. She turns back to me. "Whatever is left over will hardly be enough for school supplies, let alone college tuition."

I feel my lungs compress inside my chest like two vacuum bags getting the air sucked out of them. "Relax," she chirps. "College is just a racket for corporate brain-munchers anyway. Life is the only real school there is."

My emotions threaten to disgorge like a hundred-armed octopus all over Eric and Damien's lawn. I had a plan. *We* had a plan—Moony and I. High school, then university, then an internship somewhere with real offices and natural light. A steady job with payroll and benefits. Hard work molded into marketable skills traded for a reasonable life.

How can there be no money?

I see the tiny private New Hampshire campus I've been dreaming about for the past three years drift into a fog of doubt. The cable-knit sweaters, vegan lattes, and vintage messenger bags of my future disappear like steam through an open window.

Carefully, I tuck the tentacles of my panic back down, one by one. I can't afford to unwind, to let my guts spill out like a shaken soda can, or—like my mother—I may never recollect them all.

She has to be lying.

"I'm not going," I tell her.

Her eyebrows arch in a comical way as she rubs at her forehead and drops her purse on the lawn. "Catia."

"I'm not going with you. I don't want to live with you. I want to stay here."

"You can't stay here," she snaps. "I just told you we're selling the house."

"Then I'll live somewhere else." I cross my arms.

"Oh yeah? Where is that?"

"I don't know. Anywhere." I jut out my chin stubbornly.

She laughs and shakes her head. "You're still a minor, Catia. Have you thought about that?"

"So?"

"So they won't allow you legally to live on your own. Not yet."

"Are you threatening me?"

She raises both her hands in the air, palms out, in surrender. "I was your age once," she says after a moment. "I won't force you. But I'm asking you, Catia, to come with me. And I'm reminding you that you have nowhere else to go. I've been out there with nowhere and no one, and I'm telling you it's not where you want to be."

She digs a cigarette out of her front pocket—her jeans are so tight it's a wonder she got them in there in the first place—and lights it up.

I have a choice to make, but it doesn't feel like much of one. And I know I've made it already, made it the second I decided to dial her number. "I thought you quit," I tell her.

"I did." She takes a long drag, rolling her eyes with pleasure, and lets it back out with a groan. "Damn, I forgot how good these are." She catches me staring. "Don't look at me that way. It's been a rough day."

This is typical *her*. I find my grandmother dead. I mourn the loss of the only real parent I've ever known, and yet her day is hard. Her own mother is gone; does she even care?

"What about the police?" I say, stalling.

"I already spoke with them."

"But you weren't here. What could you tell them?"

She inhales sharply through her nose. "Cat, she was old. She was overweight. Her heart had been bad for years. It's kind of a no-brainer."

"How do you know that?" I ask suspiciously. "About her heart." Moony never mentioned a heart condition to me.

"We spoke" was all she would say.

I nod my head and start back toward the house. There is no getting around the fact that Moony is gone, and with her will go the house, and the wood floors, and the refrigerator magnets, and my future. I am underage still, by almost a year. And my legal guardian and only living relative is the woman who gave up on me nearly a decade ago. She has spent the last ten years building a life of some kind somewhere else, a life that does not revolve around me.

She is not going to give that up to settle here in Moony's shadow, drinking sweet tea and playing bingo at the Knights of Columbus hall on Wednesdays.

I step deftly around Deena's latest offering on our lawn and reach for the front door, deliberately not telling my mom about it.

From behind, I hear her curse. "There's dog shit on my shoe," she whines, her cigarette hanging from between her lips as she paws the grass with one sandal like an anxious horse. She may be my parent, and I may have to live with her now, but she stopped being my mom years ago. I pinch the bridge of my nose and try to think of her like a roommate. As I pass Moony's door, I hold my breath.

III.

THIS IS THE CLOSEST I'VE BEEN TO MY MOTHER IN AT least four years. The last time she came to see me was the Christmas of my thirteenth birthday. I have one of those crappy Christmas birthdays where everyone is all celebrated out. When I was still living with her, she would make an overly big deal out of my birthday to make me feel better. She would call our Christmas tree "the birthday tree" and wrap it in pink paper streamers. And she would pile gifts underneath it in colorful birthday wrapping with only one Christmas present among them.

As a child it didn't seem that outrageous. I didn't know she couldn't actually afford any of those gifts. I didn't understand mania then. I don't really understand it now. I still can't sort where her naturally larger-than-life personality ends and the bipolar disorder begins.

When my mom came to see me four years ago, they'd just changed her meds. Her face was puffy, and her eyes were dull. She'd put on weight. She forgot my birthday entirely. Moony said these things were a good sign. I wanted to believe her, but it was worse seeing her like that—a gelded thing, all the fight cut out of her.

That's how she was our first few visits after she dropped me on Moony's doorstep. She evened out for a couple of years, and then showed up wearing a plastic tiara and overalls, her eyes bouncing like tennis balls, her words all strung too tightly together. I didn't see her again until I was thirteen and she was back in zombie mode. I couldn't bear to look at her all through dinner. Somehow, the tiara was better. When I walked her to her car that night, I told her not to come back.

She didn't.

I press these memories deep beneath my sternum, tucking them into some unknown cavity. The softness toward her feels worse than the anger. All the fondest memories are tainted by her mental illness. I can't enjoy them without a sense of guilt at knowing her sickness made her do it.

While my mom was preoccupied with bungee-cording my stuff into the hatchback, I ran into Moony's room and snatched her vintage watch from the drawer in her nightstand. I held my breath the entire time, trying not to notice the way the mattress sunk in from years of cradling the heavy contours of Moony's body. Now, I cup the watch in my hands as we pull away from the tidy lawns and houses. Moony wore it every time she left the house. The second hand beats a steady pace around the oval face. I imagine that, as long as it keeps ticking, she isn't really dead. Somewhere, her body hums, keeping time with this watch. If I can hold on to it, I can hold on to her and what she gave me—a sense of place.

"Remember these?" I pull another rescued item from my shirt sleeve—a box of tarot cards, the only thing my mother left me the night she dropped me off and didn't come back. I remember her pressing it into my hand, the corners digging into my little fingers. Her words were fevered and breathy like dried twigs rubbing together—*Keep them hidden, Catia.*

Her eyes slide to the box, to the frayed edges of cardboard where the flap that closed over the cards has worn away. "You kept them."

Of course, I want to scream. *You made me believe they were our only link! That they were important. Like you would come back for them...for* me.

"Where'd you hide them?"

"Under the mattress," I say. I don't say that I pulled them out every night, flipping through each one, committing their archaic images to memory. Most little girls cuddle their favorite stuffed animals until the fur wears patchy and the eyes fall out. That is what the cards have become. I curled up at night with the Queen of Cups and the Emperor. I don't need to know what they mean—I just need to know that they're there.

"Did you learn to read them?" Her eyes glisten with a sort of hope.

We are sharing something. I realize she likes this and resist the urge to hurl the box out the window.

"No."

She deflates, sinking a bit into her seat.

"They're missing a card—the Moon. It wasn't in the box when you gave it to me."

She looks away. The missing card makes her uncomfortable. No doubt another superstition. "Weird."

I set the box between us, watch her shift her weight to the other side of the car. I want to ask her what they meant, why she had them, why she gave them to me. But we are uneasy together still, like strangers trapped in an elevator.

"So, New Orleans?" I finally say after a long silence.

She smiles at me, grateful for the attempt at light conversation, neutral territory. "Yep."

"How long have you been there?"

"Three years or so." She puckers her lips, thinking. "It really suits me. I can't believe I didn't go there sooner."

I can picture her wearing the Big Easy like a well-tailored suit. They share the same curse—too much character.

"You'll love it, I promise. There's always so much to do. Never a dull moment, you know what I mean?"

I shrug. I don't mind dull moments. Dull moments are safe. They're easy. They don't send people over the edge. They don't lure mothers away from their daughters or women away from their wits.

The truth is, New Orleans scares me. I picture it like a beast unto itself, this vibrant, pulsing mass of too much color and sound, where people go to lose themselves, to disappear in the euphoria. I watched a movie when I was little about a ballerina who wanted to be the best dancer in the world. She bought a mysterious pair of silky red pointe shoes that made her dance better than everyone else in the company, but when she went to take them off, they were stuck fast to her feet. They forced her to keep dancing, day and night, until she finally died from exhaustion. This is how I see New Orleans, like those red pointe shoes, a place for swan-diving over the edge. But I cannot explain this to my mother.

She glances sidelong at me. "You're doing it."

"What?"

"That thing you've done since you were little where you go all pensive and your face screws up on itself like you're untangling a wad of thoughts the way someone unwinds a ball of yarn."

I cross my arms, uncomfortable that she sees me. I'm not sure which is worse, the times she sees too much or the times she cannot see at all.

"You're lucky I'm out of school," I say, changing the subject. "This would have been a lot more complicated if it weren't summer."

Her eyes veer off in thought, and I realize this is the first time she's considered schooling. "When does that start again?"

"August. I'll be a senior." I just have to make it through one more year, and then I can get out of New Orleans and away from Mary. In the meantime, I'll try to figure out what's really going on with Moony's money because it can't be that Moony lied to me all these years or spent my future on some secret extravagance. I'll find a way to get myself to the East Coast for college. I have to.

She grins. "A senior. My little bookworm. I've told everyone all about you, shown them your picture and everything. They can't wait to meet you."

I used to want this. I used to want to meet her friends and see where she lived and be in on whatever she was doing. When she left, it was as if all the color drained from my world. But I'm not that big on color anymore. It's overrated. The lines are what really matter—nice, solid, black lines that keep everything in its place.

The inside of her Mazda suddenly feels like it's shrinking. I roll my window down, pretending it's because of the cigarette smoke.

She turns the radio on, setting it to a local Zydeco station. “That’s the spirit of things.”

Her smile is too big in the close quarters, and I flinch from the whites of her teeth and eyes as dusk settles over us. The music is rapid and maddening, a harshly happy sound that reminds me of clowns. The accordion in the radio blocks my ability to string thoughts together cohesively.

New Orleans looms closer by the minute.

My eyes are bright with tears. Tears for Moony. Tears for myself.

We are on the edge of the French Quarter in a tiny walk-up that opens onto a private courtyard. I am surprised to find her here. I’m no real estate mogul, but I know rent in this city is high. I drop my bag on the sofa and look around while she turns on all the lights.

“This is a nice area,” I say, trying to conceal my suspicion. I am acutely aware that this is something most kids don’t have to concern themselves with, but with my mother, you can never be too careful. Nothing is ever really as it seems.

She nods and grins, washing her hands in the porcelain sink in the kitchen. “I like it. It’s close to work. Close to everything. I don’t really need the car.”

Paying for a car she doesn’t drive? My ears perk up and my face flushes with curiosity. Maybe, if she can afford the French Quarter and an unnecessary car, she can afford a modest out-of-state tuition, application fees, and a coed dorm for a few years. I let hope rekindle like fireflies in my heart. “Must be nice.”

"It is. We'll have to look for something bigger, of course, now that you're here. Maybe after the house sells, we can put a down payment on something."

I want to tell her we should save that money for my school, but I know her. After the "corporate brain-munchers" speech, it's doubtful I'll convince her that college is a worthy cause. Even if she was willing, I don't think she'd manage to hold on to the money that long. And letting Mary pay means keeping Mary in my life. It means letting her embarrass me on campus or totally derail my plans. It means subsidized chaos.

I spin around, taking things in. The living room is small, but with the high ceilings, it feels roomy. The kitchen juts out from it, just one counter with a sink beneath a window, a refrigerator, and a range. A little iron patio set sits to the right of the kitchen counter, and a card table covered with colorful scarves is squeezed into a corner of the living room with two mismatched chairs. The door to the only bathroom is adjacent to the kitchen. And next to that, the door to the only bedroom. I deduce quickly that the sofa is actually my bed.

I flop down on it, cradling my head in my hands. There is a sinking sensation in the pit of my stomach as I realize I am no longer standing on level ground. It feels like the kind of haunting motion you experience after a day at the beach, when you lay down at night but your body is still rocking with the waves.

"I promise we'll find a place with two bedrooms once Edna's house sells. Okay? The sofa pulls out, and it's brand-new. I had Gary pick it up and move it in this morning while I drove over to get you."

She sits next to me and rubs my back briskly. I don't like to admit it, but the nausea ebbs somewhat with her touch.

"Gary?" I seize on the only thing that might shed some light.

"You'll meet him," she says, pulling a smile over some emotion she doesn't want me to see. "This is his place, really. I mean, I pay rent, but he owns it. He has a few properties around. He's good people."

Gary, I realize quickly, is the missing puzzle piece. I don't know the full nature of their relationship, but it's not hard to guess. He has a key if he owns the place and hand-delivered the sofa. And if he's sleeping with my mom.

I busy myself with unfolding the sofa and putting my sheets on the wide, thin mattress. Once my comforter and pillows are in place, it actually looks cozy. And I am not in the market to be picky. That we have a roof and central air and heat, a drivable car, and a Gary for everything else is a lot to be grateful for. It could be much worse considering this is my mother we're talking about—and it has been.

"Um, I need to clean up for bed."

"The bathroom is all yours," she calls from the kitchen where she is pulling things out of the fridge one at a time, sniffing them, and either putting them back in or dunking them in the trash.

We live together now, I tell myself. I say it over and over in my mind, emphasizing each word in turn, as though this will make it somehow more digestible. It doesn't.

In the bathroom, there is a small medicine cabinet over the sink with a mirrored door. I swing it open and look inside, spinning all the pill bottles around so I can read their labels. I have brought my phone with me just for this. Anything I don't recognize, I google. There are some antibiotics, a muscle relaxant, and a few Vicodin. When I get to the Haldol and the Depakote, I feel my shoulders sag with relief. In addition, there's an old half-full prescription for Lithium, one for Risperdal, and a couple of antidepressants. The fact that there are meds present at all is a welcome sign.

The room is equipped with a claw-foot tub like you see in the movies and an overhead shower. I draw a bath and climb in, settling deep into its cradle like I am curling up in the warm belly of a friendly beast. I pull the curtain and clutch my knees, enjoying the dark. Even with the water, the heavy tub, and the shower curtain between us, I can feel her in the apartment with me. And with her, all the memories and emotions begin to surface. If they rose one at a time, I might be able to manage them. But they beat against my mind like a many-headed hydra, a mounting wall of panic that will eventually topple and wash over me, dragging everything out with the tide when it recedes.

As I am climbing into the bed, I see she is back in the kitchen again, cleaning refrigerator drawers and shelves at the sink, and then slipping them back in.

"It's late," I tell her. "Can't you do that in the morning?"

She glances up at me, a sponge in one hand. "No can do, kiddo. Tomorrow's a workday. I gotta be up and at 'em early if I want to get my spot."

I calculate what day of the week it is quickly. "But tomorrow is Saturday."

"Right," she chimes. "The best day for my line of work."

And here we are, at the threshold of another question mark, an empty thought bubble I've been waiting to fill. "Which is?"

"I read cards down in Jackson Square," she supplies, like it's the most normal thing in the world.

She has always been into the fringe scene—cards, crystals, drugs—whatever is the opposite of what everyone in the normal world is doing. She is a magnet for weird. But I assumed she was limiting that to her free time. That her job was something definable with regular hours, a manager, and a printed check with a stub. This takes me by surprise even after spending ten years curled up around a tarot deck as my inheritance. I feel the fireflies of hope in my heart go out one by one. Goodbye, New Hampshire. Goodbye, college degree. Goodbye, stable future.

"Tarot?" I ask, just so we're clear. "You're a tarot reader now?"

"Well, I've always been a tarot reader, Cat. I just didn't do it nine to five before. It's in the blood, you know."

Not in mine, I think. *Not in Moony's.*

"It pays great," she continues. "Better than any bullshit retail or administrative work I might find. And let's be honest, I'm not really cut out for the desk-set scene."

She has me there.

"So," she continues, "this fits. I have a great spot in the square, and I get client calls all the time. I keep busy. And I'm good at it, you know?"

I don't know, and I don't want to find out. I'm sure she knows her way around a tarot deck, but I'm not sure anyone should be coming to her for advice. I make a noncommittal sound and settle under my covers, scrolling through memes on my phone. I consider texting my friends. What will Jaq and Gracie think come August when I don't show up in the cafeteria? Who will loan Julie Perkins lip balm every time her bottom lip splits in winter? I could tell them what happened, where I am, but the truth is, my disappearance will not disrupt their summer all that much. They might not even notice. Because, like Moony, I never let anyone close.

It takes her a good forty minutes more, but my mom finally goes to bed, and I am alone in the stillness of the room. I drag my cards out of their box and flip them around. I always start at the beginning, with the Fool. The young man stares past me at some dazzling future I cannot see. His chin is too high. His step too light. The little white dog at his heel prances like a circus animal. But this is not what catches my eye tonight. Not even the rocky crag upon which they perch, one step shy of plummeting. Tonight it is the yellow flowers of his tunic and his golden boots. I know that color. It is the color of the waistcoat on the boy in my dream. It is the color of falling.

My arms erupt in goose pimples and my heart drops a beat, as if it too cannot believe what I am seeing. Did I dream the Fool? Or did he dream me?

The fact that I cannot answer that, that I would even ask it at all, makes me feel unhinged along all the most important seams.

I quickly tuck the cards back in their box and shove them under the pillow. *When monsters sleep, it's best not to make too much noise.* That's what Moony said when I would call her into my room at night, scared that a monster was slinking through my closet or curling under my mattress.

I worry there's a monster sleeping inside me now. The very same one that hides inside my mother, that wakes up and shakes the house down to its studs from time to time. I worry that no matter how quiet I am, I cannot keep the monster from waking now that Mary has brought me to New Orleans.

I worry that the boy in the yellow waistcoat is but one of the monster's faces.

I breathe the smell of my comforter in deeply, drawing as much of my old life into my lungs as I can. I can make out Moony's favorite detergent, the chicory and coffee steam that marked every morning in that house for forty years, and my vanilla body spray that I am only just now remembering I left in the bathroom cabinet beneath the sink. But more than any of that, I smell the loss. Life as I know it has been a series of losses. I have lost my mother more times than I can count; I have lost my grandmother, my foundation, and my home. And now I feel as though I am losing myself. It is the smell between the smells, saline and sorrow.

I have no choice but to take another breath, knowing that with every inhale, New Orleans is getting in a little more. I imagine I can feel it crawling beneath me, spinning in circles like a cat chasing its tail.

IV.

SHE'S UP EARLY THE NEXT MORNING, BUT I'VE ALREADY risen. Light pours in with the dawn through the little window over the sink. It bounces off the white plaster walls, filling the whole room with a beautiful, if unwelcome, incandescence. My sleep was light at best anyway, so I decide to get a jump on the bathroom. When she wanders into the kitchen with a yawn, I am eating a plate of scrambled eggs with a side of toast, since eggs and bread were two of the only things she left in the fridge last night. We'll have to have a talk about the wonders of breakfast cereal.

She grins when she sees me, like a kid on Christmas morning. Something in her smile rubs me all wrong.

"Morning, baby. Got something to eat, I see."

"I left you some," I say with a nod toward the stove.

"Aren't you sweet?" She grabs a plate and starts filling it with eggs. "I always knew it would be great to have you here, but I never considered how helpful you would be."

She turns to me, her face glowing like the plaster walls.

That's when it strikes me. This is all one big slumber party to her. Never mind that it follows on the heels of her own mother's death. Never mind that it means uprooting me—again—from everything that fixed me to this world so I wouldn't just float away. Never mind that it is the unraveling of years' worth of plans and watching everything I was working toward blow away like dandelion fluff in a stiff wind. Like everything else, she doesn't take it seriously.

I set my fork down with a *chink* against the plate. "I'm not here to help you," I tell her, my eyes narrowing.

She sits down slowly across from me, as if sudden movements might set me off. "Catia, I didn't—"

"I'm not here because I want to be," I clarify. "I'm here because there is nowhere else for me to be. Once there is, I'm gone. And stop calling me that. I go by Cat." My voice is rising steadily, but I don't care.

She sets her plate down and leans back in her chair, crossing her arms. "I know you're angry."

"You don't know anything. You don't even know me."

"That's not true."

"It is. What's my favorite color?"

"Pink."

"Maybe when I was six. Now it's green. Dark green. What's my favorite television show?"

She shrugs. "Cat—"

"It's *Dexter*. Moony was going to buy the whole series for me even though she would have to add it to her confessional list afterward. What's my favorite breakfast cereal?"

She doesn't bother to respond. Her mouth gapes like a dying fish's.

"It's Lucky Charms because that's everyone's favorite, for Christ's sake. You could at least guess." No one can resist those colorful little marshmallows.

She takes a deep breath and blows it out through her nostrils hard and fast. "I'm not sure guessing would do much good since you seem bound and determined to prove me wrong anyway."

"I'm just making a point," I tell her.

"What? That I don't know you? Maybe I haven't been the one raising you for the last few years, but you are *my* baby, Catia. *My* girl. Even if that fact doesn't make you very happy right now."

She stabs at her eggs and takes a bite, chews, swallows. "And Catia is a beautiful name. I gave it to you because you were a beautiful child, the most perfect baby in the whole goddamned nursery. You deserved something better than Mary or Amy or Catherine. I will call you that if I want to."

I glare at her. "Ten years."

"What?"

"It's been ten years, not a few."

She ignores me.

"Your mother just died. Do you even care?"

Her eyes rise to meet mine. She looks away from me, her lips pursed.

"Right. Obviously not. This is just some fantasy to you where your long-lost daughter returns to cook you breakfast and sleep on your sofa. But I care. I loved Moony. I found her lying dead in her bedroom. I lost the only life I've ever known, the one I thought I was making for myself. That just happened...*yesterday*. So excuse me if I don't feel like painting each other's toenails and meeting all your crazy buddies down in the square. And I was never lost. You *left* me, remember?"

She doesn't answer me, doesn't even look at me. She just picks up her plate of eggs and walks stoically into her bedroom, closing the door with a soft *click*.

It takes everything I have not to throw my plate across the room.

When she emerges an hour later, the sofa is folded up with my comforter lying neatly across the back. I am curled at one end with a sketchbook in my lap, taking advantage of the good light. An open suitcase lies on the floor next to me with clothes spilling out of it. Her eyes go to the mess.

"We'll have to get you a wardrobe or something for all your clothes. I'll call Gary this afternoon."

"Yes, let's. Surely Gary will save the day." I am still smarting from this morning, still angry that she has yet to shed a tear for Moony and that she robbed me of the only closure I might have gotten by skipping out on a proper funeral. I don't care about her money excuse right now, even if it does hold water. Even if I need every penny we might have spent on a funeral to pay for a decent school. I don't care about any of her excuses.

She rolls her eyes and starts tugging on a pair of long, fingerless gloves. That's when I notice what she's wearing. If it's a costume, I'm not sure of what or who. But it's not normal clothing and definitely not business attire. Her boots are mid-calf, dark leather, and heeled. They peek out from beneath a flounce of burgundy, layered skirting. Her black corset is thick, like canvas, with tarnished buckles across the front. Her breasts rest on top like two big scoops of marshmallow crème.

She is gifted with curves that must skip a generation because Moony was simply round like a potato and I am lean and straight like an upright arrow. *You have a delicate build, Cat,* Moony would say, but the boys just called it flat.

Mary's hair is curled and cascades over one shoulder, and her lips are the same color as her skirt—too red to be purple, but too purple to be red. Her eyes are dark like mine, and they glisten beneath the weight of her heavily mascaraed lashes.

I want to crawl under the sofa with the dust bunnies, but I remind myself this is New Orleans. Everyone is larger than life here. Everyone is a float waiting to happen on Mardi Gras.

"What is this?" I ask, indicating her getup with a hand.

"Think of it like business casual." She slips a large hoop earring into one ear.

I have no words.

Something in my expression must register because she drops the smile and tries to explain.

"Everyone dresses like this or something similar in the square. It's part of the gig. If you want to get clients, you need to get attention. I do my level best."

I am sad for her all of a sudden. For the way she feels she must parade herself. I wonder if this is how Moony felt all these years—just sad for her.

When I don't respond, she gathers her things, folding up the card table and scarves, tucking what she can into a shoulder bag with silk pouches containing her favorite decks. She fills a large plastic bottle with water and ice and tucks it inside with two bananas, a bag of pretzels, and a warm can of soda.

"I'll be back tonight. I meant what I said. It would be great if you came down and met everyone. You can't miss the square—everything in the city seems to lead back to it. Just keep walking west until you see the giant cathedral." She says "cathedral" like it offends her. Like the size and scope of it are ridiculous, even in this grand city.

I don't say a word. I press my lips between my teeth and look at my sketchbook.

She opens the door to leave but stops. When she turns back to face me, I can feel her watching, but I refuse to look up.

"Cat."

I pretend to be sketching something, even though I am only running my pencil over the same lines I've already drawn.

"I know this doesn't feel the same for you as it does me, but I can't pretend that I'm not happy you're here."

When I keep my head down, she goes on.

"Not because I take joy in your misery, but because I've dreamt of some version of this day for a really long time."

At that, my head jerks up.

"I know you probably don't believe that, but it's true. I can't explain everything to you in a day. It will take time. There are so many things you don't know. But if you could just accept that I really, *truly* love you, it would make everything else a lot easier."

It's hard to take her seriously when she's in full steampunk garb. I tell myself it is the costume that keeps her words from settling somewhere deep inside me, but long after the door closes behind her, I know that the costume is not the problem. It's me. I have torn out, stomped down, and more or less destroyed all the fertile ground in me where a relationship with her could grow. I don't know how to repair that. And I'm still not sure I want to.

I glance down at the page where I was sketching. Normally, I focus on realism, on drawing and shading something so well that you start to forget it's not real. *Serious art.* More technical skill than creativity. But even this was too much for Moony. *Don't be ridiculous*, she would say. The time I told her I wanted to go to art school instead of college. The time I asked for Prismacolors for my fifteenth birthday. The time she caught me watching YouTube videos on how to put together a portfolio after lights out.

But now, quite without thinking, I've drawn the wall of dark trees from my dream. There is a break in them where the light streams through. That's where I've put him, the boy. I don't have a face for him yet, just his color—the yellow waistcoat.

This isn't realism at all. Or is it?

My tears fall like large raindrops, blurring all the lines.

V.

I'M BORED OUT OF MY MIND. I CAN ONLY SKETCH TREES for so long before I start to feel cross-eyed. There's a small television, but I can't imagine settling into a TV coma right now. Not after Moony. The image of her lying there, vacant, replays itself over and over in my mind. I sketch the flowers from her curtains and the open door, but I can't commit more of the scene to paper to get it out of my head. Maybe that's a good thing. Maybe it keeps her with me.

I move around the apartment aimlessly, opening drawers and cabinets, shuffling through things. This is the detritus of my mother's life. These things—this can opener, this collection of lighters, this unopened box of playing cards—are what she left me for, what she left me to gather. They hardly seem worth it, but then again, I'm biased.

I find myself standing before her bedroom door. I would normally never do this, never even consider it. I'm not someone who gossips or takes interest in celebrity affairs. I don't care who's sleeping with who. But doesn't she owe me some explanation? Maybe it waits behind this door, tucked away with her personal things. I place my hand on the knob but change my mind. I don't like that I am curious about her. It feels needy. She wasn't curious about me, not for the last ten years. Why should I feel something for her she can't return?

Her words from this morning echo back: *If you could just accept that I really, truly love you, it would make everything else a lot easier.*

Why should I accept that? She means it would make things easier on *her*. *How can I simplify my life? I know! I'll dump my seven-year-old on my mother's doorstep.* I don't really believe it went down exactly like that, but my memory grows thin there, like cheesecloth. Details have simply slipped through and disappeared. What I remember is standing at the window, night after night, waiting. I remember the longing, so acute it was like trying to breathe underwater, desperate and fruitless. And I remember the disappointment, like a wasp that returns again and again, stinging the chambers of my heart. I remember enough.

At the very least, I deserve to know what's happened to Moony's money, the account she said she was keeping for my college fund. If there's any chance my mother is lying, I have to try and find out. And there's a possibility Mary has money stashed away somewhere, in an underwear drawer or the heel of a boot. She hates all institutions, including banks. It would be just like her to roll her cash up and sleep on it. I know Moony would say stealing is a sin, but doesn't my mother owe me? Especially now?

I stare at her door, deliberating, wrestling with my conscience and my hunger to know more. At last I cross the room and try the knob again. Her door swings wide before me. Her room is a mess of clothes and accessories. She has a few stacks of books, mostly on occult topics, punctuated by a couple of self-help titles: *Quieting the Manic Mind: Mindfulness Techniques for Mental Health* and *You Can Fix Your Life*.

She has a long dresser against one wall. It's covered in crystals and perfume bottles and framed photos. I pick one up. The frame is shaped like two calla lilies bending together. In the photo she has on a blue wig, and there are big pink circles painted on her cheeks. Her false lashes are obscenely long and disco gold. Her smile is electric. She's wearing a hot-pink, furry bra and her neck is festooned with plastic beads in radioactive colors. Mardi Gras—parade of ghouls. I can tell she's a little drunk. I wonder who took the picture. Gary, maybe? Who is making this memory with her?

I set it down, disturbed. I move on, picking each one up in turn.

She is wearing her outfit from this morning, or something like it, her arms draped around a goateed man in a top hat and a woman with black lipstick and white-blond hair.

She is hugging someone close to her, a woman with shockingly red hair and large teeth. Their cheeks are pressed together.

She's standing next to a weird, life-size voodoo doll, laughing. It looks to be somewhere in the French Quarter.

They all seem to be from New Orleans, as though her life only began in the last three years.

At the end is a small frame with a three-by-five school picture. The girl is small, with dark, straight hair and a smattering of freckles across her nose. Her smile is crooked, unsure. She sits before a hazy backdrop, a bushel of spilled apples and some hay bales beside her. I recognize my nine-year-old self staring back at me—the plaid button-down Moony made me wear that day, the little silver ring shaped like a bow on one hand.

This picture upsets me the most. Did I want her to not care at all? Does this really prove anything, one picture in a frame out of a million missed moments? I don't like knowing I am present here beyond my will. I think the old belief that pictures steal a piece of your soul must be right. I feel captive, this piece of me a hostage in her wayward life.

I open her drawers one by one. They're full of the usual things—pajamas, underwear, T-shirts. I close the last one with a huff, disappointed. I haven't uncovered any wads of cash. I'm not sure what else I was expecting to find. Drugs, maybe? Guns? A drawer full of sex toys? Something to prove how awful she is. Something that corroborates the story in my head, the one that casts her as the villain. Only someone that heinous could ditch their daughter. I don't know how to reconcile anything else.

I rustle through the nightstand and come across the papers she took from Moony's desk. A few from the top rests a statement for an IRA account. The balance is barely $10,000. I'm no mathlete, but I know that even without a tax deduction, that won't pay for one year of school in New Hampshire. My mother wasn't lying.

I slouch onto the bed, defeated. I don't understand. Why would Moony lie to me? Why tell me there was a college fund waiting for me if there never really was? Did she just not understand how much university costs now? What was she going to do in a year's time when I graduated? What was she going to tell me then?

I'm angry at Moony. Angry that she led me on. But even angrier that she has proven my mom right. And angrier still that she has left me here with *her*, with nothing.

I look around and decide to rifle through the overpacked closet. I need a stash of cash now more than ever. I am almost done with my search when I see a disturbance in the dust ruffle. I'd nearly forgotten to check under the bed. I check below and find a plastic bin. I drag it out into the light and pop off the top. It's full of old papers—lease agreements, an old car title, stuff like that. This doesn't surprise me. Filing would be beyond her.

Beneath the paperwork are dozens of envelopes in different colors. Inside are greeting cards. I recognize Moony's handwriting on the envelopes right away. They are all addressed to Mary—some Mary Rush and some Mary Gage—at varying destinations around Texas and Louisiana. I open one and pull out the card inside. The image is of two cardinals on a snowy pine branch. There is no typed sentiment, just a picture—of me. I am about ten. My hair is pulled back into a ponytail, and I'm wearing shorts and a camisole. I am asleep on the sofa in our living room.

I turn the photo over in my hand. Moony has written *Cat napping* with the date on the back. Her idea of humor?

I pull out more. They're all the same. Blank greeting cards with pictures of me. Some have as many as three or four, most have one. In some, she has tucked a note written to my mother:

Mary,
Cat is well. She's doing good in Ms. Elmore's class. Don't worry.
—Edna

They're all brief like that. Sometimes she enclosed a picture I'd colored or drawn. I recognize the artistry of my younger self, before I learned that art should be serious, when I happily defined things on paper in a crush of color and broken lines never knowing where they'd end up. Pictures I thought I'd stashed safely under my bed or in my closet. Pictures I thought she'd taken to throw away.

In one, I find a note that reads:

Mary,

Thank you for the money. Here is a picture of Cat in her dress for Easter Mass. She has a new friend at school.

—Edna

I stuff the ridiculous card—polar bears canoodling on an iceberg—back into the envelope and toss it aside. At the bottom of the bin is my birth certificate in a large, brown envelope. I trace my fingers over the printed names.

Catia Eliza Gage born to
MOTHER'S MAIDEN NAME: *Mary Therese Gage*
FATHER'S NAME: ______________________.

There isn't even a name for the man responsible for my existence. Just a blank space where he should be. I think I should feel anger, and I do, but not at him. No matter how my brain tells me he should've been there and if he wasn't, it was by choice, my heart only blames her. She has robbed me of both parents. She couldn't even bring herself to write his name on my birth certificate.

I sit back on the floor and kick the plastic bin. It's really not a surprise. Whenever I asked Moony about my dad, she would just change the subject. I always figured she knew who he was though.

Now I wonder. Did my mom even tell her? Does *she* know? Was she seeing more than one person at the time? Is my paternity more of a question mark than a blank?

I'm not sure it matters. I remember reading a book in junior high about a girl who didn't know her father but would write him letters. By some magic, the letters found their way to her dad, who came to meet her. I remember the girl's desperation to know him. I did not feel that same desperation. It was as if my mother took up all the space I had inside—the space for loving, the space for missing.

There is one final envelope resting in the bin. This one is purple. The card inside is a Halloween image—a fortune-teller bent over a crystal ball and three upturned tarot cards. Jack-o'-lanterns surround her.

Moony ignored Halloween. She never bought candy for the trick-or-treaters or left the porch light on. There is something about this card that must be special for her to have sent it to my mom. There is no picture of me in this one, only a paper note. I unfold it.

Mary,
If you won't listen to me, maybe this.

—Edna

That's it? I flip the card to the back, peer inside the envelope. I stare at the image of the cartoonish woman, her nest of orange curls and purple turban, her glittering hoop earrings. Her table is covered in a cloth emblazoned with silver moons, and her crystal ball is perfectly round with a well-placed swoosh. But it is the three cards before her that draw me in. They are simplified, but if you look closely enough and know what you are looking at, you can just make out a devil, a tower, and a skeleton.

Was this what Moony wanted my mom to see? Why? And how would Moony have known what they were or what they meant? Moony did not traffic in the supernatural. She didn't believe in anything science couldn't prove, except the Eucharist and her weird superstitions. I hid my tarot deck from her because my mother told me to and because I knew if she ever found the cards, she would take them away. She would think they were bad. Not boogeyman evil, just *sin.* So why would she want my mother to see these? And how did she know enough about them to know that's the message my mother needed to hear?

As I slide the card back into its envelope, I check the date over the stamp—just months before my mom's final visit, when I was thirteen. It appears to be the last card Moony ever sent.

I gather the cards back to put in the bin, but when I lean over it to drop a handful inside, something catches my eye. An item remains at the bottom, inconspicuous, forgotten. I pick it up, flipping it between my fingers. A matchbook. It's funny to think that matches are still a thing. Is there something about this book that is special for her to keep it with my photos and Moony's letters, with every important document she owns? It doesn't look special. The background is white. One side reads *The Pelican Room* in a fat, cartoony font. It looks like your typical book of bar matches.

I flip it over again and notice the striker is crossed with an uneven line—just one. I open the cover to find three rows of matches, all lined up like perfect soldiers in red helmets. But in the front row, a gap shines where one match is missing. The frayed remains of where it was ripped away are soft against the pad of my finger. There is a story here, tucked in the space between the matches. I can feel the heat of it like the ghost of a fire struck long ago. And much as I hate to admit it, I am curious.

I make a mental note of the matchbook, the cards, and their order as I lay it at the bottom of the bin and cover it with heaps of colorful envelopes, arranging the papers on top the way I found them. I push the bin under the bed and frown. I don't like knowing Moony was writing her. I feel betrayed somehow, left in the dark. This secret correspondence I never knew about means what exactly?

There are so many things you don't know.

I feel like a chump, like Moony and my mom had some arrangement I wasn't privy to. Like they still do.

We spoke.

What else don't I know? The Halloween card floats through my mind.

I wouldn't call the letters loving or affectionate. I wouldn't even call them friendly. But there is a level of respect present between the lines that I can't ignore. Moony did not hate my mother. Some part of her still cared. She wanted her to know I was all right. She wanted her to listen. *To what* isn't clear. A warning of some kind.

I feel childish in light of this newly revealed sentiment between them. Like I alone have been carrying a grudge I thought we shared all this time. There's something so bizarre about it all. The hokey greeting cards...Why not just a slip of paper in an envelope? I remember those cards. Moony would get them in the mail and save them. I never knew why; she wasn't the sentimental type. I guess I thought she liked the pictures. The cuteness of the images is out of place with the fastidiousness of her words. The blank interiors are haunting. Even when she wrote, she wouldn't write on the card but on a piece of paper folded inside.

What words was she holding space for that she couldn't bring herself to say?

Moony was my special name for my grandmother. No one else called her that. Her face was round and plain—she wore very little makeup. And her white hair was smoothed perfectly around it, not a strand out of place. I didn't call her Maw-maw or Nana or any of those other grandmother names. I called her Grandma Moony at first, and then just Moony. I think she liked it. I'm pretty sure she did, but I don't really know. Because like so many other things in Moony's life, she never talked about it. She never said one way or another. She held her feelings down until they went still, the way you drown an animal.

The cards under the bed won't let me rest in this space anymore. I feel uneasy being here alone with them, reminded of all the gaps in my understanding. I make a sandwich for lunch and eat half of it. I stare out the window, debating. I could curl up with my denial in this apartment, pretend that none of this is happening and pass the time with blinders on like the carriage horses we saw driving in. Or I could try. I could look for a way to patch the gaps in my plans for a future of my own. I could go out and see what this city has to offer. I could make something of this time, no matter how much I never wanted it. I could find a job.

I take a breath and decide to leave.

VI.

THE COURTYARD OUTSIDE OUR DOOR IS QUAINT, with brick paving, a fountain in the center, and four raised beds full of ferns and a couple of small trees. The light breaks up between the leaves, casting dappled shadows across everything. There's only a handful of units here—it's a small complex. I imagine myself sitting out here drawing when it's not too hot. It's a nice thought, if impractical. It's already sweltering and barely past noon. And the smell is enough to gag on—dead shellfish and vomit.

A door opens at the far end, and an older man steps outside, shaking a cigarette from the pack in his hand. He lights it up, takes a drag, and eyes me standing near the fountain. I look away, but he's already sidling over with an outstretched hand.

"I'm Jim," he says politely.

I feel relief. *Jim.* It sounds normal enough. He looks normal enough. His cropped, white beard wraps around his chin like a bandage holding his jaw in place.

"Cat," I tell him, taking his hand in mine with a quick shake.

I feel the missing fingers before I see them, the sense that there's just not enough there to grab. I make a point not to look, but when he reaches up to scratch at his beard, they're in plain sight—the smooth, glossy knuckles that leave something to be desired. It reminds me of the cards, the space where a sentiment should be.

"Everyone calls me Butcher," he adds.

I swallow. So much for normalcy. At least that explains the fingers—I think.

"You new?" He says it like a cross between a question and a statement.

I nod to our door at the end. "Yes."

His eyes trace over our door. "You must be Mary and Gary's kid? The girl. The one upstate somewhere."

Mary and Gary. I feel nauseous. "Yeah, right. My grandma died, so I'm here now."

He nods silently for a moment, smoking. "Sorry about your loss. But welcome, all the same."

It's my turn to nod silently. It's the first time I've heard that—*sorry*. It's the first time someone's acknowledged that I lost something. My eyes start to well up, and I blink furiously to drive the tears back before they can fall. I'd rather not cry on the shoulder of someone I just met.

"Well, I'm going to go now," I say, waving an arm toward the gate. "It was nice meeting you."

"Yeah, sure thing. See you around."

I leave him standing there in the same spot, smoking his cigarette, as I hustle through the gate and down the street.

⚜

Being in the Quarter, I think I should feel something for this place. But the brick facades and delicate ironwork don't move me. My feet slap a rhythm against the sidewalk, and I tell myself I have no particular destination. I make my turns at random. Every time the three dark steeples of St. Louis Cathedral come into view, I hasten around the next corner to avoid the square. I weave in and out of tourist shops and art galleries, fingering souvenirs I have no intention of buying. The streets crawl with people.

I like the quiet streets best, at the fringes of the Quarter, full of shadowy alcoves and shuttered windows. If I stand still and close my eyes, I believe I can hear the buildings sigh. Their walls whisper secrets when I press my face against them. There is a story beneath the frenzy, a hundred thousand stories that make up this city, and now mine is among them, like it or not.

When my legs are aching and I've sweated my last drop of hydration, I make a beeline for the square, remembering that bottle of water my mother packed this morning. I could go home, but the whole day, I've been circling the square trying to work up the nerve to see her. I can't avoid who she is or what she does forever. Moony's collapse is like a dying star pulling opposing corners of the universe together.

Jackson Square is everything a tourist would expect. At its heart is the gothic palace that is St. Louis Cathedral, pristine and watchful with her one giant clock-face eye. Her shadow is long and chilling over the garden unrolled before her. Cobblestone wraps around the garden, making a wide, carless street for sidewalk vendors. It's here, in this dizzying throng of nomads and artists, that my mother keeps her office.

I wind through the people clotting the path until I see her.

Her table is a motley assortment of scarves and cards, and she sits under a black lace parasol that has been duct-taped to the back post of her chair. A woman sits across from her in a strapless top and sunglasses, rapt. Her husband stands over her, looking anywhere but the table. Every so often, the woman nods emphatically and looks up at him, and then he pretends to be paying attention.

I watch my mother work. Her face is lit with a wide, easy smile, and she leans toward her client, full of empathy. Her fingers move over each card deftly as she explains its meaning. I can see that her speech is speeding up, even if I can't hear her words. The woman in the strapless top gasps, leans back, and places a hand over her heart. I am instantly curious what my mom has said. As she rounds her way to the final card, she slows, like a windup toy losing steam. The woman grabs her hands in a gesture full of gratitude, and there is a quick exchange of money before she gets up and leaves with her bored husband.

I see my opening but hang back a moment. A man two tables down stands and stretches, then moves over to my mom. He leans over her shoulder and says something that causes her to light up with laughter. Something about their casualness with each other makes me edgy. I make my way to the table and plop into the waiting chair, exhausted. "My turn," I say, ignoring the man standing beside her.

Her eyes go wide when she sees its me. "Cat! You made it down!"

Unease and surprise war on her face. She grabs the wrist of the man standing next to her. "Clifford, this is my daughter, Catia. I've been telling everyone about you. Haven't I, Clifford?"

He is wearing a purple velvet beret, which he flips off his head and back on again in a gesture of greeting. "Indeed. You're all she talks about."

I give him a tense smile. He seems nice, but I don't know how to feel about men in eyeliner. And his fingernails are painted black.

My mom's mouth drops open with a gasp. "We should all go to lunch!"

"Lunch was three hours ago," I say blandly.

Clifford bends down and kisses my mother on the cheek. "Sorry, Mary. I have another date with you-know-who tonight."

She twists in her chair to look up at him. "Mr. Sideburns?"

He grins and nods his head.

"Is this the third one?"

"Fourth," he exclaims, unable to conceal his delight.

"Another time then," she tells him. "I want Catia to get to know everyone."

Clifford flashes me a look, but I keep my face blank. It's enough just getting to know my mother again. I'm not sure I'm ready for her friends. I watch him walk away and turn to my mother. I don't want to rehash this morning's argument, so I quickly interject. "I'm serious about my turn. What are my cards?"

She takes the peace offering for what it is and begins shuffling the deck. "You really want to do this?"

I shrug. "Sure. Why not?"

She lays them facedown in a complex pattern and starts turning them rapidly, her eyes scanning for things I can't see. She points to one. "See this? The Eight of Swords. You feel stuck, bound, even though you have more freedom than you realize. And this? The Devil card—you're a slave to your beliefs."

She swallows, and I squirm in my chair.

"This is the Five of Swords. You've lost something very dear to you. You feel defeated."

I instantly regret my decision to come here. I don't want her seeing me, seeing *into* me. But she's already moving on.

"This is Death and this is the Tower. Both indicate a shake-up in your life and a fresh start. And here, they are followed by the Lovers, a meeting of hearts."

I slap my hand over the Death card, the image of a grim reaper in rose-red robes chilling me to the bone as it carries me back to the night Moony died and my dream. I refuse to go there right now.

"You know what? Let's not do this after all."

She sits back. "Catia, you don't have to be frightened."

"I'm not," I lie. "I'm just not interested. I know what I'm experiencing. I don't need you to tell me about it."

"Okay," she says with her hands up in surrender. She spins a card around to face me—the Devil. "When you look at this card, what do *you* see?"

I shrug, not wanting to play her game but feeling drawn in all the same. "I don't know. A guy with horns and some naked people."

"What else?"

I look closer. The people are wearing something after all—*ropes*. Colorful silk cords tie them to the Devil like the horses tethered to carriages here in the square. It is a mockery of the Chariot card. I tell her as much.

"What does that mean then?" She peers at me, expectation dripping from the corners of her eyes.

"It's about power and control. In the Chariot, you have power. But in the Devil, you are under control because of your need for it."

I say it nonchalantly, with a tone that suggests anyone could see as much, but I feel the truth of it like a hum in my bones.

"Anything else?"

That she expects more annoys me. Like every teacher who ever said *there's no right answer* and then handed you a low grade because the answer you gave wasn't good enough. "No."

The light goes out of her face like a shot bulb.

"It's only lines on paper." The hum in my bones goes still.

She pulls the cards away and tucks them back in her bag. It's obvious she thought we were getting somewhere.

"I'm just tired," I tell her, feeling contrite for bursting her bubble. "I told you I never really learned to read them. You'll have to give me a lesson."

She eyes me, uncertain.

"A quick one," I add.

She nods, shuffles her deck, and lays out a few cards. "There is the major arcana and the minor arcana," she begins. She points to an image of a guy carrying a bunch of swords—the Seven of Swords. "The minor arcana is made up of four suits—swords, pentacles, cups, and wands. They make up the majority of the deck. Each suit has its own flavor, if you will. And every number carries its own meaning. So this card, for example, is a combination of the symbol of swords and the numerology of seven. It goes deeper than that, but you get the idea."

I study the cards she's turned over. "What about the major arcana? What's their deal?"

She grins and points to an image of a man and a woman holding hands before a rising sun. I recognize them instantly as the Lovers. "Think of the cards like a cast in a cosmic play. The minor arcana are the supporting cast, the extras. But the major arcana... they're the stars of the show."

I recognize the gravity of the major arcana instinctively, always have. "So what does that mean in a reading?" I ask.

She laughs and looks up at me with half-lidded eyes. "When a major arcana character shows up, you better pay attention."

I think of the boy and his wolf in my dream, the egg-yolk yellow of his waistcoat, and my arms break out in goose bumps, as if we are talking about more than just cards. I quickly swipe the cards off the table and hand them back to her. "Lesson over," I pronounce.

Her smile grows unsteady, like a wall being propped up with toothpicks. "I didn't expect to see you here," she says, gathering the cards.

I didn't expect to come. "So this is it? Your office, so to speak."

She looks around with a satisfied grin. "This is it, the beautiful square. Of course, I work out of the apartment most days, and a lot by phone. But this is where I come on weekends to find new clients."

I lean my head back until the dark spires of the cathedral come into view. When I sit back up, I feel dizzy.

"Here," my mother is thrusting her water bottle at me. "You don't look so good." Her face is pinched, calculating. It's a look I'm not used to on her.

I drink long and slow, letting the water course down my throat. "Thank you."

"Want me to introduce you around? You met Clifford already, but Bev is just down at the corner, and Wendel does the caricatures right over there."

"Later? I want to check out the cathedral before it closes for the day."

"Oh." Her eyes scale up the unforgiving, blanched facade, and I notice her stiffen.

"Come on," I say. "It'll be...well, not exactly fun, but at least interesting."

She gives me a tight smile. I can see her deliberating, staring at the walls as if she can see through them, as if she is checking for something.

I stand and stretch out my hand. "Don't you want to show me the real New Orleans?"

She takes my hand and follows me to the black iron fence and the heavy, waiting doors. But at the gate, she pulls back, rubbing her palm on her skirt. "You know what? Why don't we go grab some dinner instead?"

I scowl at her, not in anger but confusion. She is visibly nervous, even if she works in the shadow of this building every week.

She takes another step back. "It just occurred to me, you haven't even had a proper Cajun meal here yet. I know the perfect place off Royal Street. But there's always a line. We better head over there if we want to get in. Okay?"

It's as if she doesn't want me going inside but can't bring herself to say it. I see the inklings of paranoia at work and sigh. "Why don't you close up and I can meet you out here after, and then we'll do your dinner thing?"

She looks past me to the doors once more and finally nods. "Be quick."

I watch her turn and practically run back to her stand.

I look back at the cathedral, gazing up to the cross atop the middle steeple, my neck craning. It could be in a theme park, I realize. A castle for some tortured princess trapped in one of those pointy towers, all sunken eyes and cellophane skin.

I look back at my mom one last time, curious. Mania makes people fearless and paranoid at the same time. They'll take risks they never would otherwise and see demons in the most mundane of objects. But I can't dislodge the feeling that something deeper than her bipolar disorder has her shaking like a cat in cold water.

Determined to find out what, I pull back the creaking wood door and step inside.

VII.

I HAVE STEPPED INTO AN ERA THAT I CAN'T PLACE. I am somewhere between the reign of feudal lords and horse-drawn carriages on cobblestone. Even the air is thicker, pasty once you cross the threshold. Part medieval convent and part Greek temple, the cathedral was rebuilt in 1851, according to a loud-mouthed tour guide. The ceilings arch in complicated patterns, covered in ornate paintings. Fat, ivory pillars hold them up, ushering you toward the altar on the dais—a giant Mediterranean tabernacle with statues of angels and saints crowning each of its peaks, the Christian version of the Parthenon.

I make my way slowly up the center aisle, running my fingers along the tops of the polished wooden pews. I wonder if they use Murphy's Oil Soap here too and smile thinking of Moony standing beside me. She would have loved to come here for Mass. She would sit in rapt attention, her rounded back leaning hard against one of these pews. When I was little, she let me bring my coloring books to church. But it's been a long time since I sat through a real

Catholic mass. And I don't have the piety that she'd hoped I would.

I let my eyes fall slowly over the arcs and sags that define the Cathedral, not sure what I'm looking for. The longer I stand on this checkered floor, the more I feel like I am part of the attraction, like someone else is letting their eyes dance over me. People mill all around me. I try not to get shifty, to cast suspicious sidelong glances. I think that Mary's paranoia is infecting me a bit, and anyway, churches have always made me uncomfortable—too many eyes, all that breath in one room, the presumptuousness of the furnishings. I respected Moony's faith, but I nearly kissed her feet in gratitude when she finally told me to stay home on Sunday morning. Now, I start to feel pinched between the orderly rows of pews, the imposing Greek altar, and the throngs of strangers using their phones as cameras.

The saints creep me out, poised over everyone, glaring down from their posts on the tabernacle. They make me feel small—wrong. Especially the three across the top, each holding a gift like they're the Magi at the nativity. Only instead of frankincense and myrrh, there's an anchor, a cross and chalice, and two children. Their gazes pin me to the floor.

Standing here, like a miniature Alice having passed through the looking glass, I feel more my mother's daughter than I have in years. I do not understand this place. I do not understand Moony. I am losing my grip on myself.

I don't like cathedrals, I decide. I don't like steeples or churches or pews. And I especially don't like self-righteous statues. I tell myself it has nothing to do with Mary. Her opinions are irrational, likely fueled by delusion. Mine are based in fact—this room smells weird and those statues look scary.

I spin abruptly and start in the opposite direction, and that's when I see him leaning casually against the confessional—a polished wooden house with too many doors and a cross on top. It's as if he were in a student lounge and not America's oldest cathedral. He looks completely out of place in a shirt so thin I can see his nipples through the fabric, rumpled leather pants, and a shaggy goatee. One might suspect he's been out all night. Which would make sense here. He's attractive in that *Run!* sort of way. And he can't be more than a few years older than me. His eyes are green sea glass, and his skin is bleached sand. They lock on mine, and a whisper in my mind says he's the one who's been watching me all along.

I lower my head and march toward the doors, determined to get back outside where the air is fresh. But just as I near the last pew, I can't resist a glance up, and that's where he has me.

"Pick your poison."

"Pardon?" I stop midstride as he pushes away from the confessional and blocks my path.

He holds up a strand of red and purple Mardi Gras beads hanging around his neck, from which dangles a plastic shot glass. I realize there are two of them, identical in every way, right down to the alligator stamped across the red plastic. "Your poison? You know, what you like to drink?"

I look around wanting someone else to confirm the lunacy of what I'm hearing, but all the tourists are gaping upward. No one else seems to notice him at all. "We're in a church," I whisper, in case he was unaware. Maybe he rolled out of a bar at dawn and stumbled in here thinking it was just another bar.

He grins. "In this pocket...ta-da! Peppermint schnapps!" He

produces a little green bottle from his left-hand pants pocket. "And in this one...bourbon!" Only all he manages to pull out on his right side is the pocket lining. He frowns and pats his chest down as though the bourbon might be hiding on his body. "Well, schnapps it is," he sighs, and pours some into one of his waiting shot glasses. He holds the red plastic out to me.

"N-no thank you," I respond, trying to peer around him to the door.

He shrugs. "More for me."

"Excuse me," I say. "Can I? I mean, you know?" I end up just pointing over his shoulder toward the doorway.

He sips his drink and ignores me. "I was watching you."

"I know," I say with an edge of disgust.

"You look like you've got a lot on your mind."

I don't respond.

"Want to take a load off?" he asks, kicking a foot against the corner of the confessional.

"But you're not a priest," I counter.

"Who says?"

I don't know how to respond to this. I feel like I am trapped in a conversation with a character from the Mad Hatter's tea party.

He nods toward the tabernacle behind me. "What's a matter? Those pie-faced do-gooders on high got you spooked?"

I glance over my shoulder toward the three statues up top.

"Between you and me, I find them a bit creepy," he whispers. "But they're harmless." He shoots the rest of his drink and unscrews the cap from his bottle so he can swig straight from it. "You know, I know your type."

"My type?"

"Sure. Wound up like a snake eating its own tail. Unable to see the grand design unfolding all around you."

I rub at the back of my neck. "Really, my mom is waiting for me."

"Is she?" He looks over one shoulder. "I don't see her."

"She's outside."

"You just need to relax, Catia." He wiggles the little green bottle in my face. "Open your eyes. There's so much you're not seeing."

"How do you know my name?"

"How do you not know mine?" he counters.

"Are you a friend of my mom's or something?"

"Or something," he says with a lazy sideways smile. "It's too bad about your grandmother. We used to be close."

Now I know he's toying with me. He's far too young to have known Moony before I was around, and I don't remember him. "I find that hard to believe."

He shrugs.

I try to scoot toward an open pew, thinking I can go down it and around him to get out of here, but he blocks me.

"Don't you know it's customary in Louisiana if you visit someone's house to accept their hospitality?"

I laugh. "*This* is your house?"

"Of course it is," he declares. "And I'll let you in on a little secret—all the best ones are."

I scrunch up my nose, mentally kicking myself for getting sucked into this ridiculous conversation. "The best ones?"

"Churches," he says under his breath. "And this, my dear, is holy communion." He raises the bottle of peppermint schnapps high.

"Right." All I want is to get out of this ornate, oversized box and away from this hungover lunatic. "Let me see that."

He hands the bottle over, and I sniff it. It smells exactly like the mouthwash Moony used to buy me. I could hurdle some pews to bypass this guy, but I've always been a fan of the path of least resistance. "If I take a sip of your stupid drink, will you please get out of my way so I can leave?"

"But of course." He gives a little curtsy. "I'm a gentleman after all."

"Yeah, and I'm Mother Teresa." I knock the bottle back, thinking I must be crazy to give in to this guy, but it's obvious he knows my mom—it's the only way he could know about Moony—and I didn't smell anything off. Still, I keep my lips pressed tightly together, so only a little manages to make it into my mouth.

He actually says, "The body and blood of Christ," as I take my sip, just like a priest giving communion.

I hand the bottle back to him. "Happy?"

"As a clam." He slips the bottle back into his pocket and turns to one side, gesturing with his arms for me to pass.

I nearly sprint to the door. Just as I grab the handle, I hear him say, "Cat? Don't be a stranger now."

I shake my head and slip out into the waiting heat. I've had enough of this cathedral and enough of this city for one day. As the sun chases my chills away, I feel foolish. I shouldn't have taken that drink, even if I kept most of it out of my mouth. This city is getting under my skin, weakening my judgment. I remind myself that grief does funny things to people. But I still feel unchecked.

I see my mother waiting for me across the square, waving a purple scarf over her head. My temples throb and my cheeks burn. That, in there, that rush to entertain the ravings of a madman? That's a *Mary* thing. Not a Cat thing. And definitely not a Moony thing. I am prickly all over as this registers, like a mad cactus. Two days in her presence and she's already influencing me. I can't stop thinking about the cards, the letters, and the secrets in between. *Bone up, Cat,* I tell myself. *You will need skin like an armadillo if you want to keep the city at bay and survive the next year with her.* But it's the parts that have already gotten in that worry me most as I wipe the last traces of peppermint from my lips.

VIII.

WE STOP TO EAT AT A LITTLE CAFÉ. I'VE LOST TRACK of streets and turns. The Quarter is like a maze of old brick and scrolly ironwork. Everything starts to look like everything else. My mother seems to have her bearings here, which is ironic because she is a woman without bearings in general. She is quiet now, tucked behind her menu, focused. I sag into my chair with relief.

"I met your friend," I say after a few moments.

"Clifford? I know. I introduced you." She doesn't even glance up, but her voice is bright and warm like sunshine. She is happy. We are talking, having a late lunch together. We are like other mothers and daughters.

I rearrange the sugar packets in their holder. Pink. Blue. Pink. Blue. Yellow. Pink. Blue. "No. Not him. The one in the church."

She looks up, her brows coming together between her eyes. "I don't know who you mean."

"Don't you?" I lean back in my chair. "He's kind of young. Scruffy. Terrible dresser."

She stares at me.

"Bit of a lush," I add.

Her eyes flit back to her menu, and her smile tries to remedy itself. "Doesn't ring a bell. Are you sure he's a friend of mine?"

Is her voice an octave too high?

I shrug. Thinking back on it, he didn't really say as much. But he knew my name. And he said he knew Moony. "Pretty sure."

She sets the menu down, impatient. "What was his name?"

"He didn't give it," I have to concede.

"A friend of mine with no name?" She chuckles.

"Wouldn't be the first time, I'm sure." It's a low blow, but I can't help myself.

She sighs and places her elbows on the table. "Catia, I don't have *church* friends."

"Apparently, you have one." I am about to say more, but we are interrupted.

A server approaches our table, brown skin gleaming against the stark white press of his button-down shirt and black tie. His teeth, I note, line up like the matches in the book I found, in perfect rows. His eyes are the color of toasted acorns. They slide to me, and I try to pretend I don't notice. He is young. Older than me, but not by much.

"What's good? You ladies ready?"

I fold my menu and glance up casually. I order a crawfish po'boy and fries even though I don't really like meat all that much. I'm not really a vegetarian, just not a fan. The po'boy is to satisfy my mother, who won't shut up about crawfish this and Cajun that, as though I haven't been living in Louisiana the last umpteen years. I flash her a smile to make sure she notices.

She beams at me and places her own order of salad and étouffée. When the server walks away, she leans across the table on her elbows. "He's cute."

She says this with a deviant smile as though we're girlfriends. My annoyance from this morning at her need to pretend that the last ten years didn't happen begins to wind its way up my limbs. But I don't want to fight with her in public. I remember a few of those moments from before—being in a McDonald's somewhere off the interstate when the soft-serve ice cream machine wasn't working and she thought the woman behind the counter was withholding it. She started screaming so loud they had to call the police to escort us out.

"I didn't notice," I lie and decide to change the subject. "So, what was that? Back there?"

She sits back. "Not the friend thing again?"

"No." I've accepted that we're getting nowhere fast on that. I want to know what happened before. "The cathedral. That whole last-minute dodge you gave me. You looked...*scared.*"

She fiddles with the paper wrapper from her straw on the table, wadding it into little knots and unwadding it again. "I'm not sure what you're referring to."

There is something to this, I can tell. I can see it in her jittery fingers and refusal to look at me. There is a story to be unearthed here if I excavate carefully. I wonder if everyone drawn to New Orleans is like this, full of deeply buried stories, like graves. "Sure you do. You definitely didn't seem like you liked that place."

I try to change my voice, like she does, like we're girlfriends. It is higher and thinner than normal. It is inviting.

She shifts in her seat. "I don't like it, I guess."

"Any particular reason?" I ask.

She shrugs. "I spent a lot of time in churches growing up. Edna insisted. Mass every Sunday, sometimes on weekday mornings. The rosary before bed every night. Catholic school in between. It was a lot. I'm done with all that now."

The way she says *that* makes it sound like she is spitting it out of her mouth like a bad fruit. It sounds like more than the inconvenience of getting up early and dressing in scratchy clothes. There is something she's not saying. I also can't help but notice that Moony made her attend a lot more than she did me. I wonder if she was afraid I'd turn out like my mother, rebellious and unstable—if that's why she had me stop going once I reached a certain age.

"Catholic school, huh? What was that like?" I didn't even know there was a Catholic school in our town. I went to the public school ten blocks away like everyone else around us.

Her eyes meet mine, and they are different, darker than I remember.

"It was strict."

My mother has a way of describing things that even at her most lucid is a tad over the top. It's the reason I have a name like Catia instead of Ellen or Kate or Anne. The sky is dazzling or it is devastating, but it's never just blue. Her answer about the Catholic school is too succinct. I am just about to lean forward and ask for more when the server appears. She is saved by my po'boy.

"Can I get you anything else?" he asks us both, but he is looking only at me.

"Catia will have some beignets. Won't you, Cat? But don't bring those till later, when we're finished, please."

"Yes, ma'am."

My mother smiles up at him. "My aren't you a cute thing?" she says, reaching out and giving his apron a tug.

He laughs uncomfortably.

"Catia's new here—to New Orleans, not Louisiana. She's Louisiana stock through and through. How about you? Are you from here?" Her eyes skim over him in a way that makes us both blush.

It takes everything I have not to crawl under the table.

"Oh, yes, ma'am. Born and raised." He tries to shift the focus to me. "You should let me show you around sometime, Catia."

"It's Cat," I correct him, glaring at my mother. "And I'm not really 'Louisiana stock.'" I make air quotes around the last two words and literally cringe at myself. I don't know how to flirt. Mary, on the other hand, is obviously a natural.

He flashes an amused grin. "I'm Daniel."

"Good to meet you, Daniel," I say. My mother jabs her pointy boot into my shin under the table. Her eyes widen like flowers opening in the sun.

"We only got in last night," my mom cuts in. "Cat's grandmother died. Cat found the body. Well, you don't want to know all the gory details, but you get the picture."

Daniel is nodding at my mom to be polite, but I can tell he's struggling to follow her. I'm impressed at how calm he seems. She's usually unnerved most people by now. I feel sorry for him. I realize that if I don't say something, she'll just keep talking. I have to save us both.

"Are you guys hiring perchance?" I blurt.

"Uhhh..."

I instantly regret it. It's a tiny café. They can't need more than a few people on staff. My mother has come on to him and rambled like a madwoman, and now I've asked for a job. It's horrible realizing that I am the one who's rendered him speechless, not Mary. "Forget it."

"Nah," he says casually, his smile bunching on one side of his face. "I'll check."

"No, really. You don't have to. I, uh, was just thinking out loud. I don't really have the time."

He smiles uneasily.

"Don't be silly, Catia, honey," my mom cuts in. "She doesn't have any plans," she tells Daniel.

I narrow my eyes.

"Well, you ladies enjoy your meal and let me know if you need anything else." Daniel shakes his head as he leaves the table.

Once he's gone, I put my head in my hands and just breathe. "I wish you wouldn't do that," I say.

"What?"

"Tell people about Moony, about my personal life. And stop calling me Catia."

"There's no shame in it, Cat. Old people die all the time. It's part of life."

I realize she doesn't get it, never will, but at least she didn't call me Catia that time. I eat the rest of my meal in silence while she goes on and on about some of the men she met and dated when she first got here, crazy parties she's been to, and her first Mardi Gras when she got pickpocketed.

Daniel brings the check while she's in the restroom, and I can't help but think it's too well-timed to be a mistake. He hands me a sheet of paper as he puts our ticket down.

"What's this?" I ask.

"An application. You said you were interested...or something."

I nod, mortified. "Oh. Um, thanks?"

He leans over, his mouth tantalizingly close to my ear. He smells like chicory root and cypress trees. Warm blood pulses through me. "I'll give you a tip—if you don't have a job history, just write that you volunteered at your local animal shelter in the town you came from. The owner is a dog nut, and she'll never call to confirm."

"Right."

"I mean, it will mostly be seating people and bussing some tables and grunt work, but it pays," he says, straightening.

"Okay," I tell him. I could use a reason to be away from my mom several hours at a time and a way to save for New Hampshire or simply somewhere that isn't here. I could have an escape plan in place by graduation, leave NOLA and its haunts in my dust.

"Don't wait too long," he says. "Positions fill quick in the Quarter. Can't beat the tips."

"Got it." I fold up the application and tuck it in a pocket. I'll fill it out tonight while my mom is in bed.

"So, hit me up?" he says, grinning awkwardly.

"Yeah, sure." I can't imagine anyone saying no to those dimples. I watch him walk back to the kitchen.

When Mary returns, she carefully wraps up the beignets I couldn't finish in a paper napkin and slips them in her bag. I help her carry the folding table and chair all the way back to our apartment, grateful to finally see the little courtyard come into view. Butcher is sitting out front on the fountain's edge, smoking again.

"Evening," he says as we pass.

"Evening, Jim," my mother calls over a shoulder. "Have you met my Cati—my *Cat*?"

"Sure have," he responds. "Smart girl."

I'm not sure what he means by that, but it seems rude to ask for clarification on a compliment.

"Gary stopped by," he continues. "Says he'll be back tomorrow."

My mother nods. I wonder what she's hiding about the elusive Gary. When we get inside, she mutters, "He's always watching."

"He's smoking," I assure her, hoping she doesn't begin to tell herself stories about Butcher to stoke her fears. I remember her paranoid delusions often started with a little seed of discomfort—maybe a friend who turned down her invitation to dinner, or a boyfriend who stopped calling. Even as a young girl, I could see the way her mind would take this nugget of unpleasant truth and begin to weave a story around it, layer by tedious layer, moving farther and farther out to the edges of reality until she could no longer follow her way back in.

I wonder what she's hiding about a lot of things, like Catholic school, my father, greeting cards, and Moony. I wonder about Daniel and his dreamy eyes and perfect smile. I wonder about our little house sitting vacant in Moony's town and whose lawn Deena will be pooping on now. But mostly I wonder about St. Louis Cathedral and the man with the peppermint schnapps. I wonder how he can look so young and sound so old. I wonder how he knew Moony...knows me. And I wonder why I trusted him when everything I've been taught says I shouldn't.

IX.

I HAVE TURNED BACK AT LEAST A HALF DOZEN TIMES, my application pressed against my stomach. I don't know Daniel or anyone else at the café. I don't have to apply. But I need money, and I have an in there. And I am the one who asked about a job. Impulsive as it felt, it also felt good. Like I was taking charge of something. But even this inner struggle cannot push last night's dream from my mind as I wind my way through the Quarter. It hammers at my brain with relentless acuity.

I dreamt again of the boy on the cliff, my limbs grasping for purchase in a sprawl of air. I felt myself falling, only, as the wind blew past me, I realized I was not falling down but up. And then I was tumbling over a cliff's edge—not off of it, but onto it. And the boy was waiting for me there, but he had grown. He wore the face of the man with the peppermint schnapps. His hair was cropped close to his scalp and his goatee wrapped around his too-red lips. His yellow waistcoat had been traded for a jacket, leathery like the underside of a bat's wing, and his white wolf friend was now a black goat with gleaming yellow eyes and two twisting horns. He held a hand out to me and smiled. I reached for him, and he led me back into the waiting shadows of the forest. When I looked down again, it wasn't his hand I was holding but a chain of shining red silk.

I pulled out my box of cards upon waking and used my phone to shine a light over their carnival colors, flipping through until I came to the Devil. And while the devil on my card was orange and black with white horns and red wings that billowed like a cape behind him, his smile was the same as the devil in my dream and his chains were unmistakable. He may not have looked like the man with the peppermint schnapps, but I *knew* he'd smell like mint if he were standing next to me. Old and young at once. Glamour. Carnage. The Devil is liberation, but only when you are willing to see him for what he truly is.

Open your eyes. There is so much you aren't seeing.

Something sizzled in my mind like burning electrical wire. I spread the cards across the bedspread, looking for something that I would only know once I saw it: the Fool—the boy from my dream. He was as clear as the golden glow of his coat.

I have met them both in my own way. They have been keeping me company nearly my whole life. And now when I need them most, when Moony is too far and my mother is too near, they have emerged from my deck or from my mind, garbed themselves in sinew and skin, and made these streets their home.

It makes its own kind of sense. Not the kind I can explain to anyone else. Maybe not even the kind I can believe in. But as I pick my way toward the café, this nagging instinct is burrowing in my belly and laying its young. There is a connection between my cards, my dreams, and the man in the church. I am reminded of my mother and her insinuation that Butcher was watching her. Of the ease with which these small nuances of life can be ascribed meaning and strung together like pearls, blown to monumental proportions in the lens of one's own mind and contorted into monstrous, looming shapes, like shadows that stretch out and overwhelm their source. I am reminded that—like it or not—I am my mother's daughter.

I turn from this uncomfortable truth to the promise of Daniel's dimples and strong shoulders. Moony would not be pleased, I think, as I cross Chartres Street. She would not have approved of Daniel's darker skin and curly hair. She never spoke her racist thoughts out loud, but there are things you can see moving inside a person, like snakes under their skin. I do not share her sentiments, but I am haunted by the memory of this flaw in her character. After learning there was no college money, it makes me wonder what else I missed or ignored or excused. Why do we only want to remember good things about the dead?

As I pass the large picture window of a gallery, I can't miss catching a glance of myself in its reflection. I am all wrong for this city. My hair is flat, my jeans are torn, and I am too pale. Not in the pretty porcelain way either, but in an I-hate-the-outdoors way. I don't picture myself in my own mind the way normal people do. I see myself outlined in charcoal pencil and washed over with watercolors. I see myself in two dimensions, a soft and hazy replica of the real thing. It fits better with my superstraight hair and equally straight body. It fits better with the flatness of my life. But it doesn't work here. New Orleans is multidimensional. Nothing is as easy as it appears on the surface.

In the plate glass, I am taller than I remember and thin. My hair is parted down the middle, blunt cut just past the shoulders. It looks dark in the glass like a mahogany halo. My blue-and-white striped shirt is too plain, and my sneakers are too dirty. I don't know how to dress for the Quarter, so I just dress the way I always do.

I put my head down and watch my shoes, trying to tune out the bustle. I opt for quieter streets over crowded ones when I can, but it's impossible to avoid all the tourists, all the people asking for money, and the street performers. I really shouldn't be surprised when an older man with a dusty top hat and white gloves stops me in my tracks by sticking out the tapered end of his long, lacquer-black cane.

He gestures to a covered table he has set up on the sidewalk.

"No, sorry." I try to keep going, but he steps in front of me.

His face is painted black and white like a theatre mask: one half of his mouth curls up in a skeletal, Cheshire grin, while the other half turns down in an exaggerated frown. One eye is painted as if it rounds over the hump of a full, smiling cheek, while the other eye droops at the corners like an undercooked egg sliding down his skin. Only...they're mismatched. The smiling eye is poised over the frowning mouth. And the drooping eye hangs over the curving smile.

If I stare too long, I start to feel disoriented.

His cane is topped with a silver handle in the shape of a raven. He doesn't look like he has a limp. A small blackboard hangs by a white string around his neck. He reaches into the pocket of his black pants and emerges with a piece of chalk. He writes on the board: *Try your luck at a game?*

His smile behind the grease paint is friendly, and his thick, arched brows are inquiring. Maybe it's his muteness that gives me pause, or the way no one else seems to notice him. I feel sorry for him somehow, for his mixed-up face and his sad, little chalkboard. I have time—I did leave early.

He rubs at his board with a gloved hand and writes, *What have you got to lose?*

I shrug and step over. Anything that can get my mind to stop circling all its unanswered questions is worth a few minutes.

His table is set with three silvery, overturned goblets. "The shell game?" I ask.

He nods happily. His gestures are overblown like most clowns, every expression doing the work of dozens of words. He writes, *You know how to play?*

"Doesn't everyone?" I respond.

His grin grows up the sides of his face like a creeping vine. *Not like I play it,* he writes back.

He places his white-gloved hands atop two of the goblets and begins to spin the cups, weaving them in and out of a complex pattern that gradually speeds up until his hands are a blur my eyes can no longer trace. When he finally stops, he writes, *Pick one.*

I feel dizzy from watching him. I point to the cup in the middle, which is just like me—always avoiding extremes.

He picks it up, but there's nothing there. He sticks out his bottom lip in a pout and draws his fingers down his cheeks to indicate tears. *Too bad,* he is saying. *So sad.*

He writes, *Try again,* setting the cup back down.

I point to the one on the right. There stands a miniature bottle of peppermint schnapps. The glass is the color of a traffic light—green for *go*—and the label is black and white, like his face. He picks it up and sends it spinning into the air high above our heads. I watch it tumble end over end over end for an unnaturally long period of time. I glance at the man, and he taps his wrist and fakes a yawn. Then his face brightens suddenly, and he points up.

I manage to look up in time to see the bottle finally fall. I catch it just before it hits the concrete and shatters. I'm not sure I like this game.

He points to me with a sweet smile. *For you.* Then he bows, and I tuck the bottle safely in my pocket before he can send it spinning again.

There's more. Want to see? he writes, all three cups replaced on the table

I nod even though I don't really want to see. It's more that I can't look away. I notice the red-and-yellow sash tied around the band of his top hat.

With a flick of his wrist, he grabs his raven-topped cane and twirls it over one of the cups—the goblet to the right. He smiles at me and grabs the cup by the neck, overturning it. Beneath it lies a key: one of those old-fashioned, skeleton-key types with a twirly top and a fancy, one-sided end to slide into the keyhole. He points to me again. *Take it.*

"What does it open?" I ask, reaching for the key as if I expect it to bite.

He draws a question mark on his board and gives me a sly smile. He waves the cane over the goblet now in the center, and turns it over with a speedy twirl of his fingers. Beneath it is a card. And not just any card. It's a tarot card exactly like the ones in my deck. But it's not one of my cards: it's the missing card—the Moon. Instinctively, I reach for it, but he slams the goblet back down, nearly clipping my fingers.

I snatch my hand back. "Hey! That's mine. How did you get that?"

He grins at me. When he pulls the cup up again, it is gone.

I narrow my eyes at him. "Who are you?"

His answering expression is quizzical and innocent, as if I am the crazy one for asking.

"Did *he* send you?" I wiggle the green bottle of schnapps at him.

He sets his cane on the table and writes *Who?* on his board, showing it to me. He then picks up one of the goblets, taking a sip. Only a second ago, they were empty, but now the one in his hand is full of dark, cherry-colored wine.

"You know, the guy," I practically growl. "The one who drinks this stuff and talks like a gentleman though he's anything but."

He ignores my questions, continuing to sip his wine. Then, his face lights up with an idea, and he reaches behind my left ear. He pulls out a coin, a token from one of the local casinos. He flips it at me, hitting me in the cheek before it falls to the ground. Then he does the same on the right. And again on the left. And so on until the sidewalk is ringing with the sounds of falling money, and my cheeks and chest burn with so many strikes. Several nearby panhandlers run over and scrabble across the concrete to collect all the tokens.

"Stop it!" I yell, cupping my ears with my hands.

He grabs his cane and points to the sky. *Look up!*

I glance upward just in time to notice a dark, purpling cloud exploding like a bruise directly overhead. Wet blotches of rain fall in drops as big as pebbles. Every single one smells like peppermint.

And then the coins start falling, tumbling over my head and shoulders like golden hail. I cover my head with my hands and break into a run down the street. I don't look up again until I have turned several corners and can no longer hear the sound of clattering metal on stone. When I do, the sun is shining, and there is not a cloud to be seen.

X.

THE YELLOW CAFÉ SIGN IS LIKE A WELCOME FRIEND by this point. All I want is to get off these damn streets. I kept looking over one shoulder, expecting the magician to follow, but he never did. I tuck the bottle of schnapps and the key into my pockets. Outside the café doors, Daniel is waving at me. His smile is meant to be reassuring, but I don't know this boy at all. He could be an ax murderer for all I know. Doesn't New Orleans have one of the highest rates of missing persons in the US?

"Hey, you came!"

I smile tightly, trying to hide the fact that I was imagining him wielding a blood-coated blade only moments ago. "Yeah."

Daniel takes the application from me and glances at it. "Looks good. You're hired."

"What?"

He grins and shrugs one shoulder. "I know the owner. She trusts me."

I give him a puzzled look.

He laughs. "My auntie. Her name is Wanda. Come on, let's get you settled."

I follow him inside. We go over paperwork and make copies of my license, then he shows me where the trays are that I'll use to bus tables and which sink to put the dirty dishes in. We cover the counter up front, greeting new customers, menus, and how to mark the busy tables on the laminate map in wax pencil, as well as the register and ringing up tabs. He introduces me to the other server on shift today. It's all pretty obvious—no rocket science required. And it's a quiet afternoon, a good opportunity for me to practice without feeling the pressure of a rush.

I try hard to focus when he leaves me to man the counter, though I struggle to stand still. I'm grateful when a table of people clears and I can go bus it—busy my hands and mind with something other than magic tokens, greeting cards, and nightmares. But that's when I feel something brush past me, the feeling of a stranger passing too close, their energy filling up your aura. I glance back just in time to catch the scent of peppermint. And then I see him taking a seat at a rear table. He's wearing a red chenille bathrobe over tropical-print pants. Daniel brings him coffee, and he stirs it slowly as a grin spreads across his face. At last, he looks my way and raises his cup.

I jerk backward, spilling old coffee all over the table I'm supposed to be cleaning.

"Everything cool?" Daniel comes to my side.

"Uh, yeah. Sorry. I, um, thought I saw someone I knew." I start trying to corral the runaway liquid with my hands.

Daniel glances over his shoulder, but the man in the bathrobe is looking down at a newspaper. "I'll get some more towels," he says. "Be right back."

As soon as he's gone, I step over to the guy in the bathrobe—the guy from the church with the peppermint schnapps. My shadow falls over his paper. "Are you following me?"

He looks up. "Catia. Nice to see you too. Do you mind? I'm trying to read."

"Why are you here?"

"Can't a man have his morning coffee?"

I check my mental clock. It is at least four in the afternoon. "It's not morning. And I didn't think you drank *coffee*."

He produces another small bottle from his right robe pocket and grins, pouring a bit of its contents into his cup. "All gentlemen drink coffee."

I can't seem to make his words and appearance match. He speaks like he's from another century, but he looks like he just stumbled out of a keg party.

"Want some?" he asks, holding up the bottle.

"We did this, remember?"

"Have it your way," he says, slipping it back into his pocket.

"I'm going to ask you one more time. Are you following me?"

He laughs. "My dear, it is you who are following me."

My dream from last night flashes through my mind, and I can just see the glint of sun on the purple and red Mardi Gras beads tucked into the collar of his robe. "My mom says she doesn't know you."

He doesn't look up. "Does she now?"

I cross my arms, frustrated that I am not getting the answers I'm looking for. I feel his smile behind his goatee, as if my anger delights him. "No one reads those anymore," I say, slapping his newspaper.

"I'm old-fashioned." After a moment, he glances up at me, and much as I want, I can't seem to pull away from the gaze he holds me in. "You better get used to it."

"What does that mean?"

"It means if you make a scene every time we bump into each other, you're only going to make things more difficult for yourself."

I open my mouth to protest, but he cuts me off.

"Ah, ah. Your crush is heading back."

"He's not my crush," I mumble.

"Oh please, I can smell the pheromones all over you. Better scurry along."

I turn and see Daniel throwing a towel down on the table I left. I walk over before he sees me.

"I'm sorry," I tell him, blowing out an exasperated puff of air.

"Don't worry 'bout it," he tells me. "Spills happen." He looks over his shoulder, then back to me. He checks his phone. "I'm almost off. You hungry? I know a great burger place not far from here."

My stomach is way too active for food, but I don't want to be cooped up in this little room with a walking, talking version of my Devil tarot card. At least I won't have to fight down another po'boy. "I'm not really a big meat eater," I confess.

"Oh, no worries. They've got a black bean patty, plus loaded fries, salads, and a bunch of other stuff."

I exhale. This boy is beginning to win me over. And I'm also pretty sure an ax murderer wouldn't recommend a black bean patty.

"I was worried," I tell him as we sit down to our table at the burger joint.

"Worried?"

I grin bashfully. "I thought you'd want crawfish or more beignets or something. My mom won't shut up about them."

He laughs. "None of these places hold a candle to my mawmaw Barb. Not even my auntie's café. Her seafood gumbo is the very definition of New Orleans."

I instantly think of Moony and look away. She wasn't a great cook, but she was a good one. And I didn't need her to be more than that.

"I'm sorry," he says, realizing his mistake. "I forgot your mother said your grandmother just passed."

"She died," I say flatly, suddenly not in the mood for euphemisms. "And like my mom said, I found her."

Daniel leans back as if I'd struck him. "That must be tough."

I shrug, biting my lip, desperate for a change of subject. I mentally kick myself for saying anything.

"I can't imagine life without Mawmaw Barb. She's the matriarch of our family."

"Moony raised me," I tell him. "I haven't lived with my mother in a long time."

He takes this in, a pensive draw around his eyes. "So, it's kind of like you lost a mother."

"Exactly." I am grateful he can put it into words for me. I have lost and gained a mother in one blow.

I lean back in my chair and study the boy across from me. Behind his warm, inviting eyes and relaxed smile, there is tension spread like thin butter on toast. He keeps his own secrets, and I want to know what they are. If New Orleans is a city built on stories, what's his?

"Tell me something about you no one knows," I hear myself saying. *Who am I?* I think immediately. Who is this girl who asks boys about their deepest secrets? I frighten myself, but underneath the fear is another older emotion desperate to break the surface. I can't name it yet, but it feels like hunger.

He assesses me for a moment. His eyes dance away from mine, and he laughs in this low, throaty way. "Uhhh. Okay. I'll play," he says. "I keyed someone's car once."

I sit up. "Are you serious?"

He shrugs.

"Who?"

"Nah." He waves his hands. "I don't want to say."

"That's fair," I tell him. I think for a moment, then ask, "Boy or girl?"

"Girl," he admits.

"Younger or older?" I ask this time.

"Older," he says.

I narrow my eyes at him, as if squinting will help me figure out what he's not telling me. "A lot or a little?"

"A little."

"Did you know this mystery woman who was only a little older than you? I mean, before you trashed her paint job?"

He scrunches all his features up into the center of his face and then releases them. "Yeah."

I study him. "Revenge, then?"

"Sort of."

"An ex?"

"How'd you guess?" He looks like a shamed dog.

I shrug. "Hard to imagine a nice guy like you going after some random girl, and the only girls guys get angry enough to take revenge on are usually exes—bad ones."

"It wasn't my finest moment," he confesses.

"She must have yanked your chain pretty hard to get you to do that," I say.

Daniel laughs, but there's not an ounce of humor in it. "She was a pro."

"At chain yanking?"

He laughs again. "At manipulation."

I can see the hurt pooling behind his eyes. He is still not over this girl. I suck in air. "Sounds like you have real history with her."

"Not the good kind."

"I think we established that," I remind him, and he grins. "Still have feelings for her?"

Daniel cocks his jaw. "I have feelings *about* her, not *for* her."

"Ouch." I leave it alone.

"You want the long version or the short version?" he asks after a minute.

I check the time on my phone. "Better go with short."

"I thought she was *the one*. But she thought Bruno was the one... and Nick, and Tyrell, and some flonkey who goes by Wishbone."

I take a long, slurpy sip of my drink.

"She wasn't who I thought she was. It took a long time for me to see it. Mawmaw Barb spotted it right away. I wish I'd listened to her."

"Why didn't you?" I ask.

He sticks his bottom lip out, sucks it back in. "Didn't seem possible. She looked so perfect on the surface."

I think about that. It's sensitive-guy code for "hot." I look down at my slashed jeans and chewed nails and split ends. Definitely not *hot*.

I think of my mother. She wears her mess on the outside. For all her difficulty, I don't believe she actually *wants* to hurt me. She just can't help herself. Her issues get in the way. But people like Daniel's ex are predators, gravitating to the naturally compassionate to take advantage of them. I feel a little sorry for him. "She sounds like a real piece of work. At least you figured it out."

He nods.

"Do you regret keying her car?" I ask now.

He waits a moment before he speaks. "Honestly? I don't."

I'm intrigued by this deeper, uglier layer to Daniel. On the surface, he looks like he could be featured in a NOLA tourism ad. But there's something too symmetrical about him. Something too airbrushed.

"Your turn," he says now.

I want to shrug him off, but he just spilled for me.

"Something no one else knows about you." He leans over the table on his elbows with a hungry look on his face.

I take a deep breath and try to relax. *It's just a game*, I tell myself. But it doesn't feel that way now that I'm in the hot seat. "I stole my friend's credit card. Well, her *mom's* credit card."

Daniel's face breaks out in a wide grin. "Did you ever tell her?"

I shake my head, feeling the shame creep up my neck and over my chin until my cheeks burn.

"That's cold. What'd you buy?" he asks.

"Nothing."

He seems disappointed.

"I'm not even sure why I did it," I blurt, trying to keep his interest. "I mean, she had it on her at school one day. Her mom gave it to her to go shopping the weekend before. She was showing off this purse she bought that cost, like, four hundred dollars."

Daniel eyes me over his glass of Cherry Coke. "Say more."

"It wasn't about the purse. I didn't even like the purse. I thought it was kind of ugly. I can't explain it."

"Try," he urges.

"I just felt this rage bubbling up inside me, and I felt like I would explode if I didn't do something. So, when Jaq got up to throw something away, I reached in and pulled out her wallet and slid the card out. And then I put the wallet back and acted like nothing happened."

As I confess, the overwhelming taste of peppermint rolls over my tongue. I can feel the silky liquid from my run-in with the green-eyed guy washing through me. I clench my teeth so hard I nearly bite my tongue. My nostrils are cool as ice tunnels when I exhale.

"Did anyone see you?" he asks.

"No. It's something no one else knows, remember?" I try to smile but fail miserably.

"What did you do with it then? The credit card?"

I kept it. I kept it and I turned it over and over in my hands at night when I could hear Moony snoring down the hall. I rubbed my thumb over the imprint of her mother's name: Caroline Green. Such a normal-mother name. A PTA name. A bakes-cookies name.

"I cut it up," I tell him. Which I did...eventually.

He nods once and then peers at me. "You're an odd one, Cat."

"You don't have to tell me." I remember the man on the street and shiver.

He shakes his head. "I like it. Where I come from, odd is good."

The way he says it, the glimmer under the words, makes me want to know more about where he comes from.

"Your mom too. She's...interesting."

And just like that, the bubble bursts. "That's one way of putting it."

"What's her story? Why did your grandma raise you?"

I don't like that we're venturing into this so soon, but I figure it's better to rip it off like a band-aid. "My mom has bipolar disorder."

Daniel nods, undeterred. "What's that like?"

I run my finger over our tabletop. How does one describe things like mania and psychosis to someone who has never encountered them? It's like being chained to a roller coaster on Mars. It's your mother smelling like a primate exhibit because she thinks the government is using bars of soap to spy on her or picking you up from school in a car you've never seen, driven by a man she only met an hour ago at the laundromat. It is stepping so far outside the realm of logic that you're not sure you can ever step back in again. And then it's lots of seemingly normal moments peppered in between—like shopping for new shoes and making sugar cookies together and back rubs when I had trouble falling asleep—so that you can never be certain of where you stand. But all I can say is, "Scary. Weird. I don't know how to describe it. It's not the way people think it is."

"How do people think it is?" His face is open, sincere. He's not just parroting me. He truly wants to know.

I shrug one shoulder. "I think people confuse mental illness with stupidity or incompetence. They expect it to be obvious in ways it isn't, and they miss the ways it is. My mom's not dumb.

She's not a child. She's bipolar. When she's having an episode, she can't regulate herself. When she's manic, she hears things. She gets paranoid. She's convinced. She's *convincing*. When she's depressed, she's consumed. She's gone."

"And in between?" he asks.

I feel my forehead crease. There is no resting point with my mother. Even her "normal" is not like everyone else's. "In between, she's just a softer version of the extremes. She's always shifting. You never know which version of her is going to show up next. It's like a dance where you're not in the lead and there's no pattern to the steps. It's all random."

"Sounds tough." His smile is gentle.

"It's crazy making. But we haven't spent much time together since I was little, so I can't say I've been there for all of it."

His eyebrows raise a quarter inch, and I notice that his eyes are like two round toffees in the sunlight. "And now?"

"Now I'm here, like it or not."

"Seems like you don't like it very much."

He's right. I can't say I'm happy to be here, but I'm beginning to see its potential...*for someone else*. My future is New Hampshire or somewhere far, far away. On that, I'm clear. "What's not to love, right?" But my tone is flat.

Daniel laughs. "New Orleans isn't for everybody."

"Mary's not for everybody," I say under my breath.

"Don't let her be your only influence," he says, reaching across the table to move a strand of hair that's fallen in my face. "There's more to New Orleans than just your mom."

XI.

MY FEET ARE BARELY TOUCHING THE GROUND AS I STEP into our courtyard. Daniel is two years older than me and nothing like the boys back home. He doesn't play or even watch sports except occasionally. He didn't mention fishing once. He reads books and rides a bike and wants to be an architect someday.

I'll see him again during my shift tomorrow at noon. It will keep me away from this too-small apartment and my mother's too-large personality. The pay is just over minimum wage, but it's a solid start on the college fund I have to replenish. Or at least the bus-ticket-to-anywhere fund.

I have nearly forgotten all about the street performer with the cloud full of coins and the Devil from the cathedral sipping coffee at the café, when I see Butcher. I nod as I pass the fountain, my new black apron wadded up in my arms.

It hits me that this job is my first milestone without Moony. How many more of these are there to come? In a perfect world, she would be waiting up for me with warm chicory coffee and cinnamon toast. She would be smiling as I told her all about this amazing boy unlike any other boy I've met. In a perfect world, she wouldn't care what Daniel's race is.

But this is not a perfect world. Moony would not have been happy about this job or Daniel. And somehow, the fact that she isn't even here to show her disapproval is a slap in the face. The tears are already rolling by the time I reach our door and let myself in.

He's not a large man, but he still feels big in this small space. His unexpectedness makes him even bigger. I freeze in the doorframe, the black, oil-stained apron clutched tightly to my stomach. The tears hang on my cheeks, drying slowly in place.

"You must be Cat," he says carefully from across the room.

I nod but don't take a step inside.

He stands, a hand outstretched, a hopeful smile parting his shaggy, orange-and-gray-tomcat beard. "I'm Gary." He steps toward me. "Mary's beau. Your mother went to meet some clients. She should be home any minute."

Who says *beau*?

I close the door and move around him in a wide circle, eyeing his outstretched hand as if it were a striking snake. I drop my apron on the pullout. "I know who you are."

He drops his hand, and I realize he's holding a straw cowboy hat that looks well-worn. I don't trust people in hats. They seem ostentatious to me, even the broken-in ones like this. His plaid shirt has pearl snaps and is tucked neatly into a pair of dark, starched jeans. A pack of cigarettes fills the left front pocket. "Your mother has told you about me?"

"Not really," I confess. "Butcher mentioned you," I say.

Gary nods knowingly. He seems uncomfortable, stiff. He is still standing in the middle of the room as I drop onto my sofa bed.

"How long have you known my mother?"

"We met a few years ago."

It's my turn to nod knowingly.

"Do you like it?" he asks, indicating the sofa bed. "I can swap it out for another if it's not comfortable."

"It's fine." I look up at him. He has wide-set eyes and a lot of wrinkles, like someone whose face has seen too much sun. His hair is ginger, peppered with white, and his belly bulges over his belt buckle, indicating a healthy beer habit. But there is kindness in the slope of his shoulders and the thick pads of his fingers. It gathers in the crow's feet radiating from the corners of his blue-gold eyes and the coarse, overlapping hairs of his beard.

"I know this may not be ideal," he says now, his eyes rolling around the apartment. "But we'll figure something out in time."

"It's your place, isn't it?"

Gary finally finds a seat across from me. "I own the building, yes."

"So, they're all your place?"

He nods and looks away as though this fact embarrasses him. "You could say that."

"How did you meet my mom?"

Gary laughs to himself, his smile indicating a fondness for this story. "She read my cards in a bar a few blocks from here. She's not like anyone I've ever met before. Her smile outshone the Corona sign behind the bar that night. She's more alive than most people."

I can't help but roll my eyes. I am tired of people describing things in ways that are softer or more colorful—more acceptable, perhaps—than the truth. People die; they don't pass. My mother is mentally ill, not more alive. "She must have been off her meds," I say.

Gary doesn't say anything. He is a simple man. He says things like "beau" and "pardon." He drinks beer instead of wine. Gary does not match the image of a real estate mogul. "You don't look like someone who would own property here," I tell him.

He chuckles. "You mean I don't look wealthy?"

I shrug. "That's the long and short of it, yeah."

"Built my empire in concrete from a small start-up I began in my late twenties. I don't know anything about investing, but you don't have to be that smart to understand property value. So any spare money I had went into buying up whatever real estate bargains I could find. I never needed much for myself, so I had a lot to spare."

I will swallow Gary's concrete tycoon story...for now. "You were never married?"

"Oh, I have two ex-wives. One from before I started my business and one from after. Neither one stuck around for more than a few years. I work and I drink and that's about it. Women don't like that too much."

At least he is honest. "No kids?"

"A son. He died thirty years ago in a freak accident. There isn't a day that goes by that I don't think about him, thus the drinking."

"I'm sorry," I say, looking down. I feel a smidgen of guilt for interrogating this broken man. If nothing else, I think that Gary is kind to my mother. I realize I appreciate that. She may infuriate me, but I don't want anyone to hurt her. This sense of protectiveness toward her is new to me. It feels itchy under my skin, like cells generating where there were none.

"We all have our crosses," he sighs. "You're too young for yours. I'm sorry about your grandmother, Cat. I know Mary is beside herself to have you here, but there's no reconciling the how. I wish it had come about differently, for your sake."

"Thank you." I'm genuinely touched that this stranger has shown more empathy and compassion within a few seconds of meeting me than my mother has been able to since this whole thing began.

"You would have liked her," I say, feeling that to be true.

"I'm sure I would have."

I am just about to tell him about Moony, about her clockwork church attendance and the sweet, earthy smell of chicory and her round, plain face, when the front door opens.

My mother takes two steps into the room and freezes. Her face hardens in an instant like the chocolate shell I used to put on my ice cream. Her eyes slide from Gary to me as though she is putting the pieces of a very elaborate puzzle together in the space between us. "What the hell is going on here?"

Gary and I fall silent for a long moment, as though we have been caught in a monstrous act and not light conversation.

"Mary, we've been waiting for you. I was just telling Cat that we would try to find something a little more suitable for the two of you now that she's moved in."

I look from him to my mom, but she isn't budging. Her hand is still on the doorknob, and a bird keeps chirping in the courtyard—two high squeaks back-to-back. Her eyes are narrowed, and she's looking around and around the room, her vision prowling like a spooked cat. I'm not sure how to respond because I don't understand her reaction. I sit listless on the sofa bed but slowly rise to my feet as she finally closes the door behind her.

"Whatever you two think you're doing behind my back, it won't last. I see right through you." Her voice is pressed between her teeth like a hissing snake.

"Behind your back?" I mimic, totally lost.

Gary's face sags. He's heard this before. "Mary, come on. She's a child. She's your daughter for Christ's sake. Be reasonable."

I am nearly knocked to the ground with the force of the realization. She thinks we're flirting or...worse?

"Never stopped you before," she spits, striding past him to the kitchen, where she unloads her purse and keys onto the scarf-laden card table with jerky movements.

"That doesn't even make sense," he says. "Are you hearing yourself?"

She casts a glance at him over her shoulder. "I thought I told you to stop letting yourself in here?"

He sighs. "We said four o'clock. Remember? You weren't here. I texted you. What was I supposed to do, wait outside in the heat? At my own building?"

I watch them both from my position near the sofa. I feel sorry for Gary. No matter how solid a man may be when he meets my mom, she brings enough dysfunction to the relationship for both of them. Not that Gary strikes me as solid in any way but financially. He's good-hearted, I think. Soft. But broken nonetheless. I imagine that losing a child will do that to you.

"I don't care what you do. This is *my* place. You can't just come barging in anytime you like."

"But it's not," I say, unable to hold my tongue any longer.

She turns to me, and I feel her fury hit me like a force field. I am flooded with a memory from my childhood. I was six, and she'd let me go to a friend's house to swim for the afternoon in their pool. But when they dropped me off and I came in wrapped in a towel, my pigtails dripping like wet pasta over my ears, she lost it. She accused me of horrible things no child that age could understand—said I was "exposing myself" to the girl's father, called me a whore. She forced me into a shower so hot my skin was red for the better part of an hour afterward. I cried myself to sleep, never understanding what I'd done wrong but cradling a belly full of shame. The next morning, she woke me up with a smile on her face as if nothing had happened. We ate breakfast at McDonald's, and I rode the merry-go-round at the park with her until I threw up. That morning could have been a metaphor for my early life with my mother—a ride you can't get off. At first it feels fun. It makes you light in the head and you squeal with laughter; but after a while, you just want the world to stand still for a change. You are sick with the blur of it all.

"It's not your place at all," I say louder this time. I am shaking with rage. I am not that six-year-old girl anymore. I will not allow her to screw with my head.

"What do you know of it? You just got here," she snaps.

"I know you can't possibly make enough money turning cards to afford a place like this," I tell her, liking how the truth feels as it spills out of me. "I know that you are here by Gary's good graces and nothing more."

"Cat, please," Gary cuts in, but my mother turns around, pretending not to hear me.

"I know that you're lucky a man like him wants anything to do with you. I can't imagine the hell you've put him through, especially if this is any indication." I spit the words at her back like poison darts. Only yesterday, this woman was glowing with her victory of winning me back, begging me to give her a chance, stuffing me with beignets, and regaling me with the highlights of life in New Orleans. And now, here she is, accusing me of being inappropriate with a man nearly old enough to be my grandfather. Someone she brought into our lives, not me. The worst part is, I don't even have a room to go to or a door to slam.

Gary sits down and puts his head in his hands. He won't say it, but it's clear he doesn't exactly appreciate my defending him.

My mother shifts from busying herself needlessly in the kitchen to straightening her shoulders. She sets her glass of water down carefully and presses her lips together. "Well, it's clear whose side you're on," she says, affecting woundedness. "And it's definitely not mine. But then, what did I expect? It's never been mine. Has it, Cat?"

I stare at her. There is a word for this: aghast. You read the word all the time in stories, see it acted out in movies, but how many people actually get the opportunity to experience being "aghast" in real life? With Mary, "aghast" is as commonplace as peanut butter and jelly. "How is this about me?"

"Everything's about you, isn't it? *You* were abandoned. *You* were mistreated. *You* didn't get to live the life you wanted. *You* lost someone. Do you ever think about me? The special brand of hell my life has been? What I've gone through all these years—wanting you, missing you, having no way to get you back from that... that *witch*! She stole you from me. She stole my heart. She took everything and left me with nothing. And she taught you to hate *me* for it. But you're always the victim, huh, Cat?"

She does this. She twists and twists and twists some more until you can't recognize the truth. The weight of what I have lost and what I have gained descends over me like a lead veil. "That's the pot calling the kettle black if I ever heard it."

With that, she bolts to her room, slamming the door behind her. I am left standing, reeling like I've been punched half a dozen times, feeling like the mom on the outside of my willful teenager's room. "I'm sorry," I say to Gary.

"Don't be," he says quietly. "She'll cry it off for a few minutes, and then I'll go in there and calm her down. Later, we'll go out as usual, and it will be like this whole scene never happened."

"This happen a lot?"

Gary chuckles softly. "It's part of the package, Cat. I knew that going in. Don't feel sorry for me. I love your mother, and she loves me too—I know that."

"Funny way of showing it."

"She excites easily. This has been a lot for her, you know. Losing her momma and you coming here. Don't get me wrong, she's happy to have you, but anytime the pot gets stirred very much, whether for good or ill, we usually have one of these upsets. The meltdowns are just part of it."

"You'll excuse me if I don't share your enthusiasm. I didn't sign up for this like you did." I don't get a choice, not anymore. This maelstrom is my reality now without Moony to shield me from it.

XII.

HE WAITS IN SILENCE WITH HIS HAT ON HIS LAP, turning it slowly for over half an hour before he rises to some internal clock and scoots to her door, knocking gently. There is no answer, but he doesn't let that stop him. He turns the knob and pushes in, closing it behind him. I admire his tenacity, but I think Gary is either delusional or into masochism because Mary will not get better. This endless cycle of up and down will define their relationship—any relationship of hers—for the duration of her life.

I, for my part, choose to lose myself in my sketchbook. Awkward doesn't even come close to defining the last hour for me. With nowhere to go, no privacy, all I can do is direct my attention elsewhere, pretend the whole ugly ordeal isn't happening.

I breathe a sigh of relief when I finally have the living room to myself. I look down at my handiwork, truly noting my subject for the first time. It is the boy from my dream again—the Fool. He is steady on his cliff perch; his arms open to the sea of nothing swimming before him. His yellow waistcoat is like a drop of sun, and his hair is a smudge of black. His wolf looks smaller on the page, more doglike. He is the spitting image of the card in my deck but for one glaring deviation. A silk cord is wrapped around his ankles several times in a bright, dazzling red. Not the dark, easy-on-the-eyes shade of dried blood, but the ruby-rich color of freshly spilled blood. Of open wounds and thick, spewing lava and brazen lipstick. It is a grotesque color, even as it is compelling. And it undulates through the grass like an underworld snake or some kind of organ all its own.

I know this red, of course. It is the red silk chain from my last dream, the one where the guy from the church led me away into the forest. It is the red of his smile in the dark and the red of his bathrobe in the café. He perplexes me, this devil I have conjured, with his existence in my dream space. But when he steps out into three dimensions, he scares me. I don't know if I'm hallucinating or being haunted or, worse, stalked, but none of those sound good.

My eyes go to the door to my mother's room, and I bite my lip. What are the statistics for developing mental illness if you have a bipolar parent? I can't remember, but I've looked it up. They're higher, that's the part I remember. There are genetics to consider. I think of Gary in there now, picking up the pieces of their botched relationship as he has likely done a thousand times. The men my mom attracts aren't typically the most stable themselves. For all I know, I have it coming to me from both sides of my family tree. And here I am, seventeen and just this side of genuine trauma. All the variables are in place. So the question becomes this: Am I mentally ill like my mother?

The only sliver of logic standing between me and a resounding yes is that I know from experience my mother would never, *has* never, asked herself this question. The very nature of her condition prevents it. The inflated confidence and euphoric high of mania make her believe she is hypersane and that everyone else should be medicated. Never her. Until you get her medicated enough for her to see the difference, and then her grasp on her condition is slippery at best. Because even without the bipolar disorder, there is something bullheaded and unrelenting in Mary, something that will not let her see anything other than what she wants. Moony would always hang her head after the latest disturbing phone call. "You can never win with her," she would say. "Even when you're right. She's always been that way."

So, if it's not a hallucination, then a haunting? That might make more sense if it were Moony I was seeing. Then I might say she was watching over me. But I haven't seen Moony since the morning I found her. And I still can't face that I won't ever again. The boy in the dream—the Fool boy in his yellow waistcoat with his winter wolf—he is something different than a ghost. And the man with the peppermint schnapps, with his splashes of devil red and his strange talk, he is something different than a dream.

There is a third option I haven't considered. It is forming on the outskirts of my reason, like a word that perches on the tip of your tongue but refuses to be expressed.

Could they be a vision?

It's happened before to children, to young women who trek across some mountainside for spring water only to be confronted with the Mother of God in her glory. I certainly don't fit the description of a saint, living in the middle of New Orleans with my near-pagan mother and twenty-first-century education. But are all the stories that way? Can some visions be *unholy*?

None of these possibilities feel exactly accurate. It's like I'm scratching all around an itch I can't reach. Like when Moony would tell me not to scratch my mosquito bites in that tone that let me know she would check for red marks before bed and if she found them I could count on a swat for each one. I would scratch all around the welt but never touch it, trying desperately to satisfy both my maddening need for relief and my desperate need for her approval. The man in the church and café is the mosquito bite that won't fade, the mystery welt left from some fantasy bug in my psyche. I can't ignore him, and I can't swat him away. I am circling the infection but never really landing on true relief. I know *who* he is, but I don't know *what* he is.

The bedroom door bursts open and my mother is laughing now, her face cast back over a coy shoulder at something Gary has said. She's in a black, sleeveless dress with a plunging neckline and a colorful wrap. Her hair is pinned up, her lips stained the color of wine. Gary is shuffling behind her with a wide grin, situating his straw hat on his head. Whatever he has said or done since going in there, it worked. All is clearly forgiven.

I follow them across the room with my eyes. I'm reclined on the sofa bed, the blankets gathered around my crossed legs, my fingers dirty with pencil. Just as she reaches the door, she glances at me and her smile vanishes. Her eyes go hard, and she steps out without a word.

Gary is out of the doghouse, but I am still firmly inside. The unfairness of it infuriates me.

Gary gives me a sympathetic nod at the door. "I'll have her home before midnight," he says, as if I am *her* mother. Then he adds, "It'll all be over in the morning. You'll see."

I can tell he thinks this will console me.

I look away, betrayed by the sting of tears filling my eyes. I do not breathe until I hear the door click behind them. And then I throw my sketchbook, hard as I can, against it. The pages make a futile, weak sound as they hit the wood. I choke on a sob and get up, wiping angrily at my face. I lock the door before picking my sketchbook back up, the boy Fool still staring into nothing. The cardboard cover is dented at one corner, but that's the extent of the damage.

I try to get ready for bed. I brush my teeth and get a glass of water. I put an animal documentary on television, hoping it will lull my nerves. But I can't settle into the pullout. I can't stop thinking about the look she shot me as they were leaving, a look that implied I was solely responsible for this evening's drama. Gary is innocent. She is innocent. But I—*I* am not to be trusted. It makes me want to scream. The fact that she can turn so quickly and that it can impact me against my will fills me with trapped rage.

I jump up, pacing the floor. I want to damage her like she has damaged me. I stomp to her room and look around. The bed is unmade. I try not to think about what took place in here between them. I turn away and my eyes fall on her dresser, the pictures. I see my own sitting there and before I know it, it's in my hands. They are shaking, and my own face trembles back at me. I turn the frame over and quickly open the back, ready to pull the picture out and rip it to shreds. She can't have me like this without my permission. But when I go to pull the photo from inside, another smaller picture tucked behind it falls out and lands facedown on the floor.

I stoop to pick it up and turn it over. It's a polaroid photo from one of those instant cameras that snapped less-than-perfect shots and printed them straightaway. The lighting is bad, and the image is fuzzy, but it's clear enough. It's a baby. She's in someone's arms, and it takes me a moment to recognize my mother because she's so much younger and thinner. Her hair is falling across her face as she looks down, but I can tell it's her by the color, the part, the set of her jaw, and the shape of her hands.

At first, I think the baby is me. I've seen a few pictures from then. I know what kind of baby I was—the fat, cherubic kind with wrist rolls and dimples and eyes that are too round and open. Of course, newborns never look like that. They look the way people do in those hospital pictures after they've been severely beaten. Their faces are always swollen and puffy, and they are red and wrapped up like little caterpillars. This baby is like that, but her color is not the flush of birth. She is not red and blotched but ashen white, pale blue around the tiny lips. I know it is a she because her blanket is pink. It's only now that I realize my mother is crying in the picture. It's hard to make out because the edges of everything in the photo are soft and blurred, but the tip of her nose is red, and her cheek is wet and shiny with tears.

My hand is trembling now for a different reason.

This baby is not me.

This baby is not alive.

I don't understand what I'm seeing. I have never heard of my mother having another baby. Obviously, it wasn't after me or I would have known. It must have been before. Why didn't Moony say anything? Why didn't my mom?

I have—*had*—a sister.

I study the side of my mother's face—what you can see of it—in the photograph. She is unbelievably young. Maybe seventeen? My age. And for a woman who has just given birth, she looks gaunt. Her shoulder is too well-defined beneath the gown she is wearing, her cheekbone too striking.

I run to get my cell phone and snap an image of the photo before putting it back like I found it, all the fight drained out of me. I think of my mother's hard glare as she left, and it feels sad to me, this urge she has to push me away as much as she wants to pull me close. I need to get to the bottom of her story before it fades into the brickwork around me, before she becomes just another stone in the foundation of this city of the damned.

XIII.

I AM STANDING IN THE QUARTER AT A CROSSROADS. There is no one else here—every street is vacant. A soft mist curls up from the pavement. A navy shroud hangs over the buildings. The absence of sound makes my ears ache. And then I see her walking ahead of me. She shines like a piece of sky fallen to earth.

I start after her, keeping careful count of all her turns. I can see nothing but the deep blue veil she wears. It drags behind her, blackening at the edges like burnt paper. The streets grow more narrow. The city is closing in, a maze of brick and iron. I am panting in the fog. This pace burns my lungs and makes the skin on my legs crawl, but there is something she can tell me if I can only get close enough to hear.

We burst into a wide, cobbled square where the cathedral dominates the core of the maze like a giant, sleeping heart. Ahead of me, she slips into the cathedral, looking over one shoulder to be sure I am following. For the first time, I see the black falls of her hair and her skin like shifting sand, but her eyes are hidden behind her veil.

Inside, the fog is thicker, the pews all gone. The black-and-white floor is hidden beneath gray mist. The Greek tabernacle is nowhere to be seen. The normally white columns are all black down one side. Instead of the altar, there is a cradle, but no sound emanates from within, no cries of new life. I step to it carefully, afraid to look. A pink blanket is wrapped around something small and soft, and just as I am reaching for it, the cathedral ignites in a blinding flash of pale light, as if the moon has swallowed us whole. I cover my eyes with my arms. The light recedes, and I see the woman standing beside the cradle, her face shrouded in shadow, a black cat curling around her ankles.

"Are you the Madonna?" I ask her, my voice slipping out like a sigh.

"I am the book you cannot read and the voice you cannot hear. When you sleep, I am your dreams. When you wake, I am your nightmare. In the darkness, I am your light. And in the day, I am your shadow. To know me is to fear me. To love me is to die and be reborn."

I feel her words within my chest as if they are the whispers of my own heart.

"And the child?" I ask with a nod at the cradle.

"You are my child, Catia. And your mother before you. And her mother before her. I am the mother of all women and the desire of all men. You may call me Sophia, or Shekinah, or nothing at all. I am the Indwelling. My name is of no consequence."

"Why can't I see your eyes?"

With a tug of her right hand, her veil falls away and her eyes are before me. Only they aren't eyes at all but two portals swirling with starlight—she has whole galaxies trapped within her gaze. And the horror of falling into her nearly consumes me. With a sweep of her hand, she pulls her veil back down beneath the bridge of her nose.

I reach for a column to steady myself. "Why are we here?"

"I am always here," she says simply. "You are here because I called you. I have been calling you since the day you were born, Catia. I have been calling you for generations."

"I don't understand," I repeat.

"But you do," she insists. "Or you wouldn't have followed."

"Are you a friend of the man with the peppermint schnapps, the Devil I met here?" I want to touch her, but somehow I know there is no coming back from that contact. Her cat purrs at my feet, its tail twitching against my leg in soft flicks.

"I have no friends." Her lips are straight and full. Behind them, the edges of her teeth glint in the light that emanates from her eyes. "Neither does he."

"How do you know me?"

"I know everyone."

Her answers make me feel as if I am the one not making sense. I know anything I ask will be met with more answers that simply lead to more questions. I stand absolutely still as she steps closer to me. I can feel the pull of her eyes from behind the veil—twin black holes where light goes to die. It is a sucking at my mind that awakens a deep longing within me to lose myself if only so I can find myself once more.

In a hush, she speaks. "Not all chains are forged in iron, and freedom is rarely free. What are you willing to pay for truth?"

"I suppose it depends on which truth." It is the most honest answer I can give, and anything less feels unacceptable.

Her lips curve into a horned-moon smile. "Then know this—the only lie that exists is the one you hold to be true. The only power is your own."

With that, she bends and places her lips softly on my brow, leaving a kiss of stardust between my eyes, and my body erupts into tongues of glittering, white flame.

"Breakfast!" a high-pitched voice sings out. "I made waffles—your favorite."

I blink a dozen times trying to orient myself. There is light spilling in from the kitchen and a sweet, nutty smell infiltrating the space around me. I take deep breaths of it, grateful my lungs are not filling with mist and starlight instead. I check my arms. My skin is smooth and unblemished. There is the mole I've had forever, the little scar from years ago when Moony let me slice strawberries. The cold fire was all a dream. *She* was a dream. But I still feel consumed.

"Good, you're up!" My mother bustles past me, a wide Cheshire grin on her face. "I put blueberries and bananas in them. I hope you don't mind." She's opening the blinds and straightening things in the room that don't really need it. She looks busy and happy and way too awake. "I also put in pecans. You always loved that, remember?"

"What time is it?" I sit up. I feel groggy still. It must be early.

"Seven a.m. High time for you to be up and getting ready for school."

I shake my head. Did she say *school*? "Mom, it's summer. I'm not in school."

She laughs it off. "Of course. Silly me. Still, breakfast is waiting." She sings this last part in chipper notes.

I get out of bed and lower the blinds halfway to ease the transition. There's no point fighting her; I'm up now. She must have started cooking a half hour ago. "Why are you up so early?" I don't know what time she and Gary came in last night because I was asleep already, but I remember him saying something about midnight.

"Why not?"

She sits at the scarf-laden table and crosses her legs, swinging one foot a little too quickly.

I drop a soggy waffle onto a plate. They are undercooked and overbuttered. I sit across from her deciding to skip the syrup. There is enough fruit in there to sweeten seven waffles. "Fun night?"

She grins like a schoolgirl. "You could say that."

I scroll through the headlines on my cell phone for distraction.

"So, you're not mad then?" I know I shouldn't, but I can't help myself.

"Mad?"

"You know, at me or Gary. Well, it was clear you weren't mad at Gary anymore. Maybe, since you're feeling better now, you can enlighten me as to why you blamed me for your perverted paranoid suspicions."

Her grin slips like melting candle wax. "Catia, let's not start this."

"Why? Because it's not convenient for you this morning, like it was yesterday evening?"

"I don't know what you mean." She gets up and starts putting the waffles away, acting as if yesterday never happened. But there is defensiveness in every gesture.

"You don't know, or you don't remember? Or is it just that you'd rather we all forgot?"

"You're making something out of nothing."

"It didn't seem like nothing yesterday when you stormed into your room."

"Enough!" She slams the lid of the waffle container on the counter. "Gary and I have a history. We're working through it, but having you here has...*dislodged* some things. I'm sorry if I jumped to conclusions. You have to understand how it looked from my perspective."

"How did it look? Like we were having a conversation in the living room with several feet of space between us?"

"I don't want to talk about this anymore." She shoves the waffles into the fridge and slams the door. "It's over."

I pretend to be interested in a lineup of articles on my phone. I see a headline about an order of Catholic priests releasing a list of accused sex offenders working in their churches and schools in the eighties and nineties. There are over sixty names. How much longer is the list of victims? My eyes slide to my mom. I am reminded of all her weirdness about the cathedral. The Catholic high school I never even knew existed. I take a bite of banana and waffle goo and my stomach twists. "Tell me about when you were in high school."

She freezes, looks at me. "Where is this coming from?"

I turn off my phone and shrug. "Curious. You never talk about it. I just wonder what it was like for you. You said you went to private school, but I didn't know there was a private high school near Moony."

"There isn't anymore," she says quietly. "They closed down after..."

Her eyes are cast down into the sink, but she's not seeing the dishes spackled in waffle batter as she fills it with soapy water. She's looking within to some scene I can't be privy to. She drifts away from me the way a feather might on a summer wind.

"Mom!" The sink is full and the water is just reaching the edge, cresting over onto the counter, spilling down the cabinet in front.

"Oh, gosh. How clumsy." She turns off the faucet and drops to her knees with a dish towel, sopping up the sudsy mess. "I must have been distracted."

I watch her carefully. Her shoulders are rounded now, and her eyes are heavy. Her lips are drawn thin. I can see it in the lines around her mouth and hear it in her sigh. She's sad. All the waffles-and-joy exuberance of the morning has shifted, like the sun behind a cloud.

"After?" I let the word linger between us, waiting.

"What?" She looks up, the wet dish towel dripping from her hand.

"You said there isn't a private school near Moony anymore, not *after*..."

"Oh, that." Her shoulders fall back, and her eyes flatten. She's like a dog shaking off a coat full of snow. "After I graduated. They closed a few years after I graduated."

My waffle breakfast is a tumult in my stomach, and my fingers tighten around my fork. The skin between my eyes goes cold, as if the kiss from my dream last night has left an invisible scar I can still feel. "Why?"

"Not sure," she says too quickly, which is how I know she's lying. She shrugs as if it's not important. "Just one of those things."

But it's not just one of those things. Everything inside me is screaming that it's anything but *one of those things*. The dream in the cathedral from last night feels more ominous now, like a premonition of sorts. But premonitions are for the future, and this school is in my mom's past.

"Well, what was it like going to private school before it closed? Was it just girls?"

"In our building, yes. The boys' building was next door, but we shared the campus. I told you, it was strict. Boring, really. I'm sure your high school was much better."

"Did you have a boyfriend?" She was almost always willing to talk about men, except when it came to my dad. But I think of the picture of the petal-white baby, so still in her arms. Who was the father? Surely a boy at the school next door.

She looks away, but not fast enough for me to miss the grimace that crosses her face. "No," she says simply. "Edna never let me date."

I don't doubt that, but it leaves a gaping hole where said father should be. "What was it called?"

She looks confused. "What?"

Earth to Mary. Were we in the same conversation? "Your school?"

She pauses, as if deliberating. "Our Lady of Infinite Sorrows."

XIV.

I'M HALF AN HOUR EARLY LEAVING FOR WORK BECAUSE I need to get away. I hope the walk to the café will clear my head. My mind is still spinning over all I've learned—the baby, the school closing, my creepy dream. This morning, I researched Our Lady of Infinite Sorrows private school while my mom was in the shower, which led me to an obituary for a Father Terry Michaels. He was listed as a member of the faculty, but there was no mention of the cause of death or anything to do with the school itself. The black-and-white portrait showed a man with a square jaw and wide smile. Dark, rectangular glasses framed round eyes that looked light in color. And his obviously graying hair was combed back in sleek waves. He died less than five years after my mother graduated. That couldn't have been but a couple of years after the closing of the school. I'd hoped to find more, but my mother came out of the bathroom, and I hid my phone under the table.

"You okay?" Daniel asks when I get to the café too soon. "You seem edgy or something."

"I'm fine," I say to convince both of us. But one look at his face, and I crumble. Daniel has this way of looking so genuine. It makes me want to spill my guts. I think of our confessions yesterday. I've already trusted him with a part of myself I shared with no one else. "My mom and I had a fight. But I'm fine now. It's just weird with her."

"You don't have to tell me. I met her, remember?"

He's teasing, but also not. I laugh, grateful he can make me do that. "Do you ever feel like your parents are hiding something from you? I mean, not something little like the occasional joint, but something big, like a whole other family or that you were adopted or something like that."

Daniel's face broadens with surprise. "Sounds like more than a little fight going on between you and your mom."

Isn't it always? "Forget I said anything."

"No, don't do that. You got me interested now. You're going to have to spill."

I feel foolish for bringing it up. I barely know this guy, and already my family troubles are getting in the way. "It's nothing."

"Doesn't sound like nothing. Sounds big."

I sigh. He's right. There is something in my mother's past, something major, that I am only just catching wind of. Something that might explain all the crazy—not just the mental illness, but the absolutely maddening idiosyncrasies that *are* Mary—and maybe, indirectly, the collisions with weirdos I keep having, asleep and otherwise. Because I'm starting to get the sense that there is more Mary in me than Moony or I ever wanted to admit. If I can understand her, maybe I can understand what's happening to me.

"You know what my mawmaw Barb says about secrets?"

I shake my head.

He hunches over, points a finger at me, and screws up his face. "Daniel, keeping a secret is like swallowing gasoline and expecting it not to burn. Even if you manage to hold it in for a time, one of these days, it will light you up from the inside."

We both crack up.

"She does not say that," I challenge him when I can finally breathe again.

"She absolutely does," he insists.

"About the gasoline and everything?"

"Yep. My mawmaw dispenses wisdom the way candy machines dispense cavities."

"Oh my god. Does she say that too?"

He nods and we both crack up again. "She's got a saying for everything," he admits, shaking his head. "But there's always some truth in them. Anyway, I'm glad I could at least make you laugh."

I smile at him with just the corner of my mouth as a couple walks in the door. I escort them to a table near the back and return to my station, where Daniel is waiting. He is just about to head over to the couple with their menus when I stop him.

"A sister," I tell him suddenly, as if I can't hold it in another second. "That's the secret." It's at least one of them.

He looks at me and his eyes widen.

"She died."

His eyebrows raise even higher. "Yup, that's big."

"That's not all."

"There's more?" he says in disbelief.

"There's more. I just don't know what it is yet."

Daniel places a hand on my arm. "Then we'll figure it out."

The café closes at seven, but our tables don't clear until eight or so. Daniel helps me bus the final tables, and we lock up behind the last customers, sending the other server home. We count the register together, sweep the floors, refill all the saltshakers and ketchup bottles. I'm moving on to the pepper shakers when Daniel pops the question.

"So more, huh? Like what?"

I eye him over the funnel I'm using to fill the shakers up. "I don't know. It's just a feeling."

"A needle, you mean."

"A what?"

"That's what my mawmaw Barb calls those feelings—*like a needle under the skin.* She says it's the spirits pinching you."

"Your mawmaw Barb sounds...interesting." I pull a dubious face.

Daniel laughs. "She is that. I take it you don't believe in spirits."

I shrug, noncommittal. "Never much considered it. I'm not religious, if that's what you mean."

"It's not."

I wait for him to explain. It's not that I don't believe Daniel or the spirits or whatever; I just don't believe much of anything. I know what Moony believed, and it never really registered with me. I'm not completely clear on what my mom believes—though it's night and day from Moony—but it's too hard to take anything she says or does seriously when I know the illness is always there lurking. But after my run-ins of late, my dreams and whatever you call what happened in the cathedral and the courtyard and on my walk here yesterday, I don't feel like I'm in a position to be certain about anything anymore. My own sense of reality is unraveling at the seams.

"My family has a religion; my grandmother and mother and aunties all go to church every Sunday. But then we have our beliefs. They're something else entirely. Not opposed, just different. My mawmaw Barb inherited her beliefs from her mother and mother-in-law and passed them on to me. You feel me? They're older than church, deeper than religion. They're part of our faith, beyond what any priest or preacher can tell you. It's not that unusual around here." Daniel's eyebrows raise. "You think I'm crazy, don't you?"

I laugh it off. "No, of course not. Having a belief doesn't make someone crazy. Lots of very sane, very functional people have those." I think of Moony's superstitions, always making me throw one heel of the bread away without eating it. *Bad luck, Cat. Never eat both ends or you'll lose money.* Or the way she would never sweep under my feet because she said it meant I wouldn't get married.

Daniel grins. "I'm not sure if you're trying to convince me or yourself."

I toss a dishcloth at him. "Stop it."

"I guess New Orleans doesn't exactly provide a conventional upbringing."

"Well, you're in good company because I wouldn't know anything about those."

Daniel smiles at me, and this time it is full and bright and brimming with gratitude. "You're something," he says after a minute. "You know that? I've never met anyone like you."

Something gushes through me, a wave of oxytocin. I think I feel myself lifting, an instantaneous rush that is gone just as suddenly as it arrived. I look at Daniel. Is he causing this? Is this what it feels like to fall for someone?

"In all seriousness," he says, straightening. "Tell me about this feeling."

I decide I like his term better. "The needle, you mean?"

"Right."

"I guess I've always wondered what made my mom the way she is. Like, what was her original trigger?"

"Original trigger?" Daniel has moved on to the last pepper shaker at the last table. He uncaps it and holds his hand out. I pass him my funnel.

"People who suffer from mental illness, stuff like bipolar disorder and schizophrenia, they sometimes have a trigger—an original trauma—that is responsible for causing their first episode or psychotic break. It's usually something stressful. A major life change, like a death."

"Or a birth?" he asks quietly.

"Exactly." I see the image of the ghostly white baby in my mother's arms again, so tiny and helpless and gone. "Most people have their first episode in their teens or early adulthood. This thing, this *event*, happens, and if they are susceptible to the disease, it pushes them over the edge."

"So, you think your mom had one of these events and you didn't know about it?" Daniel recaps the pepper shaker, and we walk our remaining supplies back to the kitchen.

Maybe more than one. "Well, something set it off. It's not always enough just to have the genetic predisposition."

He nods thoughtfully. "I get that."

"But..."

"*But?*" he presses.

"My grandmother used to talk about my mom like she was

always sick, even when she was a kid. She never mentioned anything my mom went through or might have experienced that could have triggered her. She never shared any memories of my mom before her episodes. She made it sound like that's just who Mary was. Almost like it was to be expected."

"And was it?"

"I don't know," I tell him. "I guess that's what I'm trying to find out. The research says it isn't likely. But some people do get diagnosed as children. And for as long as I can remember, my mom has been sick. So if something did happen to her, it had to have happened before I came along. And maybe if there was a Mary *before* bipolar disorder, then there can be a Mary *after*."

It sounds an awful lot like hope, but I don't want to call it that. I don't want to know her, I tell myself. I want to know *about* her. And there's a difference. I want to see what makes her tick out of sync with the rest of the world. Like Moony's watch, I want to peek at the gears. And then I want to peel back the layers of myself and see if the same thing exists inside of me—a cog out of place, a gear too many.

We shut off all the lights, and I head for the door, but Daniel grabs a soda and slides into a table instead. I follow him, the soft lighting of the Quarter filtering in through the large windows, casting slanting shadows across every surface. "Could it have been you?" he asks gently.

"My birth, you mean?" It's something I've never let myself consider but that has haunted me since she left me at Moony's. Was I the trigger for my mom's first mental episode? Is that why she abandoned me?

He shrugs. "It's possible. It's a major life event."

I fiddle with the cuff of my sleeve. It's hard to imagine your birth that way, not the joy and celebration it should be, but a stressor from which your mother can never recover. "I guess, except..."

Daniel leans in.

"I found this photo in her room. She was keeping it in a frame behind one of my school pictures." I pass my phone to Daniel, let him see the picture I took of the polaroid.

"Wow." Daniel sees instantly what took me several moments to process. "This is the sister you mentioned?"

"Right."

"And you never knew?"

I shake my head. "Not at all. My mother never breathed a word about it, and neither did Moony."

"Moony?"

"My grandmother."

"Glad I'm not the only one with a weird grandmother name. She looks young here," he says, passing the phone back to me.

"I know."

"And you don't think maybe it's a cousin's or a friend's baby or something?"

"No. I don't have cousins. My mom is an only child. And she's obviously crying in the photo. And why would she keep it hidden with my picture like that if the baby belonged to someone else?"

Daniel sighs. "You got me."

"I think this might be the trigger."

"Makes sense."

"I know. So why do I keep feeling like there's more?"

Daniel's eyes are without shadows, and he looks directly at me when he talks. He cares in a way few people do. "I don't know, Cat. You tell me."

And I do. I tell him all about finding my birth certificate and those weird cards from Moony to my mom, the college in New Hampshire, the statement revealing the money Moony promised to me was gone. I tell him about the night my mother left me, and growing up with Moony, and how it could be so amazing and so awful at the same time when I lived with my mother before. I tell him about Gary and the fight and my mom's weirdness at the cathedral and what she said about high school. I even tell him about the tarot deck I've been hiding for the last ten years as my only link to her.

What I leave out is the man with the peppermint schnapps and the boy in the yellow waistcoat, the woman with galaxies in her eyes and the magician with the painted face. The skeletons on parade the night Moony died. The cloak full of stars. The color of falling.

Because I don't want Daniel's face to change. I don't want that expression of interest and compassion and affection to go away, to become something uncertain or fearful or distant. Because all the other things I do tell him are my mom's things, but these—these encounters I can't explain—are mine. And for the first time in my life, I cannot point to my mother's mental illness as the reason for my suffering.

When I'm finished, Daniel leans back and props an elbow up on the back of the booth. He lets out a low whistle. "That's some history you got."

I hold my breath, realizing I've said too much. I am a package deal. You never get just me. You get me *plus* the crazy mom *plus* the dead grandmother *plus*, *plus*, *plus*...All those pluses are bound to scare most people off. But Daniel looks cool as crushed ice. "So?" I finally ask. "Are you regretting getting me this job?"

He leans in. “Are you kidding me? I’m regretting I didn’t meet you until a few days ago.”

My heart flops. I eye him warily.

“Cat, you’ve been through a lot, stuff most people could never imagine, and you’re still standing. Do you know what that says about you?”

I shake my head, an embarrassing lump forming like a fist in my throat.

“You’re strong, girl. And you’re deep. You have a lot to offer *because* of your experiences, not in spite of them.”

I let out an anxious breath. “Are you sure you’re real? I’m not hallucinating you or anything?” *It wouldn’t be the first time*, I think uncomfortably.

Daniel laughs. “Nah, I’m real. I just know how it feels to stand in the middle of a shitstorm and wonder which way is up. My parents had a bad split followed by a few rough years while they processed their denial. I was young, but I remember that feeling, like it would never change, never get better, like either everyone around you was losing it, or you were already lost.” He stands up. “Come on, we gotta get you home so you can get some sleep. You got a big day tomorrow.”

“But I’m not on the schedule,” I tell him. “Neither are you.”

“I know,” he says grinning. “But as my mawmaw Barb always says, this mess ain’t gonna clean itself. I don’t know about you, but I think we should start with the tarot deck and that Halloween card you found. Seems like the easiest piece of your puzzle to place.”

I’m speechless. “Why do you want to help me?”

“Are you serious? Helping a cute girl untangle her sordid family history? Maybe if I do a good enough job, you'll think about sticking around for a while. Leave New Hampshire to the Yankees."

Cute. He called me cute. I'm so stupidly flattered I can't respond. I recall the boy at my old high school that nearly every girl had a crush on, Jared Kahn. The nicest thing I ever heard him say in two years was "nice boobs" when Chelsie McCanna flashed the entire cafeteria on a dare.

Maybe my mom isn't so wrong about New Orleans after all.

XV.

THE STORE WE'RE PERUSING IS TIGHT AND CLOISTERED. Purple-painted shelves hold row upon row of occult books, herb-crusted candles, hex dolls, and rare crystals. There is a whole section of potions for everything from finding love to curing male pattern baldness. The window hangs with stained-glass pentacles, fairies, and Celtic knotwork. And the whole place smells of nag champa and cloves. It is a hodgepodge of magical beliefs, both ancient and nouveau, all crammed into one tiny and probably haunted shop in the Quarter. And it is the fifth one exactly like it that we've been to today.

It is the kind of store my mother would love and likely one she has visited many times over. I leave Daniel fingering an assortment of ready-made mojo bags in a rainbow of organza as I home in on the selection of tarot and oracle cards they carry. Here, at least, is where this shop differs from the others. They carry three to four shelves more fortune decks than any other store we've visited.

As my vision shifts from one eye-popping box to another, I start to deflate. Even though all the decks have things in common and many of them are similar to my deck—the one my mother left with me so many years ago—not a single one is the *same* deck as mine. I look again at the box of my own tarot cards. No author name. No artist name. There is nothing to hint at whether or not one of these decks shares the same publisher or copyright date as my own. I try to determine if any of the illustration styles are close enough to assume the artist might be the same, but my deck is a bit off from all of these. And that means I can't get another glimpse of the missing Moon card beyond what I saw on the Magician's table that day.

I shudder involuntarily as his crosswise face and silver-topped cane flood my memory, the feeling of a thousand useless golden coins pelting me from above. I might have thought I'd imagined it all but for the very real bruises dotting my collarbones the next morning. When I looked at the Magician card in my deck all those years, I never imagined he'd be such a dick.

Daniel steps next to me, and I take in a deep, delicious breath of his evergreen-and-lemongrass-scented cologne. "Any luck?" he asks.

I shake my head. "Nope. Apparently, this is some kind of rare edition."

"Let me see," he says, sliding the box from my hand. He holds it up next to a couple of similarly colored boxes, but mine is obviously different. The dark navy background and red and yellow details are accented with white and black and purple. The art has more depth and shading than most, even if the colors are relatively basic. The style is like a dream of a carnival in Wonderland. Something in the corners and the angles gives it a sinister touch, unlike the frank expressions of the decks before me. And some of the cards have symbols I've never seen before.

"You got me," he says, passing it back. "It's sort of like all of these, but not."

"Right?" I sigh.

"Can I help you?"

We both turn to see a dark-haired woman standing behind us. She is not an inch over five feet, with razor-straight bangs and huge eyes that dominate her severe face. She wears a long chain with a pentacle the size of a pie plate at the end, and her purple top has a lace neckline. She blinks as if we have startled her and not the other way around, but her smile is warm.

"I'm looking for a deck like this one," I tell her, holding up my own. "But I don't see any here."

She holds a hand out and slips on a pair of reading glasses. I pass her my deck and she studies the box, delicately turning it over in her pale hands. She slides out a few cards and flips through them, then slides them back in. "Where did you get this?" she asks.

"My mom. It was hers when she was young."

She looks at me, studying my face like she did the cards, and hands the deck back over. "I've been reading professionally for many years, and I've never seen the like."

"Oh." I'm not sure what to do with that. I tuck it away to analyze later. "Maybe we should check online?"

She shrugs. "You could. Decks go out of print all the time. Some dealers continue to collect and sell them over the internet. There are also a lot of independent deck creators these days, but you said this was older?"

"Yes." Though I'm not sure how old.

"Any particular reason you're looking for another one?" She folds her glasses back up and slips them into her shirt.

"It's missing a card," I tell her.

Her face brightens. She's curious. "Which one?"

"The Moon," Daniel says before I can.

She laughs as if she and my deck are in on a joke together.

"What's funny?" I ask.

"It's fitting," she says. "The Moon is all about secrets and the subconscious. It is the dark coming into the light. It is what's buried rising from the grave."

Her words are ominous. "Really?"

"The dead don't always stay down," she suggests. "Like a lot of things we try to bury. Everything wants its day in the sun."

I feel my arms go shivery and my shoulders crawl toward my ears as if they can hide behind them.

"I'm sure the card will turn up when it's good and ready," she adds.

I look at Daniel, and he gives a small shrug. "You said you're a professional reader?" I ask her.

"Yes, it's a passion of mine and a gift. I have over two hundred decks in my personal collection."

It makes the rarity of mine all the more intriguing. If she hasn't seen it before, who has?

"What would the meaning be of the Devil, the Tower, and Death in a reading together?" They are the cards that were depicted on the Halloween card Moony sent my mom, the one with the cryptic message. I know my mother's interpretation of the last two at least—shake up plus a fresh start. But I'm curious how someone else would view them. I'm curious what Moony might have been trying to say.

Her spidery thin brows arch dramatically. "In that order?"

I nod.

"It means you're headed off a cliff," she says plainly, and I feel myself falling up through the dark as I did in my dream. I reach out to steady myself on a shelf.

"You okay?" Daniel asks with concern. He places a hand on my arm as if to keep me from falling.

"Yeah, just a little dizzy." I look at the woman again. "What do you mean by that?"

"The Devil is bondage to a false truth. The Tower is the shattering of all we've built upon that illusory foundation. And Death is the end of one cycle that another may be born to take its place." She folds her arms. "Usually people pay me for this."

"Sorry."

"You don't read for yourself?" she asks me, eyeing my weird, little deck again.

"Oh, no. These are just...sentimental."

She nods. "I see. Well, if you ever want to learn more, you know where to find me."

"Yes." I tug on Daniel's arm. "Come on. Let's go eat."

"I thought you'd never ask," he quips.

But as we near the door, I turn back with one more question. "Just so we're clear, the Death card—it's symbolic? Right? I mean, the cards aren't meant to be *literal*." Did Moony believe my mom was in danger of dying?

"Mostly," she says, leaning across the counter on her elbows. "But sometimes, on *rare* occasions"—she casts her eyes at the deck in my hand again—"the truth is as plain as their faces."

I shudder as the skeletons from my dream the night Moony died march coldly across my memory.

XVI.

WE ARE TRYING TO FIND ONE LAST SHOP—AN OBSCURE occult goods store in Mid-City listed as Fortune's Gate on Google. It has an address but no phone number, and absolutely no reviews.

Daniel has borrowed his cousin's Pontiac for this. He comes from one of those big families where everybody shares everything and is in everybody's business—the Mathis clan. Even though he's a Walker like his dad. He's been regaling me with stories. They have their dysfunctional points, but overall they sound loving and happy. Who am I to judge? Daniel's version of dysfunctional—his older sister and cousin fighting over the same guy and an uncle who consistently drinks too much at family gatherings—may as well be the perfect family to me.

"It says it should be right here. I don't understand." I stare out the window at the convenience store and barbecue joint sandwiched together. According to Google maps, it should be right in this strip. "Maybe there's a back entrance?"

"Maybe," Daniel concedes. "Let's get lunch and regroup. I'm starving. I thought we were gonna eat after the last place."

We were. But something about Fortune's Gate—the striped awning in the picture or the grand name—made me press for one last stop. "Okay. We tried."

I agree to a little diner that's just around the corner for lunch. The menu is full of homecooked favorites like fried chicken and half a dozen kinds of pie. I load up on potato salad and cornbread and let Daniel eat the chicken I can't finish. We decide to split a slice of lemon meringue. Daniel insists lunch is on him.

It's over pie and coffee that we decide to ask around about Fortune's Gate. I don't know when I'll get this chance again, and if I don't start filling in the gaps, I'll never be able to see the full picture.

Our waitress brings the check around and smiles. I can't help but notice how she eyes Daniel, and I can't blame her. She looks like she's only about five years older than we are, and Daniel is to the eyes what meringue is to the tongue. I click my teeth in irritation.

Daniel grins. "Can we ask you something?"

Kathee pops her gum. I know her name is Kathee because of the white plastic name tag. "Sure thing, sugar."

I hate it when strangers call me by some generic term of endearment like "sugar" or "honey" or "sweetie." It is an aversion I inherited from Moony.

Daniel winks at me. "We're looking for a place called Fortune's Gate. Ever heard of it?"

She chews her bottom lip and casts her eyes up. "Nope, can't say that I have."

Daniel looks defeated. He leans toward the waitress, and I watch her catch her ponytail with a finger and twirl it.

"Do you think you could ask around for me? Maybe someone else here has? It's supposed to be in the neighborhood." He flashes a boyish smile at her, and she practically skips back to the kitchen.

I roll my eyes. I doubt he is unaware of his effect on her.

"I saw a gas station next door with a tire shop in it. We can ask there too," he says.

"I don't think there will be someone like Kathee at the tire shop for you to work your magic on." I cannot miss the sting in my tone, a dash of bitters to wash the sarcasm down. I feel like my mom, small and paranoid. I instantly wish I could gobble the words from the air before they reach Daniel's ears. Instead, I shove a large bite of lemon pie in my mouth and blush.

Daniel leans back and appraises me. "Okay. I see how it is. This is a side of Cat I haven't met before. Hi, *jealous*. I'm Daniel." He laughs easily at my discomfort, and I nearly choke on lemon and whipped sugar.

I'm wiping meringue off my mouth with a napkin when Kathee returns.

"Sorry, hon. No place by that name around here. I asked everyone in the kitchen."

"Thanks for trying," Daniel says, flashing his grin at me instead of her. "Must be closed."

She shrugs her polyester-clad shoulders. "Never heard of it. You sure you aren't looking in the wrong district?"

"Probably."

"You might try Central City or Uptown," she says with a nod.

"We'll do that," he agrees.

But I know I did not read the listing wrong. We're in the right place. It's Fortune's Gate that is lost.

We get up after paying and head out the glass door to the small, pockmarked parking lot. An older woman follows us out.

"You asking about Fortune's Gate?" she says with a raspy smoker's voice.

Daniel and I turn. I give him a wary look. "Yeah. You know it?"

She eyes me strangely. Her blue-gray hair fans around her face in a halo of frizz, and her olive skin is peppered with liver spots. She's too thin, wiry with wrinkles sagging over her bones. She carries a motorcycle helmet in one hand. Her left arm is covered in a snake tattoo. Her right arm is inked with the sphinx. As I watch, they seem to move in and out of position, slithering over her like they're trapped. I shake my head to make them stop.

Where have I seen those together before? My mind whirls and my palms sweat. I switch my tarot deck box from one hand to the other as I wipe my hands on my shorts. My deck. The World card.

She looks suspicious. "How old are you?"

"Why?"

"How do you know about Fortune's Gate?"

Land on your feet, Cat. "My mom bought a deck of cards there." I wave my tarot box between us to back up my story. "But it's missing a card. I wanted to see if they had any more."

She eyes my tarot box as if deciding something. "It's around the corner," she says after a moment. "Next to Little Will's, the barbecue joint."

I shake my head again. "No, we were just there."

She looks me up and down with black marble eyes. "You must not have been looking hard enough."

I open my mouth to defend myself, but she is already stalking away. The Devil's words filter through my mind—*Open your eyes*—as I watch her climb onto a vintage orange-and-black motorcycle a few parking spaces over and rev the engine loudly. She speeds off before I can get a word out.

I turn to Daniel, my mouth still hanging open like a Venus flytrap.

"You heard her," he says. "We must have missed it." Then he rolls his eyes as if she's just some bonkers motorcycle lady. But I can't help feeling chided by her words. As if it is my fault somehow that Fortune's Gate is not where it belongs.

We climb into his cousin's car and head back the way we came. I am moping as I stare out the window when Little Will's comes into view.

"Stop!" I shout, throwing a hand against the glass.

Daniel slams on the brakes in the middle of the road. Luckily, there is no one behind us. "Cat, you nearly gave me a heart attack."

"It's there! It's there. Turn in!" I am tapping the glass feverishly, not quite believing my own eyes.

Daniel peers at me but obeys. He pulls into the lot and parks facing the street. I look over my shoulder and there, narrowly squished between the Shop Stop and Little Will's Bar-B-Q, is the black-and-white-striped awning from the internet picture. I stare as if it might vanish at any moment.

"How did we miss this?" he questions beside me.

We didn't.

"I don't know." I try pulling it back up on my phone, but now when I search for the internet listing I read earlier, it's not there. As if by appearing in the physical world, Fortune's Gate has disappeared from the online one.

"Let's go inside." I unbuckle my seat belt and climb out of the car.

As we near the store, I see the giant moon decal across the plate-glass window. It blocks our view of the store's interior. I cringe as the shadow of the awning slides over my skin with a fickle breeze. A sign over the door reads *Fortune is a strange caller*.

Daniel reaches out to open the door for me, but it doesn't budge. "Huh. Locked." He steps back.

I try it myself, as if maybe he just didn't pull hard enough, but he's right. It's locked up tight. "That's weird."

He shrugs. "Maybe they went to lunch. Maybe that's why we missed it before."

"The whole store?"

He shrugs again. "I don't know. I mean, we obviously overlooked it."

He is reluctant to believe otherwise. I don't blame him. Buildings don't just come and go like people. But I am equally as reluctant to mistrust my own eyes.

"We can try another day," he says, taking a second step back.

But I don't want to chance it. Who says Fortune's Gate will be here another day? I tap my jaw, thinking, and accidentally hit one of the bruises from my run-in with the Magician. It brings the whole encounter flooding back into my mind. But it also reminds me of something. I glance at the door for confirmation. "Hold on. Let me try one thing."

I dig deep in the pocket of my cutoffs and pull out the key from that afternoon, the one the Magician urged me to take. It slips easily into the oversized keyhole that looks about a hundred years older than the rest of the door. It turns without resistance, and when I give the door a tug, it opens wide.

Daniel stares at me.

"It's a skeleton key," I say, as if that explains it. "After you."

A cascade of bells goes off as we enter. Right away, I can smell peppermint, but laced over it is cinnamon and jasmine and patchouli, weaving a tapestry of fragrance that plucks at every corner of my aura. Instinctively, I take Daniel's hand. He doesn't draw back or act surprised, but instead laces his fingers through mine.

Tall shelves line the walls, and rows of high tables are stacked with candles in every color, figurines of old gods, talismans in odd shapes with odder sigils inscribed on them. I pick up a jar full of amber-colored oil on the first table and tilt it before my face. Glittering snowflakes seem to swirl and dance inside in a stream of purple and gold, but there's no label. No price tag. The lid is sealed with black wax. I set it back down and give Daniel a questioning glance. He shrugs and we move on.

There's a silver-plated bowl with claw feet that holds bags filled with herbs. Mojos, maybe nation sacks? But again—no labels, no price tags. There are jars upon jars of incense sticks in candy colors all jammed together. Each one smells different than the last. I recognize blackberries baking in the summer heat and antique roses climbing over a trellis, fields of French lavender and the soft crush of damp, green moss on a forest floor. But none of the jars are labeled.

There are brass oil burners and baskets full of quartz. Chicken feet curl like dead spiders next to fans made of oily black feathers. Bones in more shapes and sizes than I knew existed are sorted into wooden trays. Ribbons in every shade of the rainbow are wound on wooden bobbins as big as my wrist. And bottles of oils in slippery greens, creamy yellows, burning oranges, and ruby-rich reds line up next to one another.

There are impossible things like jars full of indescribable blue and purple light and bottles that sigh when you pop the cork. There are unusual things like mushrooms with red-spotted caps growing on stacks of old, soggy wood, and butterfly wings that are as vibrant as the day they were harvested.

I turn from the wares on the tables to one of the bookshelves. But immediately, I realize that these are unlike the books in any other store. The covers are hand bound in dyed leather or stiff linen. Some of the books are just jumbles of old parchment bound together with braids of brightly colored yarn. Others have brass or silver locks with missing keys. There are very few with titles, and those that do have them are named things like *A Story of Spells in the Seventh Tongue* or *Rainmaking for Backward Lands*. I can't make heads or tails of them.

We are alone in the store. It's dark inside, as the moon decal and awning seem to block most of the natural light. Fortune's Gate seems impossibly large once you're in it. I don't see a counter or register anywhere. Above me hang rack after rack of drying flowers, the ceiling lost behind them.

"Does this place seem weird to you?" Daniel finally leans over my shoulder and asks.

I nod, though weird is starting to become routine for me. I could see the Magician shopping in a place like this, pocketing charms and stones with his mouth and eyes smiling and frowning at the same time. "Maybe we should go. I don't see any tarot decks."

"Yeah," Daniel agrees. "This store is starting to give me the creeps." He points to a giant stone basin overflowing with nine-inch iron spikes.

Just as we turn for the door, he appears. Or maybe it's *she*. To be honest, I can't tell for certain. Which is fitting because the World card always features an intersex person—unity in the balance of opposing forces. They are waif thin and wearing an oversized tunic with hair past their shoulder blades and pale as spider silk. In one hand, they hold a bottle like the one I first picked up but without the wax seal. In the other hand is a smaller vial from which they are pouring a dark-green liquid into the first. Their eyes are trained on Daniel and me, but they never spill a drop. After a moment, they set the vial down, cork the bottle, and shake it lazily. "Looking for something?"

"Oh. We were just leaving." I give Daniel's hand a squeeze, not sure how to handle this. Our new friend is blocking the path to the door.

"So soon?" They switch from shaking the bottle to rubbing it between their hands as if to keep it warm. "But you were looking for something, weren't you? Otherwise, you never would have found us."

I drop Daniel's hand and pull out my tarot deck, holding it up. Their eyes are angled and rusty brown like a fox. They hold up the bottle they're rubbing and say, "You have to keep them moving or they lose potency."

I raise my brows.

"The Valormint blooms," they supply, as if I am really stupid not to know. "Oh, forget it. What are those?"

"Tarot cards," I explain. "I was trying to find another deck like them. You're the last store on our list."

"Here," they say, tossing the bottle to Daniel, who catches it with wide eyes. "Just keep it moving." They beckon with two free hands, and I pass my box over. "Oh yes," they say with interest. "I remember these."

"You do?" I turn to shoot a look of shock at Daniel, who is carefully moving the bottle of petals and oil up and down.

"Of course," they say, passing them back with a serene smile. "They were purchased here a long time ago, but I never forget a sale."

After a moment, I ask. "Well, do you have any more?"

"Oh no, I'm afraid that's the only deck of its kind."

"I don't understand." I look from my box to the clerk.

"I mean that there's just the one." They hold up a single finger.

"I know what *only* means," I say. "But it's printed."

"Uh-huh." They are losing interest, beginning to pick at their nails and straighten a pile of clear jelly soaps on the table next to us.

"So who would ever print just one? It doesn't make any sense."

They scoff. "Who would ever print *more* than one?" As if I am talking nonsense. "No, that deck bears no repeating. Any more would be dangerous."

"How so?"

They shrug. "The cards—*those* cards—are whatever someone needs them to be. Can you imagine? If more than one person at a time got their hands on something like that?"

They make the cards sound like a nuclear weapon, but they have only ever been cards to me. Until...I think of the Devil and shudder. Still, I can't see how this is what I need—creepy men with peppermint booze shadowing me and golden coins flying at my face? They have to be mistaken.

I shake my head. I am starting to lose my hold on the world in this ludicrous store.

"Never mind," I huff, and take the bottle from Daniel, handing it back to the clerk.

They look surprised. "Careful, careful! You don't want to upset them."

I assume they mean the whatever-mint flowers in the bottle, but I don't ask because I don't care. I just want to get out of this store before my mind implodes. My eyes begin to water, which makes me feel angry and exposed. "I just wanted to find the stupid missing card," I blab under my breath as I pass.

"Whyever didn't you say so?" they exclaim. "Fortune's Gate always has what you're looking for."

I spin around to face the clerk. "But you just said—"

"Though it isn't often the same as what you want," they add quickly.

I feel my fingers ball into fists at my side.

"Which one are you missing? No! Let me guess. Is it the Moon?" They clasp their hands, waiting for my response.

"How did you know?" I ask.

They give me a wry smile. "The Moon is tricky. Doesn't like to be nailed down. Now let me see...I know I have that card somewhere here." They are turning over mismatched goblets and spilling bowls of dry herbs and spices. "I saw it only a moon ago. Get it? A *moon* ago!"

They are laughing to themselves when Daniel smacks my arm and points out the front door.

In the parking lot, I can just make out a couple of kids leaning up against his cousin's car.

"Shit, they're trying to pop the lock." He leans away. "Bernard is going to kill me if I lose his car." And just like that, he is running full tilt through the store, out the door, and into the parking lot.

Wanting to help, I bolt after him. We reach the car in time to run the kids off before any real harm can be done, but not in time to catch them. Daniel chucks a piece of loose asphalt after them. "Don't even think about coming back, fools!" But they're long gone.

I put a hand on his arm. "That was close, huh?"

"That's New Orleans for you," he gripes, giving me a relieved smile.

I smile and turn back to Fortune's Gate, but the black-and-white awning, the moon decal, and the cascade of bells are all gone. Little Will's bumps right up against the Shop Stop as if nothing else was ever there.

I grip Daniel's arm, my nails creasing his flesh.

"Cat?"

I turn back to him. "Time to go."

"Am I missing something?"

"The strip is missing something," I respond.

"What?" he says, but climbs into the driver's seat and pops the lock for me.

"Nothing," I tell him, refusing to look back so Daniel won't. The strip *is* missing something. It's missing the store we were just in.

XVII.

THE DRIVE BACK TO THE QUARTER FEELS TWICE AS long as the one to Mid-City. I shuffle restlessly through Daniel's playlist and then finally turn the speakers off. We ride in disquieting silence for another few minutes before Daniel speaks up.

"So, do you want to talk about it?"

"What?"

Daniel sighs. "Whatever is bothering you."

"Is it that obvious?" I bite my lip.

"It's pretty obvious."

"Sorry." I twist my fingers together in my lap, then shake them out. I don't know how to tell Daniel what I saw. I don't know what I saw. It *seems* like an entire store showed up out of nowhere after some old motorcycle lady told us it would and then vanished again when we weren't looking. It seems like Fortune's Gate is not governed by the laws of physics. It seems like this city is getting under my skin and causing me to lose it.

It seems like today only provided more questions, rather than answers.

"I think I'm just processing," I say. Which is both true and not.

"They recognized your deck," he comes back brightly. "And you got some answers about that Halloween card you found. I don't know how much closer this brings you to understanding everything going on with your family, but it's more than you had yesterday."

I nod but I'm still sulking. I've done my research. I know the appropriate labels. I know bipolar and schizoaffective. I know personality disordered and psychotic and paranoid. What I don't know is how to define the experience I just had—any of the experiences I've had since getting here. Losing Moony has meant losing practical, orderly, reliable Cat. This version of me is scared of boogey men in face paint and being inside a building when it goes *poof*. This version of me is unrecognizable. I don't know her, don't trust her.

This is not the Cat I wanted Daniel to see.

"What do you think it means?" Daniel is pensive, his face drawn in toward the center. "I mean, now that you know what you do about that combination of tarot cards. What do you think your grandmother was trying to say?"

I take a moment to just breathe and shift my focus from what I can't explain to what I can. That Halloween card was posted several months before my mother's last visit when I was thirteen—the one where I told her not to come back because seeing what the medication was doing to her was almost harder than seeing what the disorder was doing to her. Moony sent it in the middle of my mother's last manic episode. "I think she was trying to warn my mom."

"Of what?"

Perhaps of men who drink peppermint schnapps. Perhaps of little boys who cliff dive and women who wear the sky. Of coming here. Of falling up.

"I guess of her lifestyle. I mean, she's always taken risks, lived fast. She didn't go to college. Didn't get a regular job. Didn't marry or settle down. She's always been...I don't know, *her*. I think there is the bipolar disorder, and then I think there is the way she lives and the choices she makes that can only aggravate the disorder. But then, that's where it all gets confusing. Is she making those choices? Or is bipolar disorder making them for her? I think Moony knew my mom was really sick and needed help, and that if she didn't get it, if she didn't change her course, something terrible might happen."

"I understand what you're saying. It's just, why would your grandmother need tarot cards to say that?" Daniel glances at me with soft eyes.

"I don't know. Maybe she was doing something different, something more than before. Maybe she knew my mother wouldn't listen to her, but..."

"She'd listen to the cards," Daniel finishes for me.

I nod. "When my mom is...at her worst, she thinks all kinds of things that make no sense. She doesn't trust the people she should, and she does trust all the people she shouldn't. She sees messages and signs where the rest of us just see a greeting card or a bird or a wad of gum on the ground. It's like magical thinking on steroids."

A lightbulb moment sends sparklers through my brain. Maybe my mom was already reading cards then. Maybe Moony thought my mother would only get worse if she opened herself to tarot—an innocent deck of cards in most hands but something more to Mary. Even then, the cards meant something different, something powerful to my mom, and Moony knew that.

"I guess this doesn't really tell you anything about your original trigger theory yet."

I take a breath. "No. I still need to figure out whatever I can about the baby in the picture." How it got there. And how it was kept a secret for so long.

I look out the window at a blur of green and gray and brown. Who is the woman I call *mother*? Is she a young girl with a dead child? Is she a good little Catholic schoolgirl, complete with modest uniform? Is she Mary, the Madonna of New Orleans, reading people's fortunes in the square for an easy buck? Is she the woman who was so happy to have me here, making terrible breakfasts and chattering like old friends? Or the one who seethed and pouted, believing I was capable of trying to steal her man? Or the one who left me at Moony's so many years ago, her cheeks wet and pallid as she backed out the front door and drove away?

And how did she come across a deck like the one I'm holding from Fortune's Gate?

I realize I don't know her at all.

"Hey, you going to be okay with all of this?" Daniel asks. His face is etched with concern. I see it riding the peak of his brows and drawing down the corners of his mouth.

"I don't know." It is the truth.

"I'm sorry, Cat. I thought knowing more would help you. This was my idea, and I feel like it's just made more of a mess of things."

I realize he is feeling almost as awkward and uncertain about today as I am. "No, this isn't on you. I'm the one who dumped my whole sordid family tale in your lap after only knowing you for... what? A few days?"

"I'm glad you told me. I know you better now. You're real. I like that."

I smile sheepishly. "Maybe you know me too well. It's a little embarrassing. I don't want you to think that...that I'm like her."

Daniel grabs my hand. "It was obvious in the first five seconds of meeting you two how different you are. Your mom, she's like New Orleans at night—all dazzling bright lights and chaotic music on the surface, but a lot of shadows lingering in between, in the dark corners we don't like to look at. And you, you're the bedrock, the brick and mortar in broad daylight that actually holds the city together. You're solid and honest and full of history."

I've never thought of us that way. I always insisted I was different from her. I needed to be different. But I recognize now that it was because I was afraid that I wasn't. Hearing someone else say it out loud puts the fear back in its box. Except Daniel doesn't know about all the things I've witnessed since coming here. And I wonder if he'd say the same if he did.

"Besides, my family is far from perfect. One night with us and you'll realize you aren't the only one with skeletons in the closet."

I can't help laughing. "Thank you. Really."

"In fact, in order to even the scales, I think you should come to dinner tonight. We'll be home just in time. What do you say?"

Mary thinks I am working a long shift today. She won't know the difference. And she had several phone clients scheduled to keep her busy. Focusing on someone else's family issues sounds like just the antidote I need. "Yeah, sure. Sounds fun."

Daniel rolls his eyes. "Oh, girl, you have no idea what you just agreed to."

We pull up to a white, shotgun-style house on a colorful street that glows in the golden evening light. The front is characteristically narrow, with a single shuttered window and a royal blue front door, a small porch with a handful of steps. Two kids, a boy and a girl who can't be older than ten, are circling in front, barefoot, on bicycles. Daniel parks at the very end of the driveway and gets out. I do the same.

"Marco, Danielle—what did Lena tell you about being out with no shoes on?"

The kids freeze, each putting one dirty foot on the pavement to still their bikes. The concrete has to be a hundred degrees, but they don't seem to notice. I marvel at the resiliency of children. I remember a lavender bicycle with purple streamers that Moony bought me the Christmas after my mother left. I never learned how to ride it without the training wheels. She finally sold it in a church garage sale.

The boy drops his bike once he recognizes Daniel and runs up to him. "What are you doing in Bernard's car?" he asks, ignoring Daniel's question. He sees me a moment after tackling Daniel around the midsection and adds, "Who is she?"

Daniel peels him off and ruffles his dark hair. "Rude much? Marco, this is Cat. Say hi."

"Hi," he complies, running back to pick up his bike. His sister stares at me with an open expression and the kind of unabashed interest only children are comfortable displaying.

"Cat, this is Marco and this is Danielle, the twins. They belong to my oldest sister, Lena." He says this last bit with a good-natured smirk. "Your momma in the house?" he asks them.

"Yeah," Marco responds, walking his bike up to the porch and leaning it against the railing. "Why is she here?" he asks now, giving me a funny look.

"You know she can hear you, right?" Daniel teases him, reaching to nudge him on the shoulder.

Marco ignores this and ducks Daniel's hand. His sister is still standing in the street, watching us. "Where's Madeline?"

Daniel grimaces. "None of your business. Now go inside and wash up before Mawmaw comes out here and catches you with no shoes on."

Marco makes a beeline for the house and his sister finally shakes from her stupor, running in behind him, but not without dodging me first.

"Sorry about that," Daniel says shyly. "No manners."

"They're kids," I say with a shrug.

He laughs. "They're half-wild, both of them."

I smile. "So, who's Madeline?"

Daniel stops halfway up the porch steps. "The ex-girlfriend I told you about. She kind of grew on the kids."

I nod and inhale deeply. *Awesome.* I am making a first impression while still in someone else's shadow.

"Now or never," he says, grabbing my hand. We ascend the steps to the porch and push the front door open, stepping inside.

The living room is bustling with people, more warm bodies than I assumed could actually fit in this space. Two men sit on the sofa, flipping through channels on a flat screen that's too low to hear. The twins are running back and forth with wet feet, fighting over a pink bath towel. A toddler in a plastic walker bumps the coffee table repeatedly, setting glasses of tea and cold beer cans vibrating. A teenage girl, maybe two years younger than me, is putting silverware on the table in the dining room with one hand while she holds her cell to her ear with the other. The kitchen is just past that, and I can see several women narrowly missing bumping into each other, as if they are rehearsing a well-choreographed dance routine. A woman charges into the room from the back, hollering at one of the men to "Watch the baby, dang it!"

I shoot Daniel an overwhelmed expression.

He grins with pride. "I tried to warn you. This isn't even everybody."

I see Daniel's warm smile in the faces around me, his soft eyes, his proud brow. But I also see so many differences, a patchwork of people held together by name and love and history.

"Daniel's here! Daniel's here!" Marco goes yelling into the kitchen after conceding the towel to his sister. "And he brought a girl."

The teenager setting the table looks up. "Hold on," she says into her phone, setting it on the table. She runs up and gives Daniel a hug, then turns to me.

"Brittni, this is Cat. Cat, Brittni with an *i* not a *y*."

"Shut up," she says, punching him in the shoulder. "It's nice to meet you, Cat."

"Yeah," I stammer. "You too." I notice her nails are flawless and long as railway spikes. I wonder how she manages to hold her phone, or text, or type, or anything for that matter. But her smile is as warm as melted butter, and she looks at Daniel the way a kid sister looks at an older brother she adores.

She ducks back to the table to resume the silverware placement. I hear her pick up her phone and say, "You are not gonna believe this," as we turn toward the kitchen.

"You know the twins already. The little one is Matthew, and that's my uncle Charlie on the sofa, and my aunt Tiff's boyfriend, Victor." Daniel points them out. Both men nod and smile in succession but don't bother with more than that.

A woman pops up in the doorway of the kitchen before we can reach it with both hands on her hips. A damp dish towel hangs from one hand, and she is squinting at us over the top of her readers. She's short and a little stooped to boot, but she seems to fill the whole doorway with her presence. "Daniel, is that you, baby?"

"It's me, Mawmaw," he says, giving her a swift hug. "I brought someone."

"I know," she replies, looking me up and down.

Marco appears behind her. "Because I told you, huh, Mawmaw?"

"No, you foolish child, not 'cause you told me. Because Brittni dropped a fork on her way to the table, that's why."

Daniel's grandmother is tan where he is brown. Her eyes are the color of a deep pond—green where they should be brown and brown where they should be green—and her hair is gathered atop her head in loose, orange curls. She wears dangling wooden earrings shaped like leaves, and a starched white blouse with a stiff collar. The frames of her readers are a bright purple. They hang on a little gold chain around her neck when she takes them off.

"And who are you?" she asks me pointedly.

"Mawmaw, this is Cat," Daniel tells her.

"Was I asking you?" Her eyes widen at him.

"No, ma'am. But—"

"But nothing. Let the girl speak for herself." She looks at me. "You have a tongue, don't you?"

I'm not exactly sure what to do here. Mawmaw Barb's not like my mother, but her directness is as unnerving as my mother's inappropriate rambling. I catch Marco's eye as he peeks from behind his great-grandmother. He sticks his tongue out at me to drive her point home.

"I'm Cat," I say a little too loudly. "I work with Daniel."

She shoots Daniel the side eye. "Do you now? Well, come on in and get comfortable. I hope you're hungry 'cause we got more food than a rooster has tail feathers."

Daniel winks at me—another famous Mathis family saying.

"Yes, ma'am. I'm starved." The lemon meringue at lunch has put my blood sugar in a nosedive, and I can smell a dozen fragrant dishes emanating from the kitchen behind her.

Daniel and I help carry several dishes of food out to the table where Brittni is waiting with her phone glued to one ear. "No, I said a *date*. You know what? Let me call you back."

She tucks her phone into the back pocket of her impossibly skinny jeans and glares at Daniel. "Why didn't you text me back yesterday?"

"I was working."

She looks at me. "Cute new girl at the café and suddenly you're too good for your cousin? Is that it?"

For the first time, I see Daniel blush. "And y'all wonder why I don't bring anyone home for dinner."

"I'm just playing. I did need that ride though."

I feel bad as it dawns on me that Daniel was ignoring a text from a family member in need because he was listening to me spill my guts over all this weirdness with my mom. "I'm sorry," I pipe up. "I think that was my fault."

She smiles at me, and I can feel the sun in it. "Don't worry about it. I just like to give him a hard time. Carlo picked me up."

"You know I don't like you seeing him," Daniel says under his breath.

"You should answer your phone then," she shoots back.

Before he can respond, the women from the kitchen all file into the dining room. Mawmaw Barb stands at the head of the table. "Everyone take hands for the Our Father."

Even Uncle Charlie and Victor shuffle over for that, and she blesses the food. "Amen." She drops the twins' hands and takes a seat. "Eat up now. There's a second wave coming in an hour or so."

"Second wave?" I look at Daniel.

"More people," he says. "Probably my cousins Bernard and Andy, Little Steph, and Emily. And my aunt Wanda and uncle Beau. And who knows who else."

"How many aunties do you have?" I ask, trying to keep it all straight.

"Four," he answers, leaning in. "Plus my Aunt Nia, who isn't really my aunt but was best friends with my aunt Patrice growing up and practically lived here."

I glop a huge spoonful of mashed potatoes onto my plate and put the spoon back. I point to the floor. "Here? Meaning, this isn't your house?"

"This is my house, honey," Mawmaw Barb butts in from her end of the table. "Daniel's momma lives a few blocks down."

"Oh." I feel stupid for not realizing.

"These are my daughters—Tiffany, Patrice, and Desiree. Daniel's momma, Irene, is working late tonight. And Wanda, who you know from the café, will be by later." They all smile and say hello in between loading their plates up with boiled shrimp, okra, rice, and sautéed peppers.

A younger woman, maybe in her late twenties, smiles at me from across the table. "I'm Angela. I'm Daniel's sister."

I see the resemblance right away—the same soft slope of nose, the dip of lashes, the strong chin. "Nice to meet all of you," I respond.

I am ten minutes into my rice and okra when Daniel's grandmother breaks the silence. "So, Cat, tell us about yourself. You live here a long time?" She asks this last question as if she knows the answer already.

"No, ma'am. I only just moved here from upstate. My grandmother passed last week."

"Last week?" Daniel's Aunt Desiree practically chokes on her corn cob.

"Poor child," Patrice says.

"You were living with her then?" Mawmaw Barb questions.

"I was. I'm with my mom now. She's been here in New Orleans for several years."

The old woman scrutinizes me. "Mmhmm."

The table falls into talk about the latest political scandal and honorary aunt Nia's on-again-off-again boyfriend. I eat my meal in silence, feeling Daniel's warm and solid presence beside me. Once or twice, he squeezes my leg under the table. I realize he is trying to reassure me. As I listen to their conversation, I try to imagine what a family this large and dynamic feels like. It has always been just me and my mother or me and Moony. Never even the three of us. I have lived my whole life on the precipice of being alone, one great loss away from having no one. Daniel's family operates like a large safety net, like those schools of fish you see in nature documentaries that all move together.

Brittni takes a chair next to me as everyone clears the table after dinner. "Where are you zoned?" she asks brightly.

"Zoned?"

She grins. "What high school will you go to?"

I feel foolish. "I'm not sure yet."

"Probably Warren Easton. But I can help you figure it out. What was your old school like?"

I'm not sure how to describe my school back in Moony's town. I never felt out of place there, but I also never felt like I fit in. "Small."

"You won't have that problem here," Brittni says with a little too much enthusiasm as her phone begins vibrating and she rises to answer it. "Let me know when you're ready to shop for school clothes. I know where all the best boutiques are."

I watch her walk away and feel a pang of longing for my friends back home. I've been so wrapped up in all things Mary and the strange visitors I keep having that I haven't even bothered to text and tell them I've moved. The fact that no one has called only reiterates what a good job I've done keeping our connection to a minimum. I wonder how long it will take them to notice my absence if I never tell them goodbye.

I will need to do better here. I will need someone else if Mary is all I have left in the world—a friend I can trust. It means letting someone in. I realize I've already let Daniel closer than any of my friends back home. I feel the warmth of him to my right and wonder when I decided he was the one.

After dinner there are peanut butter cookies, vanilla ice cream, and chocolate cream pie. By the time we are ready to leave, I am stuffed to the gills with carbs and can barely walk. Daniel is hugging his mawmaw Barb goodbye when she decides to walk us out. On the porch, she stops me and wraps an arm around my shoulders.

"You're a good girl, Cat. I can tell. You keep an eye on my Daniel now, you hear? That boy is cuter than a puppy with two tails and not half as smart."

"Thanks for the vote of confidence, Mawmaw," he fires back.

She rolls her eyes at him. "You keep him out of trouble, and you'll have a place at my table any night of the week."

"Will do," I tell her, overcome by her sudden display of affection.

She shifts away from me, a strange look crossing her face. She makes the sign of the cross and looks to the street where a sudden breeze picks up. "Never alone, are you?" she says, not expecting a reply.

"Ma'am?"

She shudders visibly and slides her readers onto her nose. "You come back. You hear me, Cat?"

"Okay," I agree.

"Daniel," she barks into the night. "You bring this girl round again. She has need of me, like it or not."

He takes my hand and begins pulling me down the steps. "You got it, Mawmaw."

"And be careful," she shouts behind us. "The spirits are restless tonight."

XVIII.

WE SIT IN THE CAR OUTSIDE MY BUILDING. I CAN SEE the lights glowing through the courtyard out my window. Their golden hue highlights the tree branches and casts jungle shadows across the brick. I can see the orange eye of Butcher's cigarette. I can't decide if his near-constant presence in the courtyard is comforting or unnerving, but I think my mom is right. He *is* always watching.

I turn away from the window to face Daniel. I'm not ready to get out of the car. "Your grandmother was different than I pictured her."

Daniel smiles and nods. "You mean because she's light skinned?"

"And short," I add. "And ginger."

"Well, what she lacks in size she makes up for in personality," he tells me. "Mawmaw has mixed heritage. Her mother descended from the Louisiana Redbones—a group of mixed race settlers who came here from the Carolinas. The details of their ethnicity are still considered a mystery. And her father was Creole—West

African and French. My grandfather was Creole too, but Haitian on that side. And my father is black."

"Your family is like a history lesson." I grin at him.

He laughs. "It's not uncommon around here. New Orleans was such a prominent port for so long, pretty much everybody who hails from Louisiana has a family tree with a variety of branches."

"Do you see your dad?" I ask him.

He shrugs. "Sure. Always for the important things—birthdays, Christmas, school events. And I spend weekends with him several times a year."

"Do you miss him?"

"Of course," he says without hesitation. "But he lives in Shreveport, and he and my mom still don't always get along. I love 'em both, but they don't know how not to give each other a hard time."

"What was it like? Before he left?" I ask.

Daniel grins. "Before the fighting, when I was real young, I thought my dad was a badass. He used to box, not professionally or anything, but *I* thought he was the heavyweight champion of the world. He would carry me around on his shoulder, like a parrot. It felt like nothing could touch me so long as he was there."

"What changed?"

"I think he tried for a lot of years. But my mom, she can be tough. Not mean, but she doesn't take crap from anyone. He loved that about her, but he also railed against the idea of this little five-foot woman checking his ego all the time. The fighting became constant. It was better and worse when he finally left."

"I'm sorry," I tell him. I know that conundrum firsthand, when it is better and worse after they leave.

He looks at me for a long moment and then asks, "How about you? Do you see your dad?"

"No," I admit. "Never."

"Never? Not even once?"

I shake my head. "He's not even listed on my birth certificate. I'm not sure my mom actually knows who it is."

Daniel blows out a long breath. "Do you ever think about finding him?"

I scrunch up my nose. "Not really. I mean, I guess I'm supposed to be all maladjusted and melancholy with daddy issues, but the truth is, I've never thought about him much. I was too busy missing my mom—hating her, worrying about her—to expend any energy on him. Does that sound harsh?"

"Nah. I get it."

"So, what was that cute-but-dumb speech all about?" I venture.

Daniel laughs uncomfortably. "Mawmaw Barb wasn't fond of Madeline. Told me I needed to stop isolating myself after we broke up. Her exact words were, *Daniel, you got to jump in with both feet, like a clean pig finding a new mud puddle*. I think she thinks that's you."

"Great. So I'm a mud puddle now?"

"Of sorts."

"Does that mean she likes me?" I ask.

"A lot more than she liked Madeline," he replies.

"I wonder why," I say without expecting an answer.

"You're nothing like Madeline. You're opposite in, like, *every* way."

It doesn't exactly sound like a compliment or an insult. I raise my brows in question.

He groans. "I'm so bad at this."

"Yes, you are," I laugh. "But I think I know what you mean."

"Madeline was high-maintenance. It was exhausting. But you're relaxed. You don't need to hide behind all that stuff. And you don't care what people think."

"How do you know that?" Maybe I didn't care what others thought of me in the usual sense, but there were parts of me Moony did not accept. Parts like my mother in me. Parts like the artist in me. Something had been unknotting inside me since I'd come here. It was making me more real. I always believed that Moony was unapologetically herself and that I'd gotten that from her. But here in New Orleans, I could see the opposite was true. If anyone was unapologetically themselves, it was my mother. So why was Moony's version more acceptable?

"It's written all over you. Don't have to be Mawmaw to see it."

I fold my hands in my lap, processing.

Daniel leans in. "I like you, Cat, not just because you're different from Madeline. I like the way you put your head down when you're thinking and your hair falls across your face. I like how quiet you seem, but when you do talk, it's because you have something to say—you're not just trying to fill space. I like how open you are about everything, even your family and your past and things other people might be too scared to talk about. I like that I can be myself with you. I don't have to perform. *And* you laugh at my jokes. You get me."

"Oh, no, I was laughing *at* you. Did you think I was laughing with you? There's a difference, Daniel."

"I see how it is," he retorts. After a moment, he leans away. "So, we good?"

"I like you too. I like working with you, and I like seeing you, and I like that you're helping me sort through some really sordid shit."

"But?"

"But nothing," I tell him, meeting his eyes. "I'm just not sure what comes next."

Daniel leans in, grazing his fingers across my cheek. I part my lips to speak, but his are on mine before the words even form. My eyes close instinctively. My breathing slows. Everything goes dark and soft, like crushed velvet around me. His lips are slow and gentle against mine. I'm only just getting going when he pulls away.

"*That* is what comes next," he tells me.

XIX.

MY FINGERS ARE ON MY LIPS, WHICH ARE STILL BUZZING, as I step into the courtyard. He's in the shadows, so I don't see him, and I'm grinning like an idiot with my eyes on my feet. I nearly fall over him on my way to the stairs.

"Careful there," Butcher says. He raises his cell phone, using its flashlight to help me see my way. "Wouldn't want you getting hurt."

I pause, embarrassed. What did he see? How long has he been out here like this? I remember the burn of his cigarette when we first pulled up. "Sorry, just tired. It's late," I mumble for an excuse.

"Mmhmm," he replies.

I start to turn away, but something about him standing there like that—one arm raised with his cell phone lighting up the courtyard, his cigarette dangling from the other hand, the navy beanie on his head, the wraparound beard of white—strikes me as so familiar that I stare uncomfortably long. I can't place him, but I know I know Butcher somehow. From before New Orleans. Before Moony died.

Our eyes meet, and I realize for the first time that his are a gray blue, like seawater. But almost one third of the bottom of his left iris is light brown, like an algae bloom creeping over the surface of a pond.

"Can't sleep?" I ask him, moving to lean against one of the decorative trees.

He lowers his phone and takes a drag. "Lifelong insomniac," he says with a chuckle.

I nod and look around our courtyard, so quietly sequestered from the commotion of the Quarter, like a little cove of calm. "Have you lived here long?"

"A couple years, give or take." He is smiling in the dark. I can tell because of the curve of his beard, but he never bares his teeth.

"Shouldn't you be someone's grandpa or something?" It is out before I can stop it, and I'm mortified at my impertinence. Mary is rubbing off on me more and more.

Butcher just chuckles. "I prefer living alone, I guess. I like the solitude. Most people can't stop talking. They love the sound of their own voices. But you only hear things of value in the silence." He drops his cigarette and crushes it beneath a shoe.

"I get that. It was just me and my grandmother before. Our lives were pretty quiet. I miss it."

He smiles kindly in my direction. "Isn't it just you and your mother now?"

I nod. "Yeah. But living with her is like living with a crowd of people all the time."

"Loneliest place to be is in the middle of a crowd," he tells me.

I think he is right. It makes me wonder how lonely my mom must be inside herself all the time. I point to his hand, the one with the missing fingers. "What happened?"

He looks down and turns it so that the nearby porchlight falls across his abrupt knuckles. "Occupational hazard," he says.

"Really?" It would make sense.

"No. But it sounds good, doesn't it? I lost them a long time ago. I grew up on a ranch in West Texas. There was an old vaquero who used to break horses for us. One day I was out by the pen, watching, when a colt got him down. I ran in to help but left the gate open. Old Bartolo was up on his feet, but the colt made for the gate. Like a fool, I grabbed the lead rope and wrapped it around my hand. Horse drug me four hundred feet before the rope slipped, taking my first two fingers with it."

I swallow hard against the tension knotting my stomach.

"I lost my taste for ranching after that," he says now. "Don't feel sorry for an old man."

"For what it's worth," I tell him as I start to walk away, "I like the real story better."

I can hear him chuckling to himself as I turn and head up the stairs.

It takes a few weeks, but Mary and I fall into a kind of rhythm, our own beats laid down over the track of the city. She always rises before me, a little too chipper to be believed, continuing her campaign of badly cooked breakfasts to try and win me over. I wake to the smells of burnt toast, half-baked banana bread, and runny eggs before I finally break down and buy my own damn box of Lucky Charms. She starts her readings around late morning or noon. Most people take their readings by phone and pay online. But more than one stray client turns up at our doorstep, sometimes frantic. At first, I find it unnerving—this broken stream of desperate people in and out. But after the first few, it stops seeming like such an invasion. They hardly even notice I'm in the room. And I take a secret guilty pleasure in eavesdropping on their sessions.

I don't like to admit it, but my mother is good at what she does. She knows her way around the cards, and she projects a confidence they need to believe in. I see it as a shadow of the grandiosity that comes with delusion and mania, but they simply see it as real. Because she thinks she knows what she's talking about, they think she does too. It's weird to me that she can be so good at this and so bad at everything else.

But sometimes I catch her staring at the cards with an intensity that makes me nervous. Her silence will stretch out unusually long, and when she finally comes back around, she'll blink over and over again, like her eyes are dried out. She's good at covering it, but I know her even if I haven't lived with her for ten years. And I can tell that it's like she just blacked out with her eyes open.

"Mom. MOM," I practically shout one afternoon when she stares so long at the cards before her she seems to forget she has a client on the phone.

She jolts, dropping her phone in the process and scrambling to pick it up.

When her reading ends, I approach her table. "Are you okay? You seem off lately."

She turns her face up to mine but won't meet my eyes. "Of course. Don't be silly."

But later that same day, I find her in the bathroom squirting an entire bottle of shampoo down the sink. "It doesn't smell right," she says defensively when I give her a funny look.

I don't argue, just add shampoo to the grocery list.

I work several days a week—a break I need for multiple reasons—and Daniel and I spend more and more time together when we're off, so most days I only have to be at the apartment to sleep. My sketchbook lays at the foot of my bed. At night I lie with the lamp on and sketch the people I see around the Quarter. I like drawing the real people most, the ones the Quarter overlooks. They are not performers or artists or staples like my mom. And they are not tourists passing through with a hunger for rich food and loud music. They are the ones that New Orleans has forgotten. Some are just kids. Others are older, with yellowed eyes and deeply etched wrinkles that I imagine could tell their story if you ran your fingers over them like grooves in a record. They ask for money, or they ask for coffee, or they just watch you pass with looks that follow you for blocks.

And in between all these are the other sketches—the ones of the people I see but shouldn't. The Magician and his tricky face. The man in his bathrobe, so young and old at once. The woman with her covered eyes, the light hiding beneath her veil. I am careful now. I don't wander. I don't get caught alone. Even my dreams have been quieter. But sometimes I feel them watching me from under a streetlamp or on a balcony. I keep my head down when that happens. I walk fast. At night, in my bed, I turn the box of tarot cards over in my hands, but I don't open it. Not since Fortune's Gate.

Moony's watch is still ticking under my pillow where I've hidden it. I give up on folding up the sofa bed every morning.

Mary doesn't complain and Gary, for all his promises, still hasn't made good on his search for a real bed or a place with two bedrooms. More than once, I hear him whisper to her about moving into his place, but she deflects the offer again and again, and while I don't relish the idea of living with Gary full-time, I can't help but wonder what's holding her back. My mom may look like she's standing on her own two feet, but people with her condition—they need others. *A good support system* they call it online. Mary is better at pushing people away than keeping them close, but she needs Gary. And whether I like it or not, she needs me.

It is evident in the small things—little oversights and oddities that have begun happening since I arrived, like the shampoo. Like when I wake to the refrigerator light because she has left it open. Or the clients she forgets about because she is shopping or stops for coffee or gets engrossed in a conversation with a saxophone player on Royal Street. Or the third time she ordered pizza delivery but didn't have any cash. There are other things too. Bigger things. Twice she has brought a stranger home, men with hard eyes and lean throats, who seem as if they have no intention of leaving. I called Gary on the first. I called the police on the second. And one night I woke to an open front door and found her wandering the courtyard.

"What are you doing?" I whisper-yelled down the stairs as I rushed to her side.

She had her earbuds in, but I could still hear the candy rock sounds of "We Own the Night" several paces back because she was playing it so loud.

I wrapped a hand around her arm and tugged. "Mom, it's too late for this. It's four a.m. Come inside."

She grabbed my free hand in hers and started dancing with me.

This is Mary's version of high-functioning. Some would simply see it as carefree. Or absentminded. But I see it for what it is: tendrils of disease breaking through the medicinal crust, trying to gain any kind of ground. Like invasive vines that must be hacked back again and again, that keep rising no matter how many times you pour gasoline on their roots. Even with the best doctors and the best meds and the best circumstances, I cannot ever forget that my mother is bipolar. And I cannot let her forget it. Or it will overtake her—*us*—completely.

XX.

DANIEL TAKES ME TO THE MOVIES AND THE AQUARIUM and his favorite places to eat, most of which are actually outside of the Quarter. He even takes me to the Museum of Death. My vision dances over the skeletons and coffins and memento mori in a kind of fit, afraid to land anywhere too long. I pause in front of a shrunken head, feeling as if all the eyes in the room are following me. The skeletons in my dream are a whisper at my back, and then they are gone. And just as quickly, we are bursting out onto Dauphine Street, the afternoon sun melting the chills that were riding my spine and pushing the familiar mirage back into the recessed corners of my mind.

We go to his favorite coffee spot in City Park more than once. When we can't find something else to do, we hang out at the park near our favorite bridge and just talk. We circle the family stuff, focusing instead on the chance to get to know one another. It's nice to talk about other things. I learn that Daniel hates tomatoes but loves ketchup, which I tell him makes no sense. I learn that he won his third-grade spelling bee but got bullied for it so much that he deliberately threw the next one in fourth grade. He spelled *laughter* with an *f*. Even his teacher knew what he was up to. I learn that he loves the Avengers movies and Lizzo and—secretly—girls with tattoos, and that he has had six girlfriends since the ninth grade.

In exchange, I tell him about my passion for breakfast cereals and true crime shows and nineties music—can you really top a decade that gave us a girl band like the Breeders? I don't think so. I regale him with Moony stories, like the time she told off the police officer who pulled us over for not having been to mass in over a month. The poor guy was so shaken he forgot to write our ticket. I show him pictures on my phone of Deena, the cockapoo next door, and Moony standing over a pot of homecooked chicken and dumplings in the kitchen, a wooden spoon in one hand. But today, I've saved the best for last. Today, I brought my sketchbook to show him.

He flips through the first few pages tenderly, like a librarian handling an archived text from centuries ago.

I bite back a laugh. "You can handle it like regular paper. It's not that fragile."

Daniel grins but doesn't take his eyes off the page. "I don't want to smudge anything."

There are sketches of all kinds of random things. A hibiscus bloom. Moony's favorite coffee mug. The old Cadillac owned by Mr. Whitley from down the street. Rain over the tree line at the end of Sawmill Road. There are sketches of people, too. Some of Moony. Some of me. A couple of my mother done from memory or pictures I dug out of Moony's desk. One of our neighbor Eric. One of Father Fontenot. Two of Janice Brune, my closest friend until she moved away three years ago. And all the new ones from the Quarter.

Daniel pauses on a self-portrait. In it, I am looking over my shoulder at an imaginary horizon. My hair is spiked with lilac highlights and my eyes are soft, almost sleepy. "This is you?"

I nod, suddenly feeling all too exposed, like those dreams where you look down and realize you're nude.

"It's incredible," he says, tearing his eyes away to grin at me for a moment. "But you don't see yourself, not like I do."

"How so?" I'm touchy about criticism when it comes to my drawing. I try not to show how his comment stings.

"Your color choices. You're all washed out, like a reflection in the water."

I hold my arm up in front of his face. "You do see this paleness, don't you?"

He smiles. "That's not what I mean. It's as if you're afraid to define yourself too strongly. As if you're not sure you're fully here."

"Time for another one," I chime with an eye roll, turning the page before he can read any more into my self-portrait. When I draw, I don't think too hard about the choices I'm making. They are intuitive. But analyzing them after the fact like this makes me feel like a butterfly trapped in a shadowbox under pins.

I'm in such a rush to get past the awkwardness of my self-portrait that I don't think about what the next picture will be until I see it. It's a drawing I did of the boy from the forest—the Fool from my dream. The trees are dark and angry, drawn in hard, slanting lines that seem to shriek onto the page. He cuts them down the middle, as though the forest is bleeding yellow. A small figure that is decidedly human but void of all identifying features except that damn waistcoat, and the giant white wolfdog at his side.

"Who's this?" Daniel asks.

"No one," I say.

He looks at me for a long moment and then gives up. He turns the page. Moony's curtains bloom yellow. Her open doorway yawns. All else is blank.

"I don't like that one," I say quickly and turn the page again, regretting it the instant the next drawing comes into view.

It is the man from the cathedral and the café. His garish red bathrobe is unmistakable. The smug smirk on his face. The five o'clock shadow around his goatee. The paper he is not reading. His eyes bore into mine from the page, and I can smell the peppermint already.

"I remember this guy," Daniel says.

I bite my lip. In the last several weeks, I'd let the strange appearances slide to the back of my mind. I didn't forget exactly, but I put them away for a while. It was easier to do that than keep questioning what they were, why they were showing up in my dreams and my life. All the time I was spending with Daniel seemed to hold them at bay. He'd begun to feel like my own personal talisman. Now, I worry this little bubble I've been living in will burst.

Daniel looks at me.

"I know."

"He's from the café that day you spilled the coffee."

"I know."

"Why? Did this guy...*do* something to you?"

"Not really. I mean, it's hard to explain," I offer lamely. "He's hard to explain."

Daniel turns the page. The boy with the yellow waistcoat is back. He is poised to cliff dive with only a red bungee to save him. He turns the page again. The cathedral looms across the paper.

It is engulfed in purple-white flames. A woman waits in the doorway—one door black, the other white. Her blue veil glitters with stardust. He turns the page again. The man with the peppermint schnapps has taken the woman's place. He is not in a bathrobe but his goatee and expression are clearly the same. Daniel turns the page again and the man is curled inside a green bottle, hugging his knees in a fetal position, like one of those babies in formaldehyde.

Daniel looks at me. "These are...*interesting*."

I stare back, fearing what comes next. "But?"

"But why have you drawn this guy so many times? And the boy? Who are these people, Cat?"

"I didn't want to tell you."

"Tell me what?" He looks concerned, but I can see he's trying to keep an open mind.

Good old Daniel. Sweet, trusting, kindhearted, car-keying Daniel. How open can his mind be? I'm about to find out. "It sounds crazy. And you met my mother. I didn't want you thinking *like mother, like daughter*."

"What are you talking about?"

I puff my cheeks out, blow off steam. "I see him sometimes. All of them."

"The man from the café?" He is so lost. I know the feeling.

"Yes. And the boy in yellow. And the woman in blue. And a few others. At first, it was just in dreams, but since coming here, it's happened when I'm awake also."

"Your first day?"

"Was the second time I met the man in the bathrobe. The first was at the cathedral."

Daniel's eyebrows raise, and his expression is incredulous.

"I'm sorry. Maybe I should have told you, but we'd just met. And I can't really explain it. I don't know what he is. I don't know why he keeps showing up. It all started after Moony..."

"Who." Daniel gives a little shake of his head. "You said *what*."

"Hmm?"

"You said you don't know *what* he is, not who he is."

"I know *who* he is," I say carefully.

He closes the sketchbook. "You're losing me here, Cat. Has something like this ever happened before?"

I duck my head. "No. Never."

"And you think—"

"I don't know what I think." I swat at a mosquito on my arm. "Maybe I'm having an episode like my mom, but I don't have the other symptoms. I'm sleeping. I'm saving most of my money from the café. I'm not engaging in reckless behavior. I'm not experiencing delusions. I don't think I'm Jesus or you're from the CIA or anything like that."

But I think about the fear I feel when I'm alone in the Quarter, the way I don't dawdle anymore, the feeling that sometimes they would be there if I just looked up, and so I keep my head down. Is that paranoia? My eyes water no matter how I tell them not to.

"Would you know if you were?" Daniel asks me. "Having those symptoms?"

"Maybe." I want to fold into myself and hide from this conversation. Did my mother know she shouldn't be in the courtyard listening to music at four a.m.? I tell Daniel about my fears, about how I avoid spending too much time in the Quarter and how I've stopped looking at my tarot deck. I tell him I am uncertain. About everything. About myself.

"Cat." Daniel is gentle as he takes one of my hands in both of his. "Whatever this is, I don't think it's that. I get why you would think so, but you're not like that from what I can tell. Maybe you're a little spooked, but who wouldn't be in your shoes?"

I want to believe him, but the fear will always live inside me—that at any moment I could lose all sense of reality, find myself doing and saying things only I can understand. "If it's not that, then what is it?"

Daniel blows out a long breath. "I mean, you know this is New Orleans, right? This city has a very long history of strange and unusual events—a very long history of bloody and scary events. I don't want to rattle you any more than you already are, but this is a weird place full of weird people. And we like it that way. But that comes with some baggage. There's a lot of crime, a lot of poverty, and a lot of..."

"What?"

"I was going to say a lot of troubled minds."

If I could wrap my arms any tighter around myself, Daniel might hear my ribs cracking.

"Sorry, poor choice of words. I don't mean you, and I don't mean to criticize your mom. I'm just saying, people come here from all over. Creative people and inventive people and passionate people. And sometimes disturbed people. I think maybe you've just bumped into some of them."

"Maybe," I say. But it doesn't go down easy. It doesn't sit well in my gut. "What about my dreams though?"

Daniel rubs my arm. "You've been through a lot. Would it be so strange of a coincidence for you to experience nightmares around the same time that you run into these people? I mean, you haven't actually met anyone from your dreams on the street, have you?"

"The man with the goatee. The one from the café."

"But you only dreamt about him *after* meeting him, right?"

"Yeah, I guess." I know Daniel is trying to make me feel better, and it should be working. But it's not. I only feel crazier for reading anything into this at all. "What about Fortune's Gate?"

"What about it? It was a really weird store. New Orleans is full of them."

Do I want to explain what I *think* I saw? I bite my tongue. He's so sincere with his wide, square teeth and frank, brown eyes. I don't know how to not agree with him.

"If you're not having an episode—which I don't think you are—then what else could it be?" he says.

I swipe at the tears as they fall. "Ghosts. Apparitions. That's all I can come up with. I mean, isn't like 75 percent of this city supposed to be haunted anyway?"

He laughs. "You got me there. But why would they be haunting you? And why so many?"

I shrug. "Any other theories I come up with just make me sound less stable."

Daniel sighs. "Things aren't always as simple as they seem on the surface. Mawmaw is always saying there's more to this world than meets the eye." He gets to his feet and holds his hand out to pull me up.

"You sound like one of those conspiracy theorists." I massage my knees for a moment as I stand next to him.

"Come on."

"Where are we going?"

"To see Mawmaw Barb. It's time I bring you round again."

XXI.

WHEN WE PULL UP THIS TIME, MAWMAW BARB IS comfortably wedged into a rocker on her front porch. She has a colander in her lap and a plastic bag full of green beans. She snaps the ends off before breaking each bean in two and dropping it in the colander. She doesn't wave as we approach or miss a beat in her bean routine.

"Mawmaw, you off today?" Daniel asks as we linger on the steps.

She eyes him over the top of her readers. "I'm here, ain't I?"

He laughs. "I brought Cat over again like you asked."

Now she pauses. Her hands are smooth skinned with big, fleshy veins running over them like earthworms. They hover mid-bean over the colander as she appraises me. After a moment, she drops the bean in and grabs up the bag. "Come on then."

She hands the colander to Daniel and starts for the door. "May as well put you to work if you're going to be here underfoot."

Daniel tosses an eye roll over his shoulder at me as we follow. But I don't mind. I like the way she says "underfoot" as if we are no bigger than the twins. I like her take-charge attitude and domestic authority. She reminds me, in ways that make my heart ache, of Moony. Behind us, the front door closes with a slam. Unlike the last time I was here, her living room is empty and quiet today. It's early yet. The dinner crowd won't arrive for several hours.

Mawmaw Barb installs us at the dining room table. She takes the colander from Daniel and places it in front of me along with the rest of the beans. "You ever pop beans before?"

"Yes, ma'am," I tell her. I used to love doing it for Moony.

With a nod she moves into the kitchen and returns with a bag of potatoes, a peeler, and a large plastic bowl. These, she hands to Daniel. He moans. "Why can't I do the beans?"

She sets him with a glassy stare. "Boy, you know better than to act like that in front of company."

Begrudgingly, he takes up the peeler and his first potato, stripping the skin in long, steady strides.

Taking her own seat, she turns her attention to the celery she's chopping over a sunny yellow cutting board. "Now then. What do you want with me?"

Daniel starts slowly. "Cat...has a problem."

Mawmaw whacks at a celery stalk with her butcher knife. "Honey, we all got problems."

"Hers is *unusual*."

She sighs, exasperated, and sets her knife down. "Child, I wish you'd just spit it out."

"A stalker, Mawmaw. Or a few of them. Cat thinks they might be ghosts."

She grunts. "Some would call seeing ghosts a gift, not a problem."

"They're not very nice," I pipe up finally. "They aren't mean exactly, except for one." I think of the Magician and shudder.

"Well, that *is* different. What makes you think they're ghosts?"

"They're just...*off*," I try to explain. "I mean, I don't know *what* they are. They look like people—*weird* people—but they don't act normal."

"No one in New Orleans acts normal." She is grinning now. "You said you don't know what they are. But do you know *who* they are?"

I don't look at Daniel when I answer. I haven't told him this part yet. "Yes. I mean, I think so. I think they're the characters from my tarot deck. Can a ghost haunt more than one place? Like be part of my deck but also in a church or a café?"

Mawmaw's grin falls. "I see you've got ahold of this idea like a six-toed cat with a field mouse." She eyes me for a moment, then says, "It depends. Ghosts can be attached to anything. They haunt by attachment. So if they're attached to a place, they haunt only that place. And if they're attached to a thing—like an old piece of furniture, say, or a tarot deck—then they'll haunt anywhere that thing goes. And if..." She suddenly gets a cold look and drops her eyes into her lap.

"*If* what?" I press her.

"Well, if they're attached to a person, then they'll haunt anywhere that person goes," she says carefully.

I take a breath. The one thing all these strange apparitions have in common besides the deck, dream-bound or otherwise, is *me*.

Mawmaw aims her knife at me. "Anyone else see these strangers?"

"I don't think so. I mean, sometimes they're just in my dreams.

But the ones on the street, everyone just kind of passes them by. Except Daniel did see the man at the café."

She looks at Daniel. "How'd he seem to you?"

Daniel shrugs. "I don't know. Pretty normal, I guess. I mean, he was dressed kinda weird."

"Might be characters from your deck; might be masquerading as characters from your deck. Might be ghosts. Might be something else entirely." Mawmaw Barb is pensive.

"Like what?" I ask her.

She gives a little shrug and sets her knife down. "There's a lot more to the spirit world than just ghosts, honey. There's *haints*. They're the ghosts of those gone too soon who desire to cause harm to the living. And there's the *feu follet*, a nature spirit that haunts the swamp and leads folks to a watery grave. And there's more besides. Those things we have yet to name. But a spirit will usually let you know it's a spirit, even if it appears as a full-body apparition."

I stare over the beans at Mawmaw. "How?"

Her lips twitch on one side. "They may look human, but there will always be something out of place. Something that doesn't make sense in our world."

"Like how ghosts are usually all white or see-through? Or how they're always wearing clothes from another time? Like that?" Daniel asks.

"Not always that obvious. You have to be a good observer. Sometimes it's just a little detail. Maybe their eyes are a tad too big to be real. Or their fingers a touch too long. They might be missing something, like ears or—"

"Or their voice?" *Or a couple of fingers?*

Mawmaw looks at me hard. "Could be."

I think about the little boy with the too-large dog and the man who sounds so old and looks so young, and the woman with galaxies for eyes, the magician's twisted face, the biker lady's moving tattoos. The smell of peppermint. The feeling of falling. The vanishing store. There's something unusual about all of them. And yet, they're easy to explain away.

"Could just be imagination," I say at last, exhausted from trying to make heads or tails of it.

"Could be," she agrees. "But it ain't."

I frown. How does she know that?

"You don't strike me as the imaginative type," she supplies without being asked. I realize Mawmaw Barb can read me, with or without her glasses, better than most people can read a book.

"Sometimes my mom sees things. She has to take medicine. It's an illness. I'm the right age for symptoms. I've wondered if—"

Mawmaw Barb cuts me off. "You ain't sick, honey. Now that other one he brought home before you, *she* was sick. Crazy like a half-starved fox in an unguarded henhouse. That's a sickness of the will. Spreads its damage from one generation to the next like a vine creeping underground. What your momma's got is a sickness of the heart. And that's something else. It invades the mind, makes her do and say things you might never understand, but it ain't catching."

I want to ask how she knows all this, what makes her so sure, but I don't. Because something in me laps at the pool of her simple wisdom. There is comfort in her words, whether I believe them down deep or not. And I realize comfort is something hard to come by in my world these days, and something I desperately need.

"I've seen a couple of them near the cathedral. I wondered if maybe they're apparitions." I don't mention that one was in a dream of the cathedral, the Quarter maze ending in white mist and cold flame.

"Describe one," Mawmaw demands.

I look at Daniel, and he nods as if to encourage me. The first that comes to mind is the woman from my dream. "She's dressed all in blue and lit up from inside."

"Go on."

"Her voice comes at you from all directions. And her eyes are full of stars." I swallow, a little embarrassed to say this last part. "She frightens me in a way I've never felt before."

Mawmaw Barb pitches her chin down and stares out over the rim of her readers at me with arched brows. Her silver earrings swing on either side of her heart-shaped face. "That sound like the blessed mother to you?"

It feels foolishly obvious the way she puts it. "No, ma'am."

"When did you see one of these visitors for the first time?"

"The night my grandmother passed." The skeletons...*Death*.

"Mmhmm. It's as I expected. You got a hanger-on—a few of 'em by the sound of it."

"A what-what?"

"Your grandmother's passing left a hole in you, and something has moved in to fill it," she explains, as if it's perfectly obvious. She rises from the table, takes my arm, and spins me toward the front door.

Daniel follows. "Where we goin'?" he asks as we step into the nostril-stinging twang of the afternoon air, a daylight moon already dangling like a curved blade overhead.

"Ain't good to cook much less eat on a troubled stomach," she says, patting my hand. "Only one person I know can put this right."

"Izora Jo?" Daniel asks.

"Izora Jo."

Daniel grins at me. "Welcome to the real New Orleans."

"Where does she live?" I ask.

"Two blocks that way," he tells me. "You can't miss it. She and Mawmaw Barb go *way* back."

I nod, trusting, because what choice do I have?

"Mawmaw Barb knows her way around the spirits," Daniel says to me in a low voice to stay out of earshot. "But Izora Jo does the heavy lifting."

I give him a fearful look.

"Hexes, curses, possessions—stuff most people are afraid to touch," he explains. "She's what we call a 'rootworker,' only her magic is as unique as her heritage—West African, Spanish, Caribbean, and Irish."

Daniel is right. The second the house comes into sight, I realize this must be the place. A black rooster and two hens, round and orange as pumpkins, are pecking about in an herb garden behind a rusty iron fence. The shotgun house rises behind it like a jagged tooth from the ground, painted a deep purple with black-and-white trim. Several large jars of brown liquid litter the steps, their contents a mystery of sediment at the bottom. As if on cue, a fat, cawing crow lands on the peak of the roof as we enter the gate. And a chicken foot swings from the front doorknob, which opens before Mawmaw Barb ever gets a chance to knock.

A heavyset woman with hair as dark and glossy as her rooster's feathers stands in the entrance wearing a white sundress. Her smile is wider and curvier than the moon overhead and just as bright, framed by red lipstick and a face full of makeup. The sag of skin beneath her eyes alludes to many years, as do the folds over her eyebrows and around her mouth. But there is something behind her face that is exuberant. It is a face that is quick to laugh. "Barbara? I thought that was you coming up the street."

Daniel's grandmother gives her a quick hug and turns to show her we're in tow. "We need your expertise, Izora Jo. We got a haunt that won't break."

The woman looks from her to Daniel and then to me. "Better come inside."

I pick my way through the brown jars on the steps and whisper to Daniel, "What are these? Potions?"

"Tea," he whispers back, amused.

I step over a brown tabby curving around our ankles as I make my way inside, my fingers laced through Daniel's. The living room is full of overstuffed chairs and dark-stained shelves with row upon row of tightly wedged books. Their spines show dust and wear and call out with strange titles like *American Conjure*, *A Rootworker's Guide to Hexes & Spells*, and *When Bones Speak*. I'm not sure where to sit, so I just stand shoulder to shoulder with Daniel in the middle of the room while Barb and Izora Jo each pull up a chair at the tiny mosaic dining table.

"Now then, what seems to be the problem exactly?"

I let Mawmaw Barb tell most of my story, adding my own bits when she pauses for me to fill in. All the while, Izora Jo nods knowingly, her brown cat rubbing against her large calves.

"Come here, girl," she says to me when we're finished.

I take a step closer.

"Give me your dominant hand. Let me take your measure."

I do as she asks, flashing Daniel a *WTF* grin. He bites his lower lip.

But Izora Jo's fingers are soft and cool against my palm as she traces the lines there. I begin to relax beneath them. After a moment, she clasps my hand between both of her own and closes her eyes. I wait, wondering what I'm waiting for exactly, when her lids flap open and her eyes begin to roll back, flashing white. Panic rises in me, but Daniel places a hand on my shoulder. Her lips move in mouthless words, her grip on my hand growing tighter by the second, until at last she lets go and gasps for breath like she's been underwater.

"Well?" Mawmaw Barb asks. "Did you get anything?"

The older woman blinks and looks at me. "This bond is too strong to be broken by a simple conjure. It's blood that ties them, not water. And something else."

She peers at me and my legs feel weak.

"Something inside the girl that won't let go," she finishes. "Not yet."

I rub the palm of my hand on my jeans as if I can rub away what she's seen.

"Is she in any danger?" Daniel's grandmother asks.

Izora Jo inhales sharply. "How long has this been with you?"

Even though I can't say what "this" is, I know the answer to her question. "Since coming here."

She nods. "New Orleans is unlike any other place in the world. Here, you stand in one of the oldest cities in this country, on some of the youngest land. The river birthed the delta, and the delta birthed the basin, and the basin birthed the city, and it's anyone's guess why."

I smile weakly at her.

"It's a crossroads of its own kind," she continues. "And strange things always appear at a crossroads. Some of 'em good, and some of 'em not so good. Places like this are what they used to call *betwixt*."

"Betwixt?" Daniel asks beside me.

"Like where the land meets the sea."

"You mean the shore?" he says.

"I mean betwixt," she insists.

"So what does that mean for me?"

She shrugs. "Maybe nothing. Maybe everything. You got salt in the blood, so probably more of the latter."

"I'm sorry," I tell her. "I don't know what that means, *salt in the blood*."

"It means you're a bit like this city. You're a bit betwixt yourself. You've got a touch of the spirits inside you. The world's always gonna look a little different through your eyes."

I flash to the woman in my dream giving me the kiss of white flame and feel my heart pick up. I don't want that inside me. I am reminded of the ways people talk about my mother when they don't want to call her disorder what it is. This feels like that: a soft word for a hard fact.

Izora Jo grabs a large mason jar like the ones I saw outside off a shelf. She takes it to the kitchen and pours some of the liquid into a smaller, clean jar. To that she adds a host of ingredients I don't recognize—herbs, powders, and what may or may not be animal bones—as well as a few that I do—salt, brandy, and what has to be Tabasco sauce—and all so fast that I can't keep up. When she seems satisfied, she screws the top on tight, gives it a good shake, and lights a black candle, dripping the wax all around the edges to seal the jar. "You place this under your bed where you sleep, got it? That'll keep you safe while this mess plays itself out."

"I don't understand," I tell her.

But she ignores me, looking to Mawmaw Barb instead. "This one ain't for us to meddle with. You hear me, Barbara Mathis? Your boy's part of it now. Can't be helped. He sees what she sees because your blood, your salt, is running through his veins. Make him a mojo for protection and leave it at that. No real harm should come to him."

Mawmaw Barb gives a quick nod of her head and turns on her heels. "Come on, you two. Dinner ain't gonna cook itself." She heads for the front door.

Daniel and I traipse behind without a word, but at the front door, I turn and look into Izora Jo's plump face. "You never said," I tell her. "You never said if I was in danger."

"Honey, this is New Orleans," she says with an easy laugh. "We're all in danger."

I want to ask a dozen more questions, but my mind is tripping over her words, spinning in sickly circles as I try to understand. And Daniel is already at the gate, following his grandmother home.

I don't know if I actually believe all this hoodoo bullshit. But a few months ago, I wouldn't have believed in coins falling from the sky or that my mother had another baby or that my grandmother had frittered away my college money. I'm in no position to argue. Instead, I just nod and run out into the sun, a jar of herbs and brandy sloshing in my hand.

XXII.

I CAN HEAR THEIR VOICES BEFORE I EVEN FINISH unlocking the door. Izora Jo's jar is tucked into the sticky skin of the crook of my elbow, but I doubt it works on my mother's kooky clients. I pause a moment at the threshold, listening. One of the voices is excitable, high-pitched and talking much too fast. Surprisingly, it's not my mother's. By contrast, her voice is low and soothing, her tones even as she tries to settle the woman who's come to see her.

I swing the door wide and stride in. My mother's client is sitting with her at the little card table. Her curly, peanut-colored hair is frizzed around her face from the humidity, and her nose is red and puffy, her cheeks streaked wet. She toys with a wad of tissues in her lap. They both glance my way, and the woman seems nervous, but my mother reassures her. "That's just Cat, my youngest. She won't interfere."

My breath hitches at her use of the term *youngest*, but I turn my face so she won't notice. I flop my sketchbook on the sofa bed and rack my memory. Have I ever heard her call me that before? I mentally shuffle through the handful of visits at Moony's and what I can recall of the years before. I come up blank. Is this confirmation that the picture I found is exactly what I think it is? Is it coincidence or a Freudian slip? I settle myself in one corner of pillows and grab my sketchbook and pencils, pretending to draw even though I'm really just going back over the lines of an earlier piece.

"It'll be just like before," the woman confesses, a hiccup breaking her voice. "And then he'll leave me. I know he will."

My mother leans in, stroking her arm. "Don't panic, Nan. You don't know that."

She pulls away and shuffles her cards while the woman nods, crying softly. She throws several out, face up, across the table after she's had the woman blow on the deck. "See there?" she tells her. "The Empress followed by the Two of Wands. This is a new beginning for you, Nan. And see here? The King of Cups. This baby is happy news for him. Have you told him yet?"

I dare a glance over my shoulder. The woman shakes her head. "I can't. I'm too scared. If—if it doesn't last, like before...I don't think he can take the disappointment."

My mother now holds up the Page of Cups. "You need to tell him, Nan. You can't do this alone. This is a new start for the relationship too."

"Are you sure? Because I'd rather just know if it's going to be like last time. I'd rather you just tell me now."

"It's not," my mother assures her. "Let's pull one more to be certain."

She has the woman pick a card from the deck once it's all

fanned out. Nan hands it to her, and she turns it over. Her mouth twitches into a smile. "The World. See? What did I tell you?"

For the first time, I see the woman—Nan—crack a smile, her body puddling in relief.

"Tell him. Okay? And come back in six weeks, on the house. We'll pull cards every month if we have to so you can get through this," my mom offers.

I turn back to my imaginary drawing, thinking the reading is over, but the woman begins to sob into her Kleenex.

"Shhhh, Nan. It's going to be okay."

"I know, you keep saying that. It's just, I don't think I can take another one. You know? It's so hard."

"I know. I do. I've been there."

I turn ever so slightly and see my mom leaning toward her client, one hand on her shoulder.

Nan meets her gaze. "You have?"

My mother nods. "It was a long time ago, but you never forget."

"No," she responds. "Not a single one." She tucks a few bills into my mom's hand.

After a couple of minutes, Nan gets up to leave and my mom follows her to the door. She gives her a final hug before closing the door behind her. She takes a deep breath and lets it out slowly, her eyes squeezed closed, before heading back to the table to gather up her cards. I watch her bend over the cards with squinting eyes, watch her pinch the bridge of her nose and then shuffle the cards together quickly.

"You okay?" I ask her.

She tosses her hair over a shoulder and straightens her spine, letting out a breath. "Fine. Better than."

I don't really believe this, but I don't want to press it. "A little hysterical for being a new mom. What's her story?"

My mom glances at me and slides her cards into their silk bag. "Nan? She's had a hard life. Good news isn't always good news, Catia. Know what I mean?"

I let the name thing slide in the interest of gathering information and jump up and follow her into the kitchen. "Not at all. Hard how?"

"It's Nan's story to tell, not mine."

I find this whole buttoned-lip, integrity routine a little difficult to buy coming from a woman who once told our neighbor his wife was cheating on him with the FedEx guy. It is still the only time I've seen a man cry. Of course, she was manic then and beginning to get paranoid. She thought the FedEx guy was undercover for the CIA and that the man's wife was a secret arms dealer. "Right. It's just, and I hope you don't mind, but sometimes I listen in because, well, you're so good at it, and I'm trying to learn how you read the cards."

She turns to me, a genuine smile lighting up her face, and I feel a little like mud. "Oh, baby, all you had to do was ask. I can teach you all about the cards."

Wrong answer. I swing again. "You told Nan that the World card meant everything would be okay. But I don't really know what that means if I don't know *how*. Like, what her question was."

My mother bites her bottom lip. "Okay, but don't go around telling your friends or whatever."

The only friend I'd tell is Daniel because he's the only friend I have right now. And I doubt he's interested in all of Nan's problems. "Pinkie swear."

"Nan's a sexual assault survivor. It's taken a toll on her body. She's already had three miscarriages, and the last one left her so depressed her husband almost walked out on her because she kept refusing help. She was afraid the drugs would interfere with her ability to get pregnant again. Of course, I told her then, 'It won't matter if you don't have a husband to hold up his half of the bargain anymore.'" She runs her hands under a splash of cold water at the sink and rubs them over her face.

I feel a sudden rush of concern. Nan should be consulting with an obstetrician, not a fortune-teller. "You told her everything would be fine."

"Because it will be," she says.

"How do you know that?" I try to keep the angry edge from my voice. "I mean, if she's already miscarried so many times."

"The Empress and the World in one reading? Come on. You can't pay to have the deck shuffle out like that. This one's gonna stick."

"It's not velcro, Mary. It's a baby," I can't help but snap.

"I know that, Cat. It's my job to read the cards. That's what I do."

I take a deep breath and force my face to relax. "You told her to tell him. Did you mean her doctor?"

"No, her husband. She was afraid he'd freak when he found out. Probably because she'll have to get off her medication now. Well, she already is technically." She grabs a dish towel to dry her hands.

I nearly bite my tongue in half trying not to react to the fact that my mom is counseling people to get off their medication and never once, in her entire reading, did she mention seeing a doctor. I comfort myself with the thought that Nan is probably on her way to the nearest ob-gyn office as we speak. "So, you had one too?"

"One what?" She looks alarmed by my question. The color drains from her face.

"A miscarriage." Did she think I meant a sexual assault?

Mom drops her dishcloth. She didn't realize I'd heard. "Once." Her voice is pinched, like air slowly escaping a balloon where the end is being pressed together.

I think of the picture. Sure didn't look like a miscarriage to me. "How far along were you?"

She shakes her head. "I don't know. Far. It was a long time ago."

"Before me."

"That's right," she says quietly. "Before you."

If I'd wanted confirmation the baby in the picture was hers, I think I just got it. "Was it…I mean, did we have the same father?" I venture.

Her eyes cloud over. "No." Her lips pinch around the word, clipping it off.

There's something about this baby that pains her above and beyond its loss. Something she is not saying. "It's just, I don't really know anything about my dad."

She looks at me with a serious expression. "Neither do I. I remember him—how tall he was and how good he smelled and the way he spun me around the dance floor of the honky-tonk where I met him. We had a glorious night together. And that was it. And then came you. I never knew how to find him. Never even knew his last name. I'm sorry I didn't tell you sooner."

Her face lights up on the word "glorious." She smiles in spite of herself. I like knowing he is a good memory at least. "Was it the same with the other baby—the one you lost?"

She shakes her head. Her brow closes in on itself. "No, I knew the father then. He was...*before* your dad. He wasn't a good man. In the end, we were better off."

I notice she used the word "man." Not "boy" or "guy" or "kid." It seems out of place for how young she was in the photo. A lump fills my throat. How bad was he that she believed his child was better off dead? "Still, it's kinda weird, you know?"

She is slowly starting to wash dishes, but her movements are stiff and robotic. "What is?"

I shrug one shoulder. "Just thinking that I might have had a big brother or sister."

Her lips twitch into a smile on one side.

"Guess I really am your youngest then."

She doesn't seem to register what I'm saying anymore. She keeps rubbing her hands together under the water. After a few minutes, she stops and wipes them on her pants.

"Mom?"

"Hmm?"

"Can I ask you one more thing?" Ever since Fortune's Gate, I've been waiting for the right moment to slip this in, the right conversation. Now that I have her on memory road and talking about cards, this seems ideal.

"Sure, baby." Her voice is thin, like runny paint. I'm not sure how engaged she is anymore.

"The deck you gave me—the one I brought from Moony's—where did you get it?" I cross my fingers under my leg.

"I found it," she says softly. "A long time ago." Her eyes are staring into the distance, trained on something only she can see.

"Where did you—"

"I'm tired. I think I'm gonna go lie down." She cuts me off as if I hadn't even started speaking again.

"Oh. Okay." I watch her walk slowly to her room and close the door, feeling guilty that my digging has uncovered her pain.

She doesn't come back out for the rest of the night.

XXIII.

FOUR DAYS PASS AND I AM STARTING TO WORRY. She shuffles out to use the bathroom every morning and night, and she makes her way to the kitchen for food once or twice a day. Small things only, like a banana or half of a peanut butter sandwich. But mostly she just sleeps, hour after hour behind the closed door to her room. When I question her late afternoon on the fifth day, she claims she has a virus.

"What kind?"

"Hmm?"

"Your virus, Mom. Like a stomach bug or what?"

"Right. A stomach bug," she parrots, filling a glass with water and grabbing a snack-size bag of pretzels.

"Funny," I say to her back as she turns toward her room again. "Because you aren't using the bathroom much for someone with a stomach bug."

But she just waves her hand at me muttering, "I'll be fine," and closes the door with a soft *click* behind her.

I can't help but recall our conversation after Nan's reading and wonder what role it's playing in her mystery illness.

On the evening of the sixth day, I score a lucky break when she leaves her cell phone on the kitchen counter. I glance toward her bedroom—no sound—and tiptoe to the front door, slipping silently into the courtyard with her phone in hand. Once outside, I seat myself on the edge of the fountain, knees tucked against my chest, and begin flipping through her contacts. When I find Gary's number, I press the call button. He answers on the first ring.

"Mary?" His voice sounds strained.

"No. It's me, Cat."

"Cat? Why are you calling on your mother's phone? Is everything all right?"

"There's no emergency," I tell him. "It's just...Mom's acting weird."

"Uh-huh. Weird how?"

"I don't know. She says she's sick, but she doesn't look it. She's been in bed for days. She just sleeps and barely eats anything. I even tried to get her to watch a marathon of Shark Week reruns with me, but she said she was too tired." I've learned my mother is a big Shark Week fan since moving back in with her, even though she can't swim and is absolutely terrified of bodies of water larger than this fountain.

Gary is silent on the other end.

"Hello?" I say after a moment, wondering if the call dropped.

"Yeah, I'm here. Just thinking. I wondered why she wasn't returning my calls."

"I don't know what to do," I admit. I've been around Gary enough at this point to know he's a functioning alcoholic. So reaching out to him for advice feels a little desperate. But I don't know anyone else who also knows my mother. Where is Moony's good sense and decisiveness when I need it?

"Should I come over there?"

"I'm not sure. Will that really do anything, you think?"

"Probably not." His voice is low, resigned. "Cat, honey, your mother...she's a complicated woman."

I sigh into the receiver. Here we go again. She's *complicated* instead of sick. I regret reaching out to him already.

"In my experience, she rides these storms out all on her own if you just let her. Sometimes it takes a couple of weeks or so, but she comes around. Usually, something happens to pull her out of it."

"Right. Okay. Well, thanks for nothing." It doesn't seem to dawn on Gary that my fate is in the hands of a woman who only last week wanted to chuck everything and move to the Andes to study with a shaman—I'd found her comparison shopping airfare—and today cannot drag herself from the bed long enough to eat a legitimate meal or brush her goddamned teeth. I also hate it when he calls me "honey."

"Listen, don't be mad. Do you need me to bring groceries or anything?"

I take a breath and remind myself that Gary is not the enemy. He is a kind, if broken, man who is solely responsible, from what I can tell, for my mother having made it this far without ending up on the streets or dying of starvation. A therapist would probably call him an enabler, but without his generosity, my mother wouldn't be able to keep a roof over her head. "No, I'll figure it out. Can I ask you a question though?"

"Shoot," he says.

"Do you know anything about a baby my mom had before me?"

Gary *uhhhhhs* on the other end. "You should really ask your mom about that," he says.

I don't want to admit I already did and that may be precisely why we are in this predicament. But this line of thinking has brought another idea to mind. "One more thing, Gary."

"Sure, Cat. Anything."

"Do you know if she has, like, a psychiatrist or anything? Like, does she see someone—a therapist or a counselor?" I haven't witnessed her making appointments or going to see a doctor, but then again, I haven't been home much, and somebody has to be prescribing her those meds I saw on my first night here. I've checked them since, and one of the bottles seemed like maybe it was less full, so I thought she was taking her meds. But I don't really know, and I haven't stayed on top of it like I'd intended to.

He thinks a moment. "She used to talk about a Dr. Angela," he finally says. "But it's been a long time since she's mentioned her."

"Okay." I feel a little deflated, but it's better than nothing. "Thanks."

"Cat, I mean it, anything you need. I know I'm not your parent, but I love your mother and she loves you. I take that seriously."

"I know," I tell him and hang up.

I scroll through her contacts in her phone again until I see a name that might be the one Gary mentioned: an Angela Murray. My thumb hovers over the call button. Do I do this or not?

It's late, after 8:00 p.m. It's doubtful she'll even answer. If I leave a message and she calls back but my mother answers, what then? If my mom's her patient, can she even talk to me? I know I'm her daughter, but it's not the same as being a parent.

Gary sounded concerned but not panicked. I remind myself

that, in some ways, he knows her better than me. I may remember the Mary of my early childhood, but Gary knows this version of her, the version she has been for the last several years, far better than I do. If he's seen her cycle through this and come out the other side, then maybe it won't be that bad. As far as I know, she's on meds. How low can her low get?

I am just hitting the *send* button to text Angela's contact info to my own phone when a shadow falls across the screen. I look up into the mismatched eyes of Butcher, his phone's flashlight beaming past me into the gently moving water of the fountain. He smiles over me, and I am reminded again of that sense of familiarity I had during our last talk. Where have I encountered this man before? He takes a seat next to me on the fountain, and I lower my legs, turning the phone over in my lap. I promise myself I will call Dr. Murray if Mom is not improving by the end of next week.

"Cigarette?" he asks, shaking one from his pack and extending it toward me.

"No, thank you. I don't like the smell," I say. Butcher feels easy to talk to, and I don't want to go back inside yet. Our tiny apartment is stifling now that Mary's gloom is filling up all the corners.

"He's good people, Gary is." Butcher lights up next to me, taking a long drag of his cigarette.

"Yeah, he is." I didn't want to like Gary at first, but he's grown on me.

"It's a shame about his boy," Butcher adds in a soft voice, blowing out a long stream of smoke into the damp night air.

I know Gary lost a son but not much else. "He told me."

"It was an accident," Butcher says now. "He was drunk and left the top off the hot tub."

I want to ask how Butcher knows that, but I don't. It's no wonder Gary drinks every day. I feel fresh heartbreak for the man who has kept my mother safe for the last few years, kept her fed and sheltered. I register with a cold wave of shock that they have this in common, the loss of children they can never replace. I wonder if Gary knows my mother's secret about the baby since he didn't really answer me. I wonder if that's what drew him to her.

"Do you think people get what they deserve, Cat?" Butcher asks me.

I look up to our apartment door, where somewhere behind it my mother is lying in bed under the weight of her blankets and her guilt, and I try to imagine if this is what she deserves. Even with all my anger, all my disappointment in her, in what she can or can't manage, I cannot picture this as what she or I *deserve.* I cannot picture the kindness in Gary's heart being repaid by years of unending grief, cannot imagine a world where one night of intoxication is punished with the death of someone you dearly love.

"No," I say quietly. "I don't think it works that way."

He nods. "No," he says. "I don't think it does either."

XXIV.

I AM SURPRISED A FEW DAYS LATER WHEN I WAKE to the smell of something burning. My mother is in our tiny kitchen humming over a frying pan.

I push myself up on my elbows and squint in the light. "Whatever you're cooking, it was done ten minutes ago." Even though I told him not to worry about it, Gary sent a grocery delivery to our place the day after we spoke.

"But you said you don't like your eggs runny," she whines.

"Yeah, well, I don't like them burnt either." I sit up fully and watch her try to plate the fried eggs that are now black around the edges. She's barefoot and wrapped in a short, kimono-style robe. Her hair is still wet from a shower, and her toenails are a bright canary yellow, which means she painted them. Something has flipped the switch if she's managed this kind of turnaround—bathing, shaving, cooking—just like Gary said it would. I wonder what it is.

"It's good to see you're feeling better," I tell her as I pad to the bathroom to brush my teeth and wash my face.

"What was that, love?" she asks when I return. Her voice is high and bright. She seems unaware of the fog of depression she has just crawled out of.

"You know, your 'stomach bug'?" I make air quotes when I say it, but they go right over her head.

"Oh, yeah, *that*. No fun at all. Must have been something I ate. Or maybe Nan gave it to me."

"Morning sickness isn't contagious," I say with an eye roll. We both know she wasn't sick.

She ignores my snide remark and pats the chair next to her. "Come, sit and eat. We need to plan."

I slide in next to her and push my plate away. "I told you already, this whole Andes idea is ludicrous. You've never even been out of the South, let alone out of the country. What if you get altitude sickness, huh? What then?"

"I'm not talking about that," she says, brushing me off. "And you have no idea where I've been."

I glare at her a solid five seconds before she realizes her slipup. "Whose fault is that?"

She takes a breath. "Let's not do this again. Okay?"

The only reason I let her off the hook is because I don't want to send her back to bed for another nine days or more. "Fine."

"The realtor called this morning," she says with a barely concealed smile. "They sold the house. Isn't that wonderful?"

My heart sinks to the bottom of my stomach like a dead fish. *The house sold.* She means Moony's house—my home. This is the event that got her out of bed, the switch-flipper. I feel nauseous. I don't say a word.

"And she got a much better price for it than we expected. Turns out, small-town Louisiana is a hotter commodity than we thought. And you know, Edna kept that place cleaner than the pipes on a church organ."

I listen with one ear while the other tries to make sure my heart is still beating somewhere down in my bowels. I knew this was coming, or so I tell myself. But thinking of someone else living in our little house, looking out my window with the red hibiscus, cooking in Moony's kitchen, mopping her floors, mowing her grass...it leaves me hollow inside. And the hollow slowly fills with fire—the flames of envy and anger that come with thinking someone else will be living your life, the one you loved and cherished until it was taken away.

The tears slip down my cheeks, but Mary doesn't notice. She's prattling on about interest rates and property values and a lot of other things she actually knows nothing about. I try to tell myself this is good news, that maybe I can talk her into sharing a little of the money for my tuition. If I can get her to sponsor even one semester, I can get out of here and figure the next one out when I'm there. I remind myself that I have some kind of life here now. I have Daniel and the café, and I wouldn't want to go *back*. Forward is a different story. But without Moony, the house is nothing but a carcass anyway. She was the spirit that made it home. There's nothing else for me there.

"Hey, hey," my mother says, leaning in. "Why the tears?"

I don't get how she can understand her clients' emotions, but she can't understand mine. "I know Moony didn't mean anything to you, but I loved her," I snap, pulling away.

It's unfair and I know it. Moony did mean something to my mom. I know that from the greeting cards I found under her bed.

She sighs. "I can't do this with you," she says, getting up from the table. "I know what you think of me, Cat, but I'm not heartless. I'm not glad she's dead, you know. I just can't pretend we had something we didn't. However you felt about each other, it wasn't like that with us. *Ever*."

It is the word "ever" that keeps ringing through the air between us after she stops talking. It is the word that says the most. It means their relationship wasn't just strained when she got older—when she was in high school or when she took off, when she had me or dumped me, or any of the points that would obviously lead to a breakdown in the relationship. It means it was strained long before that, when she was young, when it should have been easy for Moony to love her and easy for her to love Moony back. The way it was for Moony and me.

I don't know what to do with all the questions and possibilities contained in that word. I don't know where to begin unraveling the history they shared that I am not privy to. My mind is racing over plausible explanations. Could my mother have developed her mental illness early? The way some kids are diagnosed with early-onset schizophrenia before they even turn thirteen? Was she just willful or stubborn or precocious or rebellious or any number of other traits that are used to describe difficult children? I can't understand what would put a mother at odds with her daughter straight out of the womb. I can't understand why she would use the word "ever."

"Why?" My voice is small, frayed at the edges. Fringed in black like Mary's burnt eggs.

She folds her arms over her chest like a blockade and shrugs. "Sometimes people are just different."

"But she's your mother."

She looks away, her jaw set. "That isn't always enough, Cat."

Don't I know it. "I'm so sick of all your secrets. She was your mother, and she loved you. And all you ever do is act like she barely existed, like she's just a loose end you have to tie up now that she's gone. But she took care of me when you wouldn't. She did your job for you. She picked up the pieces you left behind."

"Cat, you don't know what you're saying."

"Yes, I do. Because I lived it. I was one of those pieces. I was *in* pieces. You did that. And she stepped in when she didn't have to." My voice is loud enough for the neighbors to hear by now, but I don't care.

"You make her sound like such a martyr. She's not some saint you learned about in nursery school. She took you from me, Cat! Not the other way around." My mother's chest is heaving and her neck is blotchy, like she's allergic to confrontation.

"Bullshit."

"Catia, do not speak—"

"Bullshit!" I slam my hand on the table. "Why were you the one driving away then? Huh?"

"Fine." She seethes. "You want proof? I'll get you proof." She darts into her bedroom and back out again, slamming a stack of papers against the table in front of me. They slide across the surface like an open fan.

"What are these?" I ask, picking up the top one. It's a pamphlet, unfolded and smoothed flat. The top line reads THERE IS HOPE in red block letters. Beneath that, a wine stain of a logo and then the line, *Gamblers Anonymous*.

"The agent found them hidden in your grandmother's desk. I asked her to send me anything that might explain where the money went in that account you talked about. This pretty much says it all." She crosses her arms, defiant.

My mind spins, and I drop the paper like it's on fire. There are signs plastered all over Louisiana with hotline numbers and warning signs and words of encouragement. Almost as many signs as there are machines. It's not just the casinos. They're in every bar, half the motels, truck stops, and gas stations. But the image of Moony sidling up to one of those gaming machines, her face alight with bright colors as she plays with my future, is so surreal it turns my stomach. I think of how much she loved bingo and her game shows. And I remember times when I would get home from school and she wasn't there. She'd come in later, claiming she was at the store or running errands, but more than once there'd be no groceries. I feel sick.

My mother tugs at the lapels of her robe, clutching them over her chest in a tight fist. "We're leaving tomorrow morning for me to sign some papers. Hopefully we'll be back by sundown."

"I have work tomorrow," I say, backing up from the fan of pamphlets and information sheets before me.

"Find someone to take your shift. If you want your grandmother's ashes, you'll be ready to leave by seven."

Suddenly, betraying Moony's final wishes doesn't seem so wrong. She was betraying me all along.

The car smells of old smoke from our last ride together, turning my empty stomach. I got up on my own, dressed in jeans and an oversized T-shirt for road-trip comfort, and tucked myself into the passenger seat without speaking a word. As we roll out of New Orleans, I reread Daniel's text from last night.

I'll cover for you. This is your chance. Find some answers.

I hate how right he is, how sometimes I can't see these things until someone else points them out. Like Moony's guilt, and the bubble I've been living in for ten long years. I hate knowing I'm too close to it all to be clear. Even though I'm furious with Moony, I'm still angry at my mom. No matter how much I want to be free of her, no one has ever been able to pull my emotional strings like she does.

I plug my ears with earbuds and fade into the nonsensical lyrics of the Pixies while my mother listens to a podcast next to me. Even though we are sharing the car, we may as well be in separate cabs for the first couple of hours. She might have forced me to come, but she can't force me to like it. And determined as I am to broadcast that message with every gesture, my stomach betrays me and begins rumbling sometime after nine o'clock. So when she pulls into a roadside drive-thru for "brunch," I don't have it in me to refuse.

I tug at the cord to my earbuds and let them fall into my lap. "Get me anything with scrambled eggs and too much cheese."

She smiles and nods, but I don't return it. She orders us breakfast burritos and fries and orange juices, and we chew and slurp in silence until we're both too stuffed to even think about food, let alone eat another bite.

As we pull back onto the highway, I toy with my earbuds but don't return them to my ears. I'm tired of fighting, tired of carrying the weight of this grudge through the years, tired of being at odds with her over everything. Her words from yesterday bounce around inside my brain like pinballs, the Gamblers Anonymous logo seared into my brain.

"Yesterday, you said Moony took me from you. What did you mean?"

She looks sideways at me. "Cat, I don't think—"

"Please don't shut me down. You wouldn't have said it if you didn't want me to know. I want to know the truth," I tell her.

She is quiet for a long moment before she responds, so long I begin to worry that she's not all right, that perhaps my inquiry has forced her back into her protective, depressive fog. But when she finally does speak, her voice echoes as if it is reaching me from another time. "I didn't want to leave you there."

I want to rage at her. I want to shake her and slap her and force her to swallow those words. I have lived years believing she didn't want me anymore. I know what to do with a mother who doesn't want me. Anger is a shield against her, a weapon that protects me from the world. But it only works if she left me willingly. It only works if I can see her as callous and careless and useless to me now. If she is anything else, even a fraction of her, it will melt in the face of my empathy. It will change everything.

I think of Daniel. He would counsel me to stay calm. "Why did you?"

She takes a deep breath and lets it out slowly like someone about to wring the truth from their lungs. "She had me over a barrel, Catia. I didn't have a choice. And I was...I was getting worse."

I feel her words like sandpaper in my mind, scratching out my memories of Moony—the Moony I knew. That Moony did not hold people she loved "over a barrel." She did not leave them with no choice. *Just because she says it doesn't make it true,* I tell myself.

But that Moony also didn't gamble tens of thousands of dollars away in secret. And a thing like that, once it's out, does its damage with or without your permission. It plants seeds of doubt. It makes you break trust with your own perception of reality. It wreaks havoc in the halls of your memory. I can already feel my tenuous grasp on the story—her story, my story, *our* story—slipping.

"Worse?" It is the only part of the story that feels safe to handle.

"Sicker," she says with a tremor in her voice. "Here." She places a finger to her temple. "You remember?"

"Yes," I admit. I remember. I remember the spinning, like a force with no gravity, a whirl with no center. It becomes a vacuum. It sucks all sense into the void. The world pitches on its axis, and the person who is your safe place becomes a nest of snares. That is how it feels when you are four, five, six—a carnival ride you cannot get off, living inside an upset stomach.

She nods. "She wanted me to get help."

That sounded like a mother who wanted her daughter to be well, not a kidnapper.

"She promised to keep you safe if I went for treatment, if I voluntarily admitted myself."

Everything slows down around me and becomes viscous, as if we are moving through honey. I didn't know she had been committed. I didn't like to think of her in a place like that, even if it was what she needed at the time.

"So, I did. I kept my end of the bargain. *Bargain* isn't really the right word."

"Just tell me."

"If I got help, she would keep you safe and give you back to me when I was well again."

"And if you didn't?"

"She would have you taken away. She would report me to Child Protective Services, petition to get custody, and I would never see you again."

The eggs and peppers and french fries lurch in my abdomen, but I hold them down. *This is what you wanted,* I tell myself. This is truth. It is ugly and twisted and full of corners and angles where people and things get stuck and lost. This is not my Moony, not cinnamon-roll, gameshow Moony. This woman who makes threats against her own. But Moony is proving to be someone I didn't know. I comfort myself with the belief that she did it to protect me, to help my mom, that she was desperate to save us both. Sometimes, the ends really do justify the means. Don't they?

"So, you left me *for me,* is that what you're saying? Does that mean I'm supposed to be okay with it now?"

"I'm saying I didn't see another way at the time, Cat."

"And did you get better?"

"I did," she says quietly. "For a time."

"I don't understand."

"I was clear and focused and working even. I quit drinking and smoking. And I came for you."

"Bullshit."

She purses her lips. "I know this is hard for you to hear."

"You don't know anything about me. Don't pretend like you do." I don't know why I'm suddenly so angry at her. I don't want to hear more, but there's no stopping now. It is spilling from her like fire ants from a disturbed mound.

"I came for you, Cat. I promise. I tried. But she lied. She wouldn't give you up. She told me you were better off with her, happier there, even though *I* was your mother."

"Why? Why would she say that? You're lying."

"I'm not. Not about this. I know you have no reason to trust me, but I'm telling you the truth. I wanted you, Catia. You are everything I've ever wanted. I've spent my whole life wanting you. And I will never forgive myself for letting her take you from me."

I shake my head back and forth to deflect the sound. I cup my ears and tuck my chin. I hear a high-pitched *eeeeeeee* noise and realize it is me. I am sobbing into my oversized shirt. I hate this story that is us. I hate it more than the story I have been telling myself for the last ten years. In my story, there was one person in the entire world I could trust, and that person died. But in this story, I am not even left with that much. In my story, I am unwanted. It is painful, but it is what I know. It makes its own kind of sense. In this story, I am over-wanted. I know how to be the abandoned girl with the crazy mom. I do not know how to be the stolen girl with the manipulative grandmother.

"But you were better! You said so yourself. How could she stop you?"

"I was young and alone and scared. I had every reason to believe her," she says. "And regardless of what people think, mothers aren't always awarded custody. Especially when there is a history and another alternative within the family."

I see how tightly her hands are gripping the steering wheel. "Did she give you a reason? Did she say how she would keep you from taking me back?"

Her eyes slide to me and then back to the road. "She just said she would tell them things about me. Things I did when I was sick."

"What things?"

"I don't know, Cat. I don't remember much from before my time in the hospital. It got pretty bad. What I do recall is...well, it's hard to separate fact from fiction."

They say that the body stores trauma the way a computer stores information. That the memories are downloaded into our cells, hardwired into our very DNA. They say we never actually forget anything, but that the brain holds on to every detail of every moment of our lives, filing it away into recesses we can't reach. I don't know if she really means it, if she truly can't recall, but I know that it is inside of her—the things bipolar disorder made her do. I know those traumas are part of her, part of me.

"You said that you only got better for a time." Maybe it was for the best, what Moony did. Maybe she knew that another episode was inevitable.

"When I couldn't get you back, I gave up. The medicine made me tired. It made me feel disconnected, like I was wearing a glove over my brain. I gained a lot of weight. I started drinking again. I was young still. I wanted to go out. I wanted to find someone. You weren't there. When I came home at the end of the day, when I woke up in the morning, all I could see was the absence of you. I didn't want to live. Not like that. It wasn't long before I met someone I thought I could trust. We left together, tried Texas on for size. Away from my doctors, I let my prescriptions run out. I stopped therapy. None of it seemed to matter anymore. If I wasn't doing it for you, why would I do it at all?"

"For yourself."

"Maybe. I hated her for a while. And then the hate turned inward, and I hated myself more. I was never enough of a reason."

"So, what changed?"

"What do you mean?"

"You're obviously better now. You take meds, right? You have a doctor? I wasn't in the picture. What changed?"

She smiles in a sad, soft way. "You were getting older. I knew someday you would turn eighteen. You would leave home. I wanted you to find me ready. I wanted a chance to be your mom."

It settles over me like sawdust, piling up on my head and shoulders, itchy and suffocating. I am what rests between her and madness. A firewall for mania. It is a responsibility I don't want. With Moony gone, who will be my firewall?

XXV.

WE PULL UP TO THE CURB IN FRONT OF THE TINY HOUSE I called home for the last ten years, and I am amazed at how little has changed. I almost expect to walk in the front door and hear the television playing, smell pot roast on the stove, and see the gleam of freshly polished floors. The realtor is waving from the front steps, her smile too white to be natural and her hair unmoving in the breeze. We get out and I skirt the car, take two steps onto the lawn, and freeze.

My mother practically skips up to the realtor with an outstretched hand. "Shelly! Hi! Thank you for meeting me here."

"Oh, no, don't be silly. The pleasure is all mine. Shall we go in? I'm gonna need your John Hancock on a few of these." She waves a stack of papers at us.

"Yes, absolutely."

Shelly holds the front door open for my mom, but still I don't move. After a second, Mary sticks her head back out. "Cat? You coming?"

I will my feet to step closer, but they refuse. I don't think I can ever go inside that house again. I cannot relive that last morning. I cannot stand in there now, on those carefully polished floors, without thinking how every step I ever took in that house, in that life, was at least in part a lie.

"I'm good," I say. I point next door. "I think I'll just pop over and visit with Eric and Damien. You can get me when you're finished. Yeah?"

"You sure?" She looks a little uncertain, but aside from the realization that going inside that house will only serve to retraumatize me, I see an opportunity I can't pass up. Eric and Damien are the town's biggest gossips. If there is anything to know about my mom and Moony, about the baby in the picture and maybe even my tarot deck, they would be the ones to know it. I wonder if they also knew about Moony's gambling—if anyone did.

"I can't," I tell her truthfully. "I thought I could, but I can't."

She nods. "Okay. I'll swing by when we're all finished."

"Everything okay out here?" Shelly is at the door, her glassy eyes darting between Mary and me.

"Fine," my mother tells her. "Cat is just a little tired from the drive up. She's going to rest next door. Let's get started."

The realtor nods and they both disappear behind Moony's front door—only it's not Moony's anymore. I have to keep reminding myself of that.

I make my way across the lawn to Eric and Damien's place. I knock twice and wait on the porch, praying somebody is home. Eric swings the door open and breaks into a ginormous smile. He's in cutoffs and an unbuttoned shirt, with Deena tucked under one arm and a Swiffer Duster in the other. I can see I caught him off guard.

"Catbird!" he sings, a nickname he made up for me that only he understands.

"Hi. Can I come in?"

He looks out around me and spots my mother's car.

"The house sold. We're here to sign the contract. I just—I can't go back in there, you know?"

"Oh my gosh, of course!" he says, pulling me into a one-arm hug. "Come in, come in."

I feel a weight lift as the door closes behind us. I follow Eric to his kitchen, where he puts Deena down and gets out two mugs. "Tea? You look like you could stand to unwind. I've got a delicious lavender and green tea blend. Had to cut back on the coffee, you know. The caffeine was killing my blood pressure."

I nod and take a seat at their dining table—a turquoise-and-white vintage set that Eric nicknamed Polly Esther. He nicknames everything.

"So," he says, eyes sparkling after he sets a mug and saucer before me and sinks a tea bag in it. "How's NOLA treating you? How's life in Mary's world?"

I laugh. "It's been...interesting."

"I can only imagine."

"It's not all bad though," I confess. "I met someone."

"Really?"

I pull my phone out and show him a picture of Daniel. "He's actually really great."

Eric takes the phone and gives Daniel a thorough inspection. "Mmmhmm, he looks pretty great."

We sip our tea and make small talk for a while. I tell him all about hanging out with Daniel, our place in the Quarter, and my new job.

I tell him about Gary and a few of mom's clients. He hangs on every word. And then he tells me about the new couple moving in next door. They're young, buying a starter house. Fell in love with the property the second they laid eyes on it. "They sell essential oils or something online," he says with a dismissive wave of his hand.

"That's good," I say, unable to hide the sting in my voice completely. "Some new life in there will be good for the place."

"Oh, honey," Eric says, reaching for me. "I know it's hard. She was your whole world for many years."

The tears come unbidden then. But as soon as I can, I wipe at my face and take a deep breath. I didn't come here to cry on Eric's shoulder. I need his help. "Actually, I wanted to talk to you about something," I confess.

"What is it? Anything for our little Catbird, huh, Deena?"

On cue, Deena jumps on my knee and gives a small bark.

"It's just, since I've been living with my mom, some things aren't making sense. I mean, I've learned a few things, and I get the feeling that there's a lot more under the surface, but she's not exactly forthcoming, and Moony isn't here to ask." *And apparently couldn't be trusted to tell the truth anyway*, I think before continuing. "I know you haven't lived here as long as some people, but you've always had your finger on the town's pulse. I just thought, if anyone knew anything, it would be you."

"Catbird, you have come to the right place," he confirms. "And I am nothing if not discreet. This little convo will stay right here between you, me, Deena, and Polly Esther."

I'm pretty sure the dog and the dining table aren't gonna spill. And as long as Eric doesn't tell my mom we spoke, I don't really care who else he talks to about it. "Thank you."

"Of course," he says with a hungry grin.

"So, here's the thing," I begin. "My mom says that she tried to come for me several years ago, but Moony wouldn't let her take me. Something about things she could tell the authorities. I just... I don't see Moony doing that, but I don't think my mom is lying about this. Sometimes she remembers things wrong, she gets... *ideas*. I don't know. I thought maybe you knew more than me."

Eric leans in. "I know your grandmama meant the world to you. And she was a good neighbor—quiet and kept her property up, even if she did look at Deena like she wanted to run her over with her car. But it's no secret in this town that Edna Gage could be—how should I put this? *Rigid.*"

I know he's right, and I sigh into my lavender tea. Moony intimidated people sometimes. She had a certain way of being and a certain way of believing, and she didn't make a lot of room for anything else. "I know the effect she had on people."

"Then you know she could be hard to get along with."

I nod.

"Is it any real surprise to you that she and your mother butted heads?"

When he puts it like that, I feel foolish for thinking otherwise. It seems inevitable they would have had their struggles. "No, I guess not."

"I like your mother, Cat. She's had her troubles, sure, but who among us hasn't? She's trying. And from what I hear, her road hasn't been easy. I may be new to this town, but Damien grew up here. And people talk; they can't help themselves."

"You mean about her bipolar disorder?"

"I mean more than that," he says, leaning over the table. "From what I understand, her road got rocky long before a diagnosis. In fact, most people here think all of that turmoil had something to do with her breakdown. They feel sorry for her."

"What turmoil?"

"You never met your grandfather, did you?"

I shake my head. "No. He died before I was born."

"Well, let's just say it wasn't a happy marriage. Edna kept her troubles to herself, but there was speculation."

"Speculation?"

"Rumors of an affair. Maybe even more than one. Mary was the apple of her father's eye. A real daddy's girl. They were a house divided."

I let that sink in. I can't imagine a man brave enough to cross Moony.

"But you know, that's Catholics for you. Unhappy as they were, they never would have considered divorce. By the time Mary got to high school, it was well-known that the only person Moony had a harder time getting along with than her husband was her daughter. Harold was the buffer between those two. When he passed, your mother had no one."

"You make it sound like Moony was abusing her or something."

"No, not physically. Nothing like that. But she was controlling, overbearing, and she could be cold at times, cruel even."

That is not the Moony who raised me. She was no-nonsense, but she was never cruel. "And Damien told you all this?"

He shrugs. "Not just him. I hear things, you know. I talk to a lot of people in this town. Small towns are like their own reality shows."

I knew Eric had no shortage of people to shoot the shit with around here.

"And then there was that unfortunate incident her senior year."

"What incident?"

"She disappeared for a while. Everyone was real tight-lipped about it, most of all your grandmother. No one really knows where she went or why, but the speculation is that she was hospitalized, had her first breakdown."

"How long is 'a while'?"

He shrugs again, leans back in his chair and feeds Deena a piece of cookie from the plate he set in the middle of the table. "At least four months."

My teacup begins to tremble in my hands. I set it down and bury my hands in my lap.

"She wasn't the same when she came back, that I know for sure. Never really recovered, did she?"

I shake my head. No, she didn't. "And after?"

"She came back, graduated, but kept to herself. She left shortly after. Finally ran." He takes a loud sip of his tea. "And then there was the scandal—or nearly so. And they ended up shutting the whole school down a few years later."

"Scandal?"

"One of the teachers—a nun—accused one of the priests of... how shall I put this? Misconduct with a minor." He rolls his eyes. "The school was aptly named Our Lady of Infinite Sorrows."

I almost gag on my tea, the obituary I found for a priest from the school's faculty flashing through my mind. "What are you saying?"

"I mean, they never proved anything. The woman quietly disappeared up north somewhere—Sister Margaret Scott. She was the real tragedy if you ask me. A few years after she left the order, they found her body. She'd been shot while out walking her dog. Her case eventually went cold."

I take this in while I sip my tea. It is another name I can add to my online search.

"But the damage was already done. They shipped the priest off to another school or some distant monastery—wherever the Catholic church puts their bad seeds. And then the building caught fire; the whole thing burned right down to the foundation one night."

"Fire?"

"Oh, don't worry. It was empty, fortunately. The fire department claimed it was arson, but no charges were ever pressed. They closed up shop after that. Chose not to rebuild. Which screams of guilt if you ask me."

My mind flips through the filing drawer inside my head and pulls an image of a white matchbook with one missing match. *The Pelican Room*. She would have been gone by then, according to Eric. But still, I wonder...

"People around here have all kinds of crazy theories about that fire. Some still believe the ground is cursed. Rumor has it that multiple girls came out against the priest, all claiming the same things, and they were paid off. If anyone had reason to burn that place down, it was one of them."

I think of my mom saying she and the baby she lost were better off without the father, that he wasn't a good man, and I squeeze my hands together under the table.

"You okay, Catbird?" Eric looks at me, his brown eyes full of concern. "If this is too much, we can stop."

I take a breath, forcing the muscles in my neck and shoulders to unknot. "I'm fine. My breakfast just hit me wrong on the way over. So, you were saying she ran away after this scandal?"

"Yep. Everyone saw it coming. Everyone except for your grandmother, that is. Seemed to take her by surprise. To say they were contentious after that would be an understatement. But really, they were always contentious."

I try to let these new details settle next to the eggs and cheese from earlier, but it's hard to swallow all of this at once. Breakfast really is threatening to come back up.

"You know," Eric says thoughtfully. "I think we have an old yearbook lying around here. Damien never could resist a guy in uniform."

He gets up and leaves me with my thoughts and a cooling cup of tea. When he returns, he lays an old yearbook with a crimson, leatherlike cover in front of me. *1999* is stamped across the bottom in gold, and it's embossed with one of those weird Catholic symbols that's half cross and half coat of arms. "Told ya," he says. "Take your time. I'm going to clean up and change. Damien and I have dinner plans. Back in a few."

I open the cover and begin flipping through pages of black-and-white faces, all plastered with sweet, fake smiles. I find the senior class at the rear of the book and look under G. But there are no Gages listed. They must have taken these while she was away. Disappointment stings like lemon juice in a paper cut.

I check the index instead. *Mary Gage* is listed with two pages next to her name. I flip to the first and see a picture of several students stacking boxes and cans into paper bags. My mother is looking down, standing behind the girl the picture is clearly of. But her hair is swept to the opposite side, and I can make out her profile, so like the image in the photograph I saw with the baby. *Fall Food Drive* reads the caption. This would have been the start of the year, before the "incident" that took her away for several months.

I flip to the second, and there is a picture of a small class of girls, all perfectly uniformed. Their teacher, a young nun who couldn't be more than thirty, is standing to their left, a winning smile on her face. She looks radiant with the glow of doing what she clearly believed was important work. I see my mom kneeling in the first row. The other girls are smiling, but her face is soft and blank, like cheese. Her eyes are rimmed in shadows and cast to the side, as if there is someone standing just off camera she is watching, or maybe who is watching her. *Sister Margaret Scott and Third-Hour Class* reads the caption.

The nun Eric mentioned. Perhaps this photo was taken after the first. It's hard to say. My mother's face is puffy. I wonder how far along she is. If she even knows yet.

I decide to flip to the index again. This time, I look under *M* for *Terry Michaels*. He has quite a few page numbers listed by his name. I flip to each one in quick succession, taking in the details of him on different days, looking for something that will tell me where he fits into this story. Here is Father Terry reading in the teacher's lounge. And here he is at a track meet. And here he is laughing with two of the nuns who teach there. And here he is in line in the cafeteria. All very banal. But the last image, the photo of him with his arm around a young student, someone listed as *Sabrina White, sophomore*, strikes a chord in me, like a bell ringing through my bones.

He is pulling her into his right side with a jolly expression, one that could easily be interpreted as fondness. But the tension in her body is unmistakable. The familiarity with which he handles her does not sit well on her face. Her smile is one-sided, falling nearest to him. And her eyes are wider than they should be, her brow tense, her fingers hanging too straight at her side. The shadows I read in her face remind me of the picture of my mother with her class, looking off, haunted.

I slam the book closed with a loud *thump*.

"Did you find her?" Eric calls from a back room.

"Yes," I respond. As much as I'd like to squeeze Eric for more info, I don't think I can stomach any more truth today. When he comes back into the room, I make my apologies and decide to wait in the car.

At the door, I pause and turn to him. "You never knew Moony to gamble, did you?"

"That one? Gamble? Other than the weekly bingo game, I think she'd sooner let hell swallow her whole than be seen participating in anything as immoral as that," he says with a good-natured laugh.

I know he's right. Not about Moony's gambling, but about whether she'd let herself be *seen* gambling. Whatever machines she frequented must have been far enough away from here that she felt certain she could keep up her pious image.

I thank Eric again, head for the car, roll the windows down, and bury my earbuds in my ears, laying the seat back for a nap.

When Mary finally makes it outside, she spots me straightaway. "Wake up, kiddo!" she practically sings into my ear. "We got what we came for. Next stop, the crematorium." She announces this like one of those tour guides forever wandering the Quarter.

I sit up, a little less queasy, and slide her sunglasses from my face. "Great. Can't wait."

She pats my knee and pulls away, using Eric's drive to turn the car around. As we breeze past Moony's house, I can't resist looking back for one last glimpse of my old life. There, tangled in the blooms of the red hibiscus, I think I see a string of red and purple Mardi Gras beads.

I am turning the afternoon with Eric over in my head like a well-worn bone on our way to the crematorium. I hear the low wail for several minutes before I register the sirens. The traffic slows, and my mother begins cursing under her breath. She is suddenly anxious to get out of this town, as if the very air makes her skin crawl. We pass the little Pik-M-Up convenience store where Moony would sometimes stop for milk if she was in a hurry and the dentist office with the low roof where I had my first tooth pulled without anesthetic. We pass the garden center with their pink hanging baskets full of plants and the bank where Moony always stopped for cash. We even pass the drugstore that always smelled like band-aids and iodine.

And then we see them. A circle of fire engines clustered around the Grace Congregational Church like covered wagons pulling up for the night. Their shocking red exteriors shine like exoskeletons in the sun and almost detract from the flames. But as we come level with the church, the fire is hard to miss. It envelops the roof and steeple like waves of orange water. Most of the building is brick, so the fire seems to be concentrated in the areas where there is timber.

My mother taps her hand impatiently against the parking brake. "Why won't they *move*?" she demands.

"The church is on fire," I tell her, as if it isn't obvious.

She huffs but can't resist leaning down and over to get the full view out my window. "Haven't they ever seen a little fire before?" she asks, peeved.

But it's not a little fire at all, even if the church itself is pretty small. We are nearly at a standstill. The light ahead is blinking red, and two patrolmen are directing cars through the intersection one at a time. I stare at the hoses streaming water in violent bursts, to no avail. And as we're watching, there is a loud *crack*. Something within the belfry gives way, and a plume of dust rises through the flames. And then, with a slow and steady sway, the steeple itself lurches to one side until it is point down and tumbles to the ground below in a tumult of splintering wood and warping metal.

The Tower. I see the harrowing image from my deck in my mind. It is the toppling of all we know to be true.

My mother crosses herself—something I have never seen her do in my life—and sits back in her seat, a look of panic on her face. "We have to go," she spits. "We don't have time for this."

We are not on a deadline, and there is plenty of daylight left for our drive back. It is not time she is worried about.

Suddenly, she cuts the wheel left and pulls out to the side of the car in front of her, taking up the oncoming lane and half the city sidewalk to do it.

"What are you doing?" I clutch the armrest of my door.

"Getting us out of here."

The patrolmen have yet to notice, and by the time they do, she is at the intersection turning left and barreling down Anchor Street.

I keep looking back, worried they'll follow, but after a few blocks, I realize they can't exactly leave their posts. Pretty soon she is turning right again, and we are back on track to the crematorium with a detour of only half a dozen blocks or so behind us.

"Why did you do that?" I ask her, belatedly angry as we pull in to park. My heart is still pumping at triple speed.

"Huh?"

"You didn't have to do that," I say a little louder.

But Mary doesn't seem to hear me. She is glancing over her shoulder behind us, where the column of steadily rising gray smoke has replaced the old steeple in the skyline of our hometown.

XXVI.

I'VE NEVER HELD SOMEONE'S ASHES BEFORE. THEY GAVE them to us in a temporary box of white cardboard, all neatly folded and tucked together like an origami project, the weight of it a surprise. I resist the urge to open the box or pick at its corners. I tell myself this is Moony, but my mind refuses to believe it. I think they could be anybody's ashes. How would we know? My mom insists there's a metal tag inside with a number, and the number means it's Moony. But I don't know any number. I don't know any ashes. I know a woman of flesh and blood who baked for me and combed my hair and told me bedtime stories. And she doesn't fit inside this generic box.

We fight over what to do with them.

"I'm just saying, scattering is the most practical option. Do you know what those plots cost, Cat? We can't afford a place like that for her. She should have made her own arrangements if she wanted that."

I glare at my mother, Moony sitting squarely in my lap. "She had very specific beliefs, and you know that. She would not want to be dumped in the Mississippi like some hippie. I won't let you do that to her."

Regardless of whatever lies she told, whatever image she projected, whatever secrets she kept, as she rests against my thighs, Moony is still Moony. And I still love her. She still gave me so much. Maybe not a college fund, but the love and stability I needed for the last ten years. That counts for something. And I want for her what she wanted for herself—a stainless life, a religious end. Even if it's impossible.

Mary rolls her eyes. "Even dead, she's still the victim to you."

"Didn't you get money from the sale of the house? Surely you can spare a little to lay your mother to rest." I resist the urge to bite my own tongue, part of me knowing I should be more focused on talking her into using it for my college than anything else. But I can find another way. Moony needs this. I need this. Some kind of closure.

My mother sighs. "Cat, why is everything a struggle with you? Huh? Is there a single decision we can make without fighting about it first?"

My face burns, her words so eerily similar to Eric's. I don't want my mom and I to be a repeat of her and Moony. I want better for us, but I don't know how to get there. "I'm sure there's a compromise," I say. "I just have to find it. I'll contact the diocese tomorrow and see what they say about it."

She fixes her eyes on some distant point beyond the windshield. "No."

"What do you mean *no*?" I can't believe I'm actually trying to compromise, and she's shooting me down.

"I don't want you to do that. Just...give me some time. I'll figure something out. I don't want them involved."

The way she says "them" sticks in my ears. Like her voice goes hollow on the word, dips down, bottoms out. "What do you have against the church anyway?"

She brushes me off with a glance. "Nothing. It's not my style. Or yours. I don't need people telling me how to think. Can't you just google it or something?"

"I guess."

We drive the rest of the way in silence. I open my mouth more than once to ask a question, draw her out. But there's no way to get to the information I need to know without being obvious. *Hey, Mom, where were you all those months in high school that you disappeared?* So I shut it again every time, the weight of Moony's remains pinning my thighs to the seat.

I can't sleep that night or the next. Instead, I lie in bed feeling both the presence of Moony's ashes and the jar from Izora Jo like a warm buzz of energy through the mattress. I wait hours for my mother to finally wind down and go to her room for sleep. And when she at last closes the door behind her, I pull out my phone and start googling anything I can on church-related scandals in Louisiana between the year before she graduated and the year after. I come across the obituary listing for Father Terry Michaels again, and screenshot the obit to show Daniel. And eventually I find an article on the nun I saw in Damien's yearbook, Sister Margaret Scott. It's about her murder. They don't name the school, but it does say she was a whistleblower in a statutory rape case involving several plaintiffs that never went to trial.

My chest tightens around the word "rape."

An equation is coming together in my mind: the photo plus my mother's words, her uncanny fear, and now this. Could she have been involved in the scandal, one of a number of unnamed plaintiffs? Could that explain the pregnancy? Her secrecy?

I think about Nan sobbing into her Kleenex, the gentle way my mom leaned into her pain instead of away, the way she said *I know* as if she really, truly did. What if she understood Nan because she was a sexual assault survivor too? What if they shared more than having lost a baby? And then I remember that even in the face of that unbearable grief, she'd admitted to the belief that the child was better off dead because the father wasn't a good guy.

I refuse to let myself believe it without more proof. *I don't know. I don't know,* I repeat again and again. *I don't actually know.*

On the third night, I fall into a restless sleep after searching Father Terry Michaels's name online again. Maybe he gave a comment to someone. Maybe he knew the people involved. Maybe he was involved. When I open my eyes, I am not on my pullout sofa in the apartment in the Quarter, but sitting in a classroom full of empty desks. At the front of the room, the High Priestess is writing something on the chalkboard, something very important for me to read. Her veil is the color of the witching hour but stiffer now, like a nun's habit. I try to make out the words, but the room seems to lengthen, pushing the board and its message farther and farther away. My vision swims and blurs. The room begins to fill up with the mist I remember from my last dream. I try to rise from the desk, but something is pinning me by my shoulders to the seat.

It is then that I realize the thickness in the air around me is not mist but smoke.

I choke on hot, ash-laden gulps of it. I look up and straight into the eyes of the man with the peppermint schnapps. For a second, his breath fills my lungs with a wind full of cool relief, and then he is gone, and Father Terry stands in his place, his black frames leaning over me as he stares at me with hard eyes the color of pale stones. His smile is too wide and white to be real, and garish in its insistence. "Where are you going, Mary?" he says. "School isn't over yet."

I wake up thrashing in my sheets with my mother hovering over me in a panic. "Cat, Catia! What's wrong, baby? What's going on?"

Her hands are on my shoulders, pinning me to the bed, trying to keep me from flailing. "Let go of me!" I shout before it sinks in—what is happening, who she is, where I am.

I push her off of me and sit up. "I'm fine," I tell her, trying to catch my breath, unraveling the sheets from my arms and legs.

"Are you?" she asks, eyes full of concern.

"It was just a nightmare."

Her eyebrows pinch together as she examines me. "I forget what finding her must have been like for you. We should do something with the ashes as soon as possible. It's not good for you, sleeping over them like this. It's bad luck to keep your dead in the house."

I shake her words off. "It's not that."

Her lips press together in a thin line. She doesn't believe me.

"I'll come up with something to do with them," I finally tell her. I don't want to admit it, but keeping Moony in a box under my bed does feel like holding her spirit hostage.

She nods. "You dropped this," she says, leaning down to pick my cell phone up off the floor. As she turns it over, the screen flares to life and the color drains from her face in a retreating pink wave. She doesn't do or say anything. She just sits there, transfixed, the glare of the screen casting creepy shadows across her face.

It takes a second, but I realize my mistake. I must have fallen asleep while researching the priest from her school. "Mom?"

"What is this?" she asks quietly. Her eyes finally pull away and find mine. "Catia, what is this?"

"Research?" I supply lamely.

Her mouth opens, closes again.

"Eric said there was some kind of public scandal at your old school. And Daniel signed up for this course on local history at the community college. I thought, you know, he could write his first paper about it or something." I realize my excuse is garbage as soon as I hear myself say it, but it's the first thing I think of.

She passes the phone back to me very slowly and stands up. "I don't want you looking into this. Do you understand me?"

I shrug, uncertain how to react.

"I mean it, Catia. I don't want you researching the school or having anything to do with that town again or ever, ever speaking about this man. Do you hear me? And I want those ashes gone within the week, or I will take them down to the gulf myself and dump every last speck of her unceremoniously in the muddy, brown water."

She's not shouting, but there is force behind her words, like they are backed with brick.

"Okay, okay," I concede, quickly tucking my phone under my pillow. Without knowing it, she has told me more than any google search ever could. Because of her reaction, beyond a shadow of a doubt, I know that my mother was involved in that scandal. And what's more, that Father Terry was too.

Daniel and I both work the next day, and I am all too happy to get out of the stifling apartment where my mother has decided to cancel all her clients and kickstart an organizing campaign. As I'm leaving, she has boxes drug out across the living room from her closet, and a fresh stack of black garbage bags at the ready. But when I come home that night, very little has been accomplished. Piles of old photos, old clothes, and old papers have been shuffled and reshuffled in no certain order. A half-full garbage bag of shoes and makeup sits at the foot of my sofa bed. And Mary is nowhere to be seen.

I step lightly through the carnage, wondering how she was stuffing all this into one wall-length closet with bifold doors. And then my foot hits the plastic bin she kept under her bed. I'm surprised to see it out in the open. Surprised she would risk me finding it. In fact, looking around me, all of this seems unlike her. Mary is a woman who keeps her secrets tucked in dark corners, that much I've figured out. There is a disconnect happening if she is dragging things willingly into the light. Or maybe it's the opposite. Maybe it's that something has been connected rather than severed. A jolt of awakening. I think of her face when she was holding my cell phone. How long has Father Terry's memory been packed away in her mind like these boxes from her closet?

I notice the plastic bin at my foot is not the only one on the floor.

A nearly identical bin sits on the far side of it. It must have been under the other side of her bed. I pop the lid. More papers—an old car title, receipts for dental work, a letter of resignation from five years ago she wrote to one J.R. Washington, manager at someplace called Capital Hub, in which she accuses him of poor leadership, no vision, and sexual harassment. In that order. Which, in and of itself, tells me she wasn't totally balanced at the time.

I sift through the meaningless flotsam, wondering why she's held on to this stuff, when I uncover a manila envelope. I open it and find a thick sheet of cardstock inside. STATE OF LOUISIANA is stamped across the top in block letters. A fancy scroll of blue trails the borders. Just beneath it, *Certificate of Live Birth.* My hand begins to shake. This has to be it—the birth certificate for the other baby, my sister. I slide the paper out and begin searching with eager eyes.

CHILD'S LAST NAME: *Gage*
CHILD'S FIRST NAME: *Mary*

I know fathers name their sons after themselves all the time, but it's not really a thing with mothers, and definitely not with mine. I know how much she hates her name. We've already had that conversation.

I keep reading. The birth date is listed as *October 29, 1983*. I haven't celebrated Mary's birth in a long time, but I remember her birthday. She would never let me forget that she's a Scorpio. She has the same kind of allegiance to astrology that most people reserve for their country.

This is not my sister's birth certificate. It's my mother's.

My hand falls with a moan of frustration. It's not that I really need the confirmation. The picture speaks a thousand words. The time away from school. It's obvious my mom had a baby in her teens, a baby who died. But even so, my brain picks at the frayed edges of my theory, desperate to unwind it, to take me back to the simple *only child of an only child* story I have been telling myself for years instead of this new, sordid drama.

I start to tuck the paper back into the envelope, but my eyes stick on something like pins in a ripped hemline, waiting for my brain to catch up.

FATHER'S LAST NAME: *Gage*
FATHER'S FIRST NAME: *Harold*

But…

MOTHER'S MAIDEN NAME: *Rush*
MOTHER'S FIRST NAME: *Edna*

I hold my breath.

I never knew Moony's maiden name, which suddenly strikes me as odd. But I complained enough when my mother changed her name to Rush for Moony to have had ample opportunity to tell me. I thought my mother had changed her name to distance herself from us, from her only mother and her only—*living*—daughter. But if distance was what she wanted, wouldn't she have chosen something else? Something not connected to Moony in any way?

I slide the certificate back into its envelope and dig deeper. I am starting to come across older things now. Scratchy photographs of people I don't recognize, a baby shoe that is yellow and brittle as mummified teeth, a bundle of pressed flowers, brown with age. And then, small and tucked in on itself, a newspaper clipping. Carefully, I unfold it. It has been ripped from its original page, but some of the header remains. I can see the year *1939* printed at the top, and the letters *–ed News* left from the title. The headline reads, "Notorious Medium Committed After Brutal Attack on Spouse."

There is a black-and-white image of a woman with Moony's fair hair and round face and someone else's dark eyes staring out. Her hat nearly dips over one eye. Her hair curls close to her neck. Her smile is tight. Her eyes—intense.

I keep reading. Her name is Madora Charles. She was working as a medium and spiritualist in St. Louis at the time and had quite a following, even gaining admittance into the upper echelons of society. She was known for her card readings and table tipping, and the grand seances she held in the private homes of wealthy clients. But she was also known for being a little unhinged. The article calls her eccentric and hysterical. After a multitude of public outbursts, she attacked her husband outside a Woolworths and had to be dragged away by local police. At the end of his rope, Mr. Charles agreed to have her committed to a nearby psychiatric hospital, though it's clear he profited from the connections she established in her trade before she became unmanageable. The final sentence is on the tragic child left behind—a baby girl born only eighteen months before.

I read the article three more times, drinking it in. Finally, I look back up to study her picture, and that's when I see the important detail I'd missed earlier. She is sitting, turned at an angle toward the camera, her smart black suit forming an armor of elegance around her. It is against the dark fabric of her skirt that I can just make out a fan of cards, peeking from one darkly gloved hand. Even though I can only see the corners, they are unmistakable. I know it's my deck because apparently there's only one like it in the world.

XXVII.

THERE IS A SCRATCH AT THE DOOR AND THE KNOB TURNS. I scramble instinctively to shove all the stuff back in the bin, but the door swings open before I can get everything in. The newspaper clipping is still clutched in my right hand. My mother stumbles inside, laughing, a bevy of multicolored shopping bags dangling off her arms, Gary at her heels. I freeze.

Mary takes one look at me, and the smile drops from her face like the last autumn leaf from a tree. She releases the bags. They thud against the floor. "Cat."

I look around the chaos of the room. Wasn't she supposed to be cleaning out? Instead, she comes home with more. It's not a point worth making at the moment. I hand the article to her with shaking hands.

She takes it, looks down, and slowly folds it back up. She walks to the kitchen, sets it absently on the counter, and reaches in the fridge for a beer.

Gary looks lost, like a small child who's just been dropped off at a shopping mall all alone.

My mother takes a long drink of her beer.

"Mom?"

"You shouldn't be touching my things." Her voice strikes my heart like a shard, chilling me from within.

"I live here too. And they're kind of hard to miss."

"Don't touch my things!" she screams as if she's on fire and I am blocking the hose.

"Hey, hey now." Gary steps in, going to her side. "Cat didn't mean any harm."

I want to tell him to save his breath. *Don't be a hero, Gary.* Because this is not Mary we're dealing with. There is Mary—loud, proud, outlandish Mary. And then there are the fragments that take over when her illness is in overdrive. They cycle through quickly, coming on too strong, making no sense, like pure emotion has just been given the keys to a BMW. Go ahead, Rage, take the wheel. Pain, Lust, Fear—drive your hearts out. The road is yours.

I should have seen it coming in the boxes. The burst of aimless energy. The expression on her face when she turned my phone over, like flashes of light coming on and going out. She is like the cloak of the veiled woman and the dive of the boy fool. Her head is full of stars. She is always falling up.

This, I realize with the clarity of a capsized iceberg, is the original trigger, the inciting incident, the trauma that set it all in motion. It is Father Terry. And it is Moony. And it is the dead baby. And it is me. And before all of these, it is the cards and a heritage of mental instability that stretches back generations. The salt in our blood.

"Why didn't you ever tell me that Moony's maiden name was Rush?"

She glares at me, her eyes darker than normal, as if her pupils have swallowed the irises. "It's my name now. One small thing I could take from her after all she took from me."

But it's also mine. This story that is us, the one I am piecing together, that I hate, that begins somewhere with Madora Charles and winds through Moony and my mother like unspooled yarn—circling around Harold and Father Terry and the baby with no name and no breath and the man with the peppermint schnapps and now curling itself around my heart—it is also my story. And it is also my name.

"I thought you changed it to move farther from her, from *us*, but you did it to get closer." I say quietly.

Mary concentrates on her beer label. Hard. She doesn't confirm or deny my statement.

"I thought you were a daddy's girl," I say more to myself than her.

She looks up at me. "He loved me."

A piece of my heart breaks for her, for the little-girl way she says it. For the words hiding behind these. My grandfather, Harold, he loved her, but Moony didn't.

Rush. I think I understand the name change now, maybe even better than she does. She was closer to her dad because he was the one who was closer to *her*, not because she chose him over Moony. In the end, after everything, regardless of what she says, she chose Moony over him.

Gary is rubbing my mom's back like he can stroke the chill from her voice. I am trembling. I feel my history tumbling like old stones around my feet—reordering itself—erecting a wall of unfeeling marble, of worn and battered granite bricks spliced together, full of chinks.

"Who is Madora Charles?" I ask, pointing to the folded clipping.

Mary shrugs. "A woman. A medium. A patient. Someone who lived and died a long time ago."

"Who is she *to us*?" I clarify.

She stares at me a long moment.

"I can see the resemblance to Moony," I add, in case she thinks she can spin it any way but straight.

"She's your great-great-grandmother," she says.

"How do you know about her? Where did you get this?" I ask.

"She told me," she says smugly. "Edna. After I found the cards. After she found me with them. I must have been eight or nine years old. I'd never been whipped like that before or since. She screamed it at me and showed me this article, shaking it in my face. And then she took the cards away. But I snuck back later and stole them—the cards and the article. I hid them from her. She punished me for weeks when she found out." My mother laughs humorlessly as she remembers something the rest of us can only guess at. "She had a unique brand of discipline. She was creative, your grandmother. I'll give her that."

I shake my head as if that could keep the words from crawling into my ears and lodging themselves inside my brain. My heart is cracking open. The only discipline I ever got from Moony was a time-out. When I was young, she kept a little red stool in one corner of the kitchen, and if I was really bad—if I shouted at her or deliberately did something she told me not to—she would put me on it for five or ten agonizing minutes. When I got older, she abandoned the stool and simply sent me to my room to "cool off" or "think about things." I could count on one hand the number of times that happened and still have fingers left.

"I broke her," Mary says now, her chin lifting, her face hardening. "*I* broke her. That's why she was so good to you. Because I didn't flinch against the hardness in her until all her edges were worn smooth. I got the stone, but you got the pebble. You have me to thank for that."

I think of Moony's pale strands of corn-colored hair in old photographs. I think of her strong jaw and round head and tiny watch. My mother's hair is dark and red and streaked with colors Moony would think indecent. Her jaw is pointed, and her face has angles and contours I feel I'm only just appreciating. And all of it is making a new kind of sense—the stubbornness and resentment and refusal to give where Moony is concerned. It's less that Mary doesn't love her mother, and more that she does. Their differences are myriad, but their sameness is what really kept them apart. Their inability to fully reconcile, right up to the very end, has left my mother bitter and in stark denial of her true feelings. Why entertain a desire you can never hope to fulfill?

"I don't understand," I say quietly. "Why wouldn't she want you to see this? Why keep the cards at all if she didn't want them found?"

My mother sits at her card table and looks up at me. "She kept them because they were her only connection to her mother, Helen, when she went away."

"Helen?"

"The little girl in the article—the daughter of Madora Charles."

I look down at my hands, how every cell knits together like

so many stitches to form a chain, and all those chains tie end to end to form...*me*. The women of my family are like this, knotted together end to end. But I can't see what we are making. "Where did she go?"

"To the same institution they sent Madora to, many years before."

We are a repeating pattern, a chain of chaos. I look at my mother and see everything I never wanted to be. "Moony grew up without a mother?"

"For a time," my mother says, and it's the first time I've heard her say anything in regard to Moony without spite lacing her voice. "Unlike Madora, Helen got out. *Eventually*. But she was never really right. That place broke her."

"And Moony?"

My mother shrugs. "She believed a life of smallness and sameness would protect her from her mother's and grandmother's fate."

I swallow air. There is no comfort in it. "What was her *unique brand of discipline*?" I am afraid to ask, but more afraid not to.

My mother grins coldly. "Withholding. She did it to me my whole life. In those early weeks, after she'd ransacked my room to no avail, when she still thought she could torture the location of the deck out of me, she would withhold seemingly small things. I could only drink a teaspoon of water at a time. Or I wasn't allowed soap until the kids at school were all calling me 'Scary Mary.' Or I found the bathroom locked and wasn't given a key until I started peeing outside and became so constipated she had to take me to the ER. One week she made me eat split pea soup for every meal because she knew how much I hated it. If I puked, I had to clean it up myself."

I take a step toward her with my hand out, to touch her arm or her back, to comfort her. But she jumps up, skirting my fingers like they are the ends of a live wire.

I don't know what to say. Do I defend Moony's memory? Do I refuse to believe her? Do I apologize for being on the receiving end of everything that was best about my grandmother, while she received everything that was worst? I am racked with a kind of survivor's guilt and a relief that I am ashamed to admit. "I can't imagine," I tell her.

"No, you can't," she responds with hard eyes. "She withheld all kinds of things hoping I'd break. But mostly she withheld herself. She stopped showing me affection, stopped telling me she loved me. And then she withheld you. She still wanted to break me after all those years. But I'm stronger than her."

She laughs genuinely now, a full-throated, roaring *gaw-gaw-gaw* sound like the call of some prehistoric bird. She laughs and laughs until she's clutching her stomach with one arm and her eyes are spilling over with fat, ironic tears. "And the best part?" she finally spits out. "The best part is that I left the deck with you. She had it the whole time!"

I am watching myself watch her laugh as though I have left my body and am floating in the back of the room. I want to slap her. I want to hug her. I want to run. But I can't move. And so I just stand there, in my watercolor way, a wash of faint lines and pale colors, quivering with the vibration of her laughter, which masks her anger, which masks her sorrow, which masks her pain. I think of the Magician, with his mismatched face, and see him reflected in my mother's reaction. None of her expressions fit together right. They are all converging at once, a pileup of emotion.

She finally stops. Her gulps of air become gasps. Her roar becomes a hush. She stands spent before me, her hair a mess around her face. She wipes at her nose with one hand. "But she took you from me in the end. And you took her. And I had no one."

I gape. Like fish. Like an openmouthed baby doll. Like the dead.

"That's the punch line," she finishes. "But I'm all laughed out."

After a moment, my mother grabs her purse and keys. She kicks the lid off the plastic bin next to her, the one full of the greeting cards Moony sent. "Here, take a look at these. There are pictures in some."

I pretend I've not already seen them and pick one or two off the top, turning them over in my hands. "Where are you going?"

"Out."

"Let me drive you," Gary says, shaking me from the stupor that has allowed me to forget he was even in the room.

"I need to be alone," she tells him without looking back.

XXVIII.

I DROP THE CARDS BACK INTO THE BIN WHEN SHE IS gone. Kick it. Slide the lid back on. Her shopping bags litter the floor, along with all the crap from her room. I start to gather them, then set them down again. *Fuck it.*

Gary looks at me and picks up my mother's unfinished beer. "Not interested, huh?"

"I've seen it," I confess.

He nods, taking a swig. "I guess we better clean this place up before she gets back."

I am not keen on cleaning up another one of my mother's messes, but I figure I should give the chip on my shoulder a rest. "I'll do it. You can go home."

"You all right?" he asks now, bending some to look me in the face.

"I think." The more I learn about my family, the less I want to know. And yet, there are still things nagging at my soul. I pick up the newspaper article where she let it drop. "Did you know?" I ask him on a whim. "About that stuff she said today?"

He hangs his head. "Some of it."

I sniffle, feeling like the person outside of an inside joke. This stranger, this man who did not know Moony and until a couple of months ago did not know me, knew things about us all that I didn't.

"Things slip out when she drinks," he says matter-of-factly.

"What about this?" I ask him, holding up the newspaper clipping. "She ever show you this?"

"Nah," he says.

I stare at the picture of Madora Charles a moment longer before gingerly refolding it. "You know what this means?" I tell him. "It runs in our family."

"What does?" he asks.

I want to shake him. I want to take him by his sloping shoulders and waggle him back and forth until his brain stem comes undone. *The cards. The crazy.* "Her disorder, Gary. The mania. The paranoia. All of it."

"Oh, that," he says as if he'd forgotten all about it.

Yes, Gary, that. I bend down to fold the lids of a nearby box together and scoop it up. This one seems to be mostly full of accessories—purses and a pair of suede boots.

Gary follows my lead, closing up another box after tucking its escaping contents back inside.

"I said I would take care of it," I tell him.

He rises, pausing, fumbling with his hands. Finally, he says, "She's not like that woman in the article. She's not that bad."

"Then you haven't seen her at her worst."

Gary doesn't say anything. He turns toward the door as if to leave.

I stand and face him. "You said things slip out when she drinks. What other things?"

Gary turns around. "Cat, it's not my place."

"It's my family. If you know things about my family that I don't know, then spill."

He takes a sudden interest in the pointy toes of his boots. "I don't know much. What she told you today, about her momma. I know how hard losing her dad was on her. It got rough after that, between the two of 'em. Real rough. And she had some problems—at school."

"What kind of problems?"

He shrugs. "She won't say exactly, but she says things that make it obvious if you're paying attention."

I narrow my eyes. "What kind of things?" I know I'm making Gary uncomfortable, but I don't care.

"She calls it a *bad place*. Says they hated her there. Says they had ways of punishing her that shouldn't be allowed to happen in this country. Says they were worse than her mother ever was."

My stomach rolls. "Who? Who punished her? Did she say?"

"No," he admits with a sigh.

I close my eyes, and Moony's white hair and glowing skin swim before me, the square frames of Father Terry's glasses, Eric's mouth grinning on the word "scandal." I am nauseous with truth.

"I've tried asking," he says all of a sudden. "It's only when she's drunk and on a roll that some of this comes out."

I frown. "She doesn't like to talk about her past."

"I know you got issues with your momma," he says. "I understand. There were days growing up when I could have lit my house on fire and never looked back. My daddy was a drunk and a mean one at that. But your mom has been through a lot, Cat. And she's trying. Which is more than I could ever say for my dad."

His fire fantasy is not lost on me. The matchbook, the school. I am drawing dizzying connections that may or may not be valid, but I can't unsee them. "You don't have to defend her all the time," I tell him. "I'm not heartless. She just doesn't make it easy. You weren't there when I was little, when she left."

"I know," he says quietly, a distinctly defeated hang to his head.

"Why do you stay?"

"I love her," he says. "And so do you."

I want to argue, but the fight has fled my veins.

"When I lost my son," he starts, his voice soft like tufts of goose down, "I thought I'd never love again. I had a revolver, a Colt Special, and I sat in the dark with the barrel in my mouth many a night, thinking about how easy it would be to stop the pain. But then I'd think, if I died, so did he. Whatever was left of him would be lost. So I'd put it away and fight through another day or week or month. The first time I met your mother, I told her about Noah. Told her the whole story. And she looked at me and said, 'Every time you think of hurting yourself, you hurt your boy.' I sold my gun after that."

"I'm sorry," I tell him because I am.

He smiles a little. "I still haven't figured out how to forgive myself for what happened to Noah, but when I look in her eyes, I see the same pain I carry and then some. I know she has walked through hell and back again. But it's what happened with you, losing you to your grandmother, that did the worst damage. You may not see it, but she's worked hard to put the pieces she has left back together. For you."

I'm not sure how to respond to Gary's speech, where to start, where to end. But I know he's wrong about one thing. My mom was damaged long before I came along. Damaged by Moony. Damaged by whatever happened to her at Our Lady of Infinite Sorrows. By Father Terry. By my sister. And yes, at last, by me.

XXIX.

SHE DOESN'T COME HOME THAT NIGHT, AND I DON'T blame her. Her constant running suddenly makes sense to me. I think I would want to run also if I were her. I think I would want to feel my feet pumping beneath me, shredding ground, the world passing me by in a blur, the distance between who I am and who I am becoming growing wider with every step. But you can't outrun the story that is you. I feel that truth stirring in the marrow of my bones. I feel it creeping beneath my skin. I feel it lodged, like an unreachable kernel between the teeth, in the cavities of my heart.

And I think that is the difference between my mother and me. The belief that she can outrun herself has driven her to the edges of her understanding more than once. The knowing that I can't has held me firmly in the unforgiving grip of my truth.

I lie in my sofa bed, waiting for the click of the knob as it turns, for her to burst in laughing or crying or drinking. I wait for the bigness of her to return and push me out of this space, through the hairline cracks in the bricks, through holes in the mortar, beyond the reaches of the city. Mostly I wait to feel something. I finally got most of her boxes shoved back into her closet. I stacked her shopping bags next to her bed. More bullshit to fill the holes Moony left behind. *I* left behind.

I finger the newspaper article. I have read it a dozen times over trying to understand, trying to weave the broken threads flailing in my mind into something sensible. I stare at the picture of Madora Charles, willing her to speak. I stare until her eyes burn like pools of hot pitch and her lips curl into themselves and the circle of her face becomes dinner-plate smooth.

She never says a word.

I want to ask her, *Was it you? Or was it the cards? Who pushed you over the edge, Madora Charles? Was it the Fool? Or the Devil? Or a mother who taught you that even the most mundane of human experiences, like using the bathroom, could be turned into an instrument of torture?*

I flip through my deck and wonder, *Which one of you is responsible?*

When I land on the Hermit card, I linger. The beard. The light in the dark. The unwavering presence where there should be none.

I suddenly can't stand the feeling of my bedsheets beneath me. The room is shrinking, or my breaths are growing. The maze of my thoughts needs room to spread out or my head might collapse on itself like a red giant, erupting like a supernova.

I tug on jeans and tumble out the front door into our courtyard. Butcher is waiting by the fountain. He is always smoking. I take the steps two at a time until we are face-to-face. "I know you," I tell him abruptly. "I know what you are."

He takes a drag. "Is that so?"

I feel full of bubbles. I feel drunk. My head is light as air.

I think I could float if I tried. "I've known you a long time, but I only just figured it out."

He peers at me. "Be careful with that head of yours. The downfall of every great man has been thinking he knows more than he does."

I peer back. My bubbles start to pop. "What is that supposed to mean?"

Butcher flicks his cigarette into the fountain. "You don't know what you don't know, no matter what you do. Simple as that." He walks away, disappearing behind his apartment door.

I sit on the lip of the fountain for a long time, watching the sky. There is a pattern to the dark if you look closely enough. But I don't know if I have the stamina for finding it. I miss Moony's clockwork world. I miss the smallness of it. The way the earth felt under my feet. I don't belong there anymore. I know that. I've grown, in this city of spice and jazz and ghosts. I've been exposed. Contaminated. In the black woods of fairy tales, the trail of crumbs leads you out again. But not in my story. In my story, there is only deeper in.

When I finally go back inside, it is well after midnight. I call Daniel anyway. I must anchor myself to something.

"Cat? Is everything okay?" He sounds sleepy. I can picture him rubbing his eyes, squinting in the dark of his room.

"Come over," I blurt.

"Now? What time is it?"

"Late." Is this how my mom does it? When she drags her men back home? I have no grace for this and don't care. I am alone and don't want to be. My bed is huge in this small room. I'm tired of incremental progress. I want to surge. I want Daniel. I've always wanted Daniel. "You should come over. Stay with me."

"Where's your mom?" he asks now. He is waking up. I can hear it.

"She left," I tell him. "She won't be back. Not tonight."

"Cat." Daniel's voice changes, deepens. He becomes serious. "What are you asking me exactly?"

I take a breath. "To spend the night. With me. Here. And everything that comes with that."

He breathes into the phone.

"I want you. All of you," I say to his breath. I wait.

Finally, he says, "Give me a few. I'll be there. We'll talk."

But when he knocks on my door half an hour later, we do little talking. I let him in, pull him toward me. I taste him deeply and don't let go.

"Are you sure?" he whispers into the night, his lips at my neck just below my ear.

I am. I answer him by pressing my body into his, by pushing him into the thin mattress, by sucking the words from his lips. He doesn't ask again.

He is gentle and he is slow, as if I am made of china. But I don't break when he fills me. I grow stronger, my heart swells. My watercolor lines pulse with a new intensity of color. And when it's over, I lie curled against him like two leaves fallen from the same tree. I feel his breath on my shoulder, the *tick tick tick* of his heart against my back like Moony's watch under my pillow. There is no regret.

I fall asleep among a litter of limbs and tarot cards. I dream of a woman hog-tying a scarlet bull, and an owl wielding a sword with two blades—one dull, one sharp. I wake up just as I begin falling, wondering which end will catch me.

XXX.

THE NEXT DAY, DANIEL LEAVES EARLY FOR WORK, AND still Mary doesn't come home. By the afternoon, I'm starting to worry. I call and text repeatedly, but she never responds. I check the bathroom—all her pill bottles are there. Unless she swung by a pharmacy, she doesn't have her meds. Not that I know which ones she is taking or *if* she's been taking them. Finally, much as I don't want to, I decide to brave the Quarter, to go out looking for her. Maybe she's in the square giving readings or in one of the dingy bars. Maybe I'll see her car parked along a narrow street. It's a long shot, but it's all I've got.

I take the streets methodically, tracking my turns with the Notes app on my phone so I can be sure I cover every one. At first, it is uneventful. The streets resonate with a million feet pounding. It's bright out. The daylight makes even the scrawniest of alleyways and deepest of potholes seem cheery. I start to get bored after the first hour and a half. I wander in and out of shops. Poke my head into bars that are open early. Survey the tables at restaurants through their windows. I breeze past the café and think of going in to see Daniel, but decide not to. I don't want to be rescued. I deny my inner damsel. I'm not ready to step out of the magic of our night together into what's next. I want to hold on to the perfection of us side by side with nothing in between—no moms or grandmas or strangers—a beat longer.

When I reach the square, her presence isn't among the paintings of skeletons and cats and colorful front doors. It isn't hiding between the six-strings and the drum sets and the benches full of people. Disheartened, I turn into the garden, sticking to the outer circle. That's where I find the Devil leaning against a tree. He has one leg up, foot against the trunk, and his arms are crossed behind his back—the Hanged Man. Today he is wearing a woman's jacket with a faux fur collar and the sleeves ripped off.

I walk up to him.

"Back for more?" he asks with a wicked grin.

I roll my eyes. "You haven't seen her, have you? My mom?"

"Afraid not." He pulls a snakeskin flask from a back pocket and takes a swig, then reaches out to me, offering it.

I take it from him and swallow the cold burn, the mint lighting up my nostrils like sun on snow. I pass it back.

He caps it. "There's something different about you," he says, studying me.

"You too," I tell him. He seems suddenly shorter to me, sadder. I think I see the beginning of lines around his eyes, and the whites are pink with angry veins. Is that gray in his goatee? Maybe he's not as young as I thought he was. He's just a drunk after all.

"Why here?" I ask after a moment. "Why the church? Isn't that kind of your kryptonite?"

He looks at me for a long while, as if deciding whether to answer, and then says, "One person's devil is another's angel."

I can't argue.

Then he adds, "Do I really exist anywhere else?"

I notice the necklace he's wearing. A long silver chain with a bat hanging upside down at the end, its wings wrapped around itself protectively.

We are both stuck, he and I, hanging by a thread. Perhaps everyone is, they just don't see it. "Did you know my great-great-grandmother Madora Charles? Are you why we are the way we are?"

I have included myself in our family lineup of troubled women: Madora, Helen...Moony may not have been hospitalized, but she certainly had some deep-seated issues as it turns out. My mother is more obvious. And me. I don't know what I am yet—gifted, deranged, normal. But I am beginning not to care. Moony tried so hard not to be like her own mother that she broke herself and her daughter. I don't want to make Moony's same mistakes as much as I don't want to make Mary's. I want to make my own. I want to surrender to my fate.

He stares at me, eyes like hard candies. "I don't really have that kind of power."

"I know." It feels good to walk away.

That night, I sit by the fountain after a day of futile searching. I text Daniel. I don't ask him over again, but I blush when I remember. His text back echoes my feelings. *Dreaming of you...*

I text Gary. He hasn't heard from her. I decide to take a chance. It's the last card I know to play.

A soft voice answers on the third ring. "Hello?"

"Dr. Angela? Is this Angela Murray?"

"Speaking. Who's calling?"

"You don't know me, but I think my mom may be a patient of yours. Her name is Mary Rush. I'm her daughter, Cat."

There is a long pause and then she says, "Mary *Rush*?"

"Yes."

"And you're her daughter?"

I don't have time to repeat myself. My frustration mounts. "Yes. Her daughter, Catia. You're her doctor, right? Her psychiatrist?"

"I am," she admits. "But Mary never told me she had a daughter."

I'm not sure how to respond to that. I suck air for a moment. "My grandmother raised me. I only just came to live with her a few months ago after my grandmother died."

"I see."

"I think something is wrong," I tell her. "I don't know who else to call."

"How so?"

"My mom didn't come home last night. It's been twenty-four hours now. I don't know where she is. She isn't answering her phone," I push it out all in a jumble.

There is a pause, and then a soft, deciding breath. "Cat, I hate to be the bearer of bad news, but I haven't seen your mother in some time. Several months, in fact. She missed her appointment in April and didn't reschedule. I left her a voice mail—*many*."

My mind wheels like a carousel gone rogue. "Then how do you know if she's taking her medicine? I mean, I could check if you tell me which ones she's on. There are so many bottles in there. I don't know—"

"I have to stop you right there," she explains calmly. With that very sympathetic therapist voice. "I'm not at liberty to speak about her prescriptions with you, even if you are her daughter."

I huff, searching my mind for what I can ask her and get a response to. "What am I supposed to do?" My voice is small, shrinking with my hope.

"I suggest you call the police and report her as missing."

I thank her brusquely and am about to hang up when another question seizes me. "Wait, Dr. Angela! Can I ask you something else?"

"Certainly, though I can't promise I can answer." I detect the layer of patience she spreads thickly over her words.

"How do you know if...I mean, what are the signs if, like, you're someone like my mom?" It is clumsy of me. And desperate. It surprises me even as I ask it.

If I am bipolar, I tell myself I can make peace with that. But I don't want to live in denial. I don't want to hurt others by refusing to medicate.

I hear her breathing stop. Hear the long exhale that emanates. She is caving beneath the weight of her conscience, her responsibility, to Mary, to me. "Cat...your mother's diagnosis is complicated. There is no one contributing factor and no one emergent feature. And patients are not always aware of their own symptoms. I'm sorry, but there is no short answer to your question."

I inhale a quick sip of air. "Okay."

Then, as if on second thought, she adds, "Listen, if you're experiencing any confusing emotions or disorientation, anything that would give you cause for concern, I urge you to make an appointment. If not with me, then with another qualified mental health specialist."

It's very "good doctor" of her, but I'm regretting this conversation already. "I'll keep that in mind."

"And..." Her voice lowers an octave. "For what it's worth, if you're asking—if you're showing concern—it's a good sign."

"Thank you," I answer.

"That doesn't mean you should forego seeing someone though. You understand?"

"Yes," I assure her. "I understand." My focus may be on my mother right now, but I can't help considering the sense of her words. Daniel does keep reminding me that I've been through a trauma. Maybe once my mom is back, I will look for my own therapist.

Dr. Angela clears her throat. "How old are you, Cat? Are you a minor?"

My convivial feelings toward the good doctor wash away in a wave of paranoia. I don't understand what difference that makes. I'm suddenly overcome by the urge to hang up, so I do.

If I call the police like she said, what happens to me? I'm still under eighteen. I have no surviving relatives that I know of. The cops aren't going to just take my information and walk away, leaving me alone. Mary may not be my first choice for a roommate, but I'll take her over being a ward of the state any day.

I climb the stairs and lock myself inside our apartment, deciding against alerting the police. Surely, she'll be back tomorrow. Gary said she'd done this before. "She always comes home," he said. But he's only known her a couple of years. He is forgetting that once, ten years ago, she didn't come home after all.

XXXI.

I'M DREAMING OF MY OLD ROOM IN MOONY'S HOUSE when I first hear the laughter. It weaves itself into my dream. I am searching in the dark for something I've lost because none of my lights will come on. I pat the walls and bed; my hands slide over the mattress and brush against something cold. The kind of cold that only registers as the absence of heat where heat should be. I jerk my fingers back, knowing without seeing that it is Moony's body. And then the laughter begins. It lodges itself in Moony's throat. Horrified, I turn to run, but the door won't open. I am trapped in my old room, in my old life, in the dark, and Moony's corpse is laughing at me.

I sit up and gasp for air. After a few solid breaths, I let my shoulders slump. The apartment is calm. I switch on the lamp beside my sofa bed and rub at my eyes. Then I hear it again, and for a moment, I think the dream has not ended. But the fullness of my face in my hands reassures me I am awake. The laughter I'm hearing is distinctly feminine, but my mother's room is still empty.

I go to the front door and lean my ear against it. It is a tinkling sort of gaiety, like little bells ringing all at once.

I open the door and step outside onto the balcony. I blink as I look out over the courtyard. I hear her before I see her, the ring of her squeals. But soon enough her pink skin comes into focus, the long tangles of wet, white-blond hair. Water droplets fling upward through the night sky as she twirls and tromps in the bowl of our fountain with all the grace of a herd of buffalo.

I start down the stairs. "Ma'am...ma'am," I say in the loudest whisper I can manage. "You need to quiet down. Is there someone I can call for you? Are you in some kind of trouble?"

My concern is met with a wall of water as she whirls and splashes me full in the face.

"What the hell?" I gripe. "Hello? I'm trying to help you. Someone's going to call the police." I don't know why I'm bothering; she must be drunk. Or high on something. But I keep thinking of the night I found my mother down here dancing and how I'd want someone to be kind to her if they found her this way.

The woman's slip is soaked and plastered to her body like wallpaper. I can see the lines of her butterfly tattoo through the fabric above her hip. I'm not sure where her dress went. I see a pair of heels on one of the tables and a small bag with pearl handles. Again, she splashes water in my face.

"Hey!" I say a little louder this time. "Seriously, quit that."

I reach for her arm, but she slips away from me like a pink eel. "What's your name?" I ask, trying to get her attention.

"What's *your* name?" she echoes.

Damn this city, I think coldly. I go to her purse and open it, but there's nothing inside except a wad of twenty-dollar bills. I snap it shut again and hold it up for her. "You're going to get robbed," I try to tell her. "You can't just leave cash like that lying around here."

"Hey, that's mine," she says, stumbling toward me. At least I finally got her attention.

She climbs out of the fountain and snatches her purse from my hand, only to toss it back onto the table. She grabs my hands in hers and tries to drag me to the fountain. "Get in," she says playfully. "Get in with me! It'll be fun."

With some effort, I pull my hands out of hers. I'm not sure what to do, and I'm not sure why I care, but I do the only thing I can think of in a moment like this. "Come upstairs," I tell her. "I'll find something dry for you to wear."

She just stands there, blinking at me. I realize then how undeniably beautiful she is. Her skin is flawless. Her eyes are wide and bluer than hydrangea blossoms. Her hair reaches past the small of her back. She can't be more than ten years my senior, but she seems ageless. She's no High Priestess, but I also doubt she is just a stray.

"I have food," I say in another attempt to lure her inside.

That gets her attention. "I'm starving!" she declares and reaches for her shoes.

I climb the stairs as she drips behind me, her shoes and purse in one hand, the other clutching the banister.

I shut and lock the door behind us as she stands dripping onto the rug in the living room. I go to the kitchen and pull out the turkey and cheese, some bread and mayonnaise, and begin making the beautiful, wet stranger a sandwich. I set it on a plate and hand it to her, along with the last cold soda. She falls on it like she hasn't seen food in a year.

While she eats in the kitchen, I go to my mother's dresser and dig around. I come out with an old T-shirt and some running shorts and a pair of underwear. It'll look ridiculous with her heels, but at least she'll be dry and covered up. I decide to try again. "Listen, is there someone I can call to pick you up? You really shouldn't be walking around alone this late in the city."

She shakes her head.

I blow out a breath. I'm not sure what to do with her.

"I'm Aimee," she says around a mouthful of turkey and cheese.

"Hi, Aimee. I'm Cat." I watch her chew. "Fun night?"

Aimee swallows. "Always."

I nod. Some kind of progress is being made. "So do you always skinny-dip in fountains, or is that just a one-time thing?"

She laughs openmouthed, and I get a full view of masticated sandwich. "You're funny," she says.

And you're an alien, I think. "Do you live around here?" The Devil lives at the cathedral. The Hermit lives next door. Maybe I can walk her home, though I quickly deduce that walking back alone would not be in my best interest. I check my phone. It's 3:00 a.m.

"Oh yeah," she tells me. "I just moved."

I'll bet you did. "It's not very cool of your friends to let you wander off alone."

"I got lost." She finally finishes eating and begins slurping on her soda. "This is a nice place," she says, looking around.

"Thanks. It's my mom's." I leave it at that. No point getting into a whole conversation about Gary and Mary's relationship with someone who likely won't remember it in the morning.

I start to yawn. "So, listen, are you sure I can't call somebody for you? Or an Uber or something? I mean, it's really late and all." It feels wrong to just let her walk back out the door.

"Let me change, and I'll get out of your hair." She scoops up the clothes I brought out.

I fall across my bed when she goes in the bathroom, exhausted. I am almost dozing off when she comes out again. On her way out, she bumps into a chair with an *oof* and promptly falls to the side, bending an ankle awkwardly in the process. She erupts into giggles.

It's a slow fall. The kind only drunks can manage, curving like noodles. And no harm is done. But it's a clear indicator of her condition. "Why don't you just sit down for a bit?" I say against my better judgement. "Sober up."

She rises and flops into the chair facing me. I prop myself up in the bed, determined to keep one eye on her until I can safely send her out into the night.

Aimee pulls her knees up to her chest, and she suddenly seems small and far too young, like a little girl at a sleepover. "So you live here with your mom?"

I nod. "Yeah."

"Just the two of you?"

"Yep."

She nods. "My mom died when I was three."

"I'm sorry," I tell her.

"Don't be," she says, but her eyes have gone soft at the corners. "I barely remember her." As if to change the subject, she reaches for my tarot deck lying on the corner of my bed. "What are these?"

"Family heirloom," I mutter.

She pulls them out of the box and begins flipping through

them. “Yeah, I’ve seen these. Tarot cards, right?” She pronounces tarot like *carrot*.

“Uh, yeah.”

“Fun.” Her face lights up. “This one looks creepy.” She laughs, holding up the Devil card. She makes a monster face. “Very serious.”

I realize he doesn’t frighten her at all.

She flips some more and holds up the Death card next. “Ooooh,” she says. “I bet people don’t like it when they get that one!”

In spite of myself, I smile. “No, I bet they don’t.” She keeps flipping, and I ask her, “They don’t scare you? Some people, you know, get freaked out by them.”

She shrugs. “What’s to be scared of? They’re just paper. Besides, isn’t the whole point that they’re supposed to *help* you?”

“Yeah, but what about the meanings? Like the Death card. You wouldn’t be scared by that?”

Aimee grins. “Everybody dies, Cat.”

It’s almost creepy, the way she says it. But there’s something about her apple cheeks and big, batting eyes that puts me at ease. Maybe too much. My eyelids are starting to feel about twenty pounds heavier.

“I guess. But no one wants to.” I think of Moony and feel my chest tighten. Another yawn escapes.

“That’s because people have lost sight of the only real thing left in this world.” She scrunches up her nose, staring at a card she’s picked from the rest.

A drunk philosopher. Just my luck. “Oh yeah? What’s that?”

“Hope. Duh.”

“Hope?” I can hear my words slurring with sleep. “That’s not real at all.”

"Of course it is," she replies. "Without hope, what does anything else matter?"

I am just on the edge of drifting off when she holds up the card she'd been peering at. "This one is my favorite."

I fall asleep looking at the Star.

When I wake the next morning, light is streaming in through the window over the sink with too much enthusiasm. I squint against it, sitting up in bed. Remembering the night before, I look to the chair where I last saw Aimee, but it's empty. In her place lies the Star card from my deck. I pick it up. On the back she has scrawled *Hope* in lipstick from our bathroom. I figure I should be vexed that a drunk has defiled my family's prized deck, but there is something endearing in the gesture, like an autograph. I don't quite know how to classify Aimee—part party girl, part tarot goddess. But I know why she liked the Star. In her way, she is the Star.

I smile on my way to the bathroom, only to find that Aimee has stolen a bottle of Vicodin, my only hairbrush, my mother's new suede boots, and a six-pack of beer from the fridge.

I laugh so hard I end up on my knees with tears the size of mosquitos coursing down my cheeks. By the time I can collect myself, I'm not even angry anymore. I hope she likes the boots. I just wish she'd left the hairbrush.

XXXII.

ANOTHER DAY AND NIGHT PASS WITH NO WORD. I TEXT my mother three more times. The first text is much like the rest. *Where are you, Mary? Can't you at least tell me where you are, so I know you're okay?*

By the second, my despair is peeking through. *Mom. Please just text back.*

The third becomes personal. I type *I miss you* only to delete it, feeling angry that she's even put me in this position. Finally, I send *I'm sorry*.

I don't know what I'm apologizing for. She's the one in the wrong. But I've no doubt she's holed up, imagining some slight on my part, some offense she's invented that keeps her from replying. Maybe if I concede she'll give in and come home.

Tomorrow, the weekend is upon us. I call Daniel and make plans to drive to Moony's town to scatter her ashes. I can't think of anywhere else she'd want to be, so I decide on her own front yard.

I spend another night alone, struggling to fall asleep, and even find myself wishing Aimee would turn back up. I'm sure there's a blouse or two she could take as recompense for the company. I consider it, but I don't call or text Mary anymore. I'm tired of pandering. I'm hurt and I'm angry.

In the morning, Gary calls to say he got a three-word text from her—*let me be*. The part of me that was quietly panicking more with every day that passed finally breathes a sigh of relief. And then the rage bubbles up like carbonation, a steady fizz that grows and grows until it is flowing over my edges like a shaken soda can. I'm furious that she's put us—*me*—through this. It's childish and petty. She's probably living it up in a room at the Monteleone, drinking champagne by the Carousel Bar with a rotation of strange men while Gary and I chew our nails and beg her forgiveness. Gary says she'll come around, but I've decided to stop caring when she does. I leave a note on the counter saying where I'm going, then tear it up.

"You sure about this?" Daniel asks as I settle into his passenger seat.

I nod. "It's time. I need to be done with all this." I need to be done with her.

I tell Daniel about the conversation with Dr. Angela and my mother's text to Gary.

"At least you know she's okay," he says as we pull away.

It should be enough, but it's not. Angry as I am, for the first time in ten long years, I feel her absence more like a cold ache in the chest and less like a hot blister over the skin.

It is warm today in our small town, mine and Moony's. That's what Moony called it—"warm". *It's too warm out today, Cat, wait till evening.* Or, *How can they stand to play out there when it is so warm?* But the truth is, it is always more than warm. It is hot the way only Louisiana can be hot. The kind of hot that comes with the loud hum of cicadas and fat, stripe-legged mosquitos and a cloud of wet air. I am standing on her front lawn watching two men with giant sweat rings on their blue T-shirts that say *Guidry Moving* carry a long, pine dresser through the front door. Her box is clutched to my stomach, where it is causing my own T-shirt to stick to my skin with damp.

I cannot do this. Not with these people moving in. I'm not sure what I'll do with Moony now. I look to Daniel.

"No pressure," he says gently.

We're turning back for the car when Deena starts dancing around my ankles. I set Moony on the floorboard and close the door. Eric is standing on his porch waving. "Hey, Catbird! Back already?"

I drag Daniel over. "Hey, Eric. This is Daniel. Remember?"

He grins at Daniel with a knowing expression. "Mmhmm. Well, I can see clearly what Cat sees in you. Y'all come on in for some iced tea."

We duck inside, grateful for the blast of AC. "I didn't know that was happening today," I say, pointing a finger out the window.

Eric follows my lead and nods. "Yes. Two eager beavers, that couple. They're a little too Southern Baptist for my taste, but I think they'll keep the house up. You here for something important?"

"I wanted to spread Moony's ashes," I tell him. "In the yard. But it doesn't feel right now, seeing as it's not her yard anymore."

Eric shakes his head. "If I'd known, honey, I would have told you to come sooner."

"It's all right. We'll figure something else out." I take a breath and feel the tug of instinct in my gut. "Can I show Daniel that yearbook you showed me?"

Eric's face lights up. "Of course, Catbird. I can hook you up."

We wait while he gets it from the back. When he sets it on the table, I flip through and show Daniel the pictures I found of my mom, of Sister Margaret Scott, and of Father Terry. It's the last picture, the one of Father Terry and Sabrina White, that makes my stomach twist.

"Do you or Damien know her?" I ask Eric.

He spins the book his direction and looks at the picture. "Damien does. Only one Sabrina in this area. Must be her. She's about twenty miles north of the town limit."

"Really? Do you think she remembers anything about the school?" An idea is formulating, bubbling up from my stomach to my brain.

Eric looks at me. "I can't speak for her, but that scandal was the biggest thing to happen to this town in forty years. At her own school. I doubt she's forgotten it."

"Do you think she knew my mom?" I venture.

"Oh, Cat, everyone knew your mom."

I look at Daniel. "Do you think she'd talk to us?"

Eric shrugs. "Can't hurt to try. Here, let me draw you a little map out to her place."

⚜

We are standing on Sabrina White's front porch. Only, it's Sabrina *Wright* now, which is funny and not funny at the same time. I try not to feel nervous, and then I give up. Daniel fidgets behind me. I can feel the flutter of his hands and feet as he continually repositions himself.

"Maybe she's not home," he says again.

I do not point out the white sedan in the carport, or the muffled sound of the television we can hear coming from inside. I push the doorbell a second time and glance up into the swaying tops of the telephone pole pine trees that gather in little crowds across her property.

I am just about to turn and throw up my hands when I hear approaching footsteps. The front door pulls back and only a screen separates us. I study her face, looking for clues that this is the girl I saw in the yearbook photograph, but it's hard to say from one picture and one meeting.

"Can I help you?" Her smile falters at the sight of us. We are obviously not who she was expecting.

"Hi," I say too loudly. "Are you Sabrina? Sabrina White?"

She blinks. "Who's asking?"

I glance back at Daniel for courage and take his hand. "Um, I think you may have known my mother. You went to school together here."

Her face relaxes a little, her eyes widen, but she does not move to open the screen door between us. "Is that so?"

"Her name is Mary," I supply. "Mary Gage. She was a couple of years older than you."

Her lips purse. That's what I see first. And then she casts her eyes down at the floor. They bounce up again. And then down again. She rubs her neck. "I remember Mary" is all she says.

I sigh with relief. "I know this is strange," I admit. "But can we come in and ask you some questions about that time? It's just, my mom is sick. And, well, I'm trying to piece some things together."

More lip pursing. "Sure," she says with a tone of resignation. "Why the hell not?"

Sabrina's kitchen is like a scene from that creepy *My Obsession* docuseries. Everything that stands still long enough is covered in Coca-Cola branding. The logo, the letters, the colors are everywhere. She even has an old Coke vending machine angled cutely in one corner with little Coke tchotchkes stacked on top. It's all red and white and pale green with a dab of mustard thrown in for contrast.

"I'm a collector," she says when she catches us looking around with wide, slightly freaked-out eyes. She says this as if it makes sense of it somehow.

I nod. "Nice."

Daniel clears his throat beside me.

"You kids want something to drink?"

"I'll take something," I say. Daniel nods.

"Coke?" she asks brightly.

"Perfect." I try not to sound condescending.

Sabrina pulls three bottles out of her fridge and pops the tops. They are the fancy glass bottles and not the typical plastic ones. She hands us each one and says, "Coke always tastes better in the glass bottle."

I nod again. I don't really care, but I can hear Moony all the way down aisle seven at the grocery, griping that they have the nerve to charge twice as much for half the goods. I turn the ringer off on my phone and lay it in my lap under the table.

"So," Sabrina says. "You're Mary's girl?"

"Yeah." I smile in a way I hope is sweet. "Did you know each other well?"

"Yes and no," she says. When I don't respond, she adds, "She was older than me," as if that explains it.

We could do this all day, this little dance around the truth. But I don't have all day. Daniel and I have a lengthy drive back to New Orleans, and I still don't know where my mother is. And I never want to come back to this town again, which surprises me even as I think it.

"I don't know how to say this," I begin. "So I'm just going to say it."

Her eyebrows rise a half inch.

"Something happened to my mother at that school. And I think it has something to do with Father Terry. And I think you might know something about it."

She sips her Coke thoughtfully, as if searching for the right words. When she sets it down, she takes a long breath and lets it out very, very slowly. And then she says, "That man deserved a lot worse than he got."

I kick Daniel's ankle under the table.

Sabrina narrows her eyes at me. "I guess she doesn't talk about it."

I shake my head.

She folds her fingers together and lays them in front of her on the table. "Talking about it is hard. I didn't say a peep for almost twenty years. Can you believe that? Carrying that around with me all this time. I damn near forgot. *Repression* is what they call it. Holes in your memory like swiss cheese. And then, a few years back, I started getting these migraines. Powerful headaches that hurt so bad I couldn't move for a day at a time. And the doctor checked everything he could think of, but there was nothing wrong with me. Finally, he said, 'Sabrina, I don't think I'm the kind of doctor you need.' And he sent me to a therapist."

I think of Dr. Angela. "Did she help?"

"She did. But it took time. Still does. You don't just bounce back from something like that."

I swallow hard and ask her to state the obvious. "Something like *what*?"

"Rape." She says it very plainly with no window dressing. She does not pause or change the tone of her voice. There is no undercurrent of hysteria, no tears or heavy breathing. She says it as if she just said "influenza" or "homework" or "sandwiches."

But she did not say those things. She said *rape*. And the earnestness and familiarity with which she said it makes me squirm in my seat. Because that is a word to be whispered, like "devil" or "death." It is a word to be carried like a rumble in the chest, not spoken out loud like dinner conversation. And I am immediately ashamed of my squeamishness and aware of my own conditioning against myself as a woman, which shames me more.

"He raped you?" I ask, stumbling only a little on *he*. "Father Terry?"

"Not just me," she says with a pointed look.

I feel myself swimming in midstream. I feel all the *o*'s in *Coca-Cola* staring at me from around her kitchen with round, accusing eyes. I feel my mother's story unroll like a heavy, velvet drape above my head and drop over me, full of dust and cobwebs and tiny, menacing spiders. Somewhere inside myself, I sneeze. And then, in that same deep place, I wretch.

It is Daniel's hand squeezing mine that reminds me where we are and why. "How do you know he...*did that* to my mother?"

Sabrina inhales. "Father Terry was careful. He picked girls who were troubled. Girls who came from broken families or bad homes. He picked those girls because he knew they were less likely to be believed, more likely to be ignored. At least, that's what my therapist says. My dad was a drunk who liked to wake me up with a swift kick to the mattress every morning. You understand?"

"I think so."

"Your mother, and don't take this the wrong way, but when it came to troubled girls, she stood out."

That does not surprise me.

"She was outspoken and quarrelsome with the sisters. And she smoked behind the gym between classes. Her dad had died, and everyone knew she was grieving."

I nod. I know this part.

"I think she might have been one of his favorites."

My eyes water, and I place a hand over my mouth.

"I don't have to keep going if you don't want."

I shake my head, wipe my hands over my face. "No, please. I'm sorry. Keep going."

She looks concerned, but after a pause, she continues. "We knew each other—the ones he had chosen. We would see each other leaving his office, and we just knew. We could smell it on one another, I guess. Sense it. We would sometimes give each other looks when we passed in the hall. Looks of sympathy, looks of knowing."

"How many of you were there?"

"At least four, maybe seven. Maybe more. Your mom, she... *stepped in* for me more than once."

"Stepped in?"

Sabrina nods. "I think she was trying to protect me because I was younger. A few times she found me in the hall with a pass to his office, and she would calmly, without saying a word, take it from my hands and go in my place. I never got to thank her for that."

A sob lodges itself below my thyroid gland, squatting like a toad in the throat.

"And then she went away," Sabrina says softly. "And no one could protect me after that."

I close my eyes and press my lips together to keep the toad from escaping. "She was pregnant," I tell Sabrina.

When I open my eyes, Sabrina is crying without sound. Nothing about her face, her demeanor, has changed except the wetness around her eyes.

"I always wondered," she says. "She'd been acting strange, more impulsive than usual. She turned a desk over in one of her classes. Two of the nuns had to carry her out of there, kicking and screaming. Everyone whispered that her mother had packed her away to an institution, a nuthouse for troubled girls. But when she came back a few months later...well, I thought that theory made a convenient cover. That's all."

I try to think of my mother—shattered beyond repair from a dead father, a psychologically abusive mother, repeated rape, unwanted pregnancy, and stillbirth—somehow finding the strength to walk back into that school and face all the girls who thought she was crazy for crazy's sake and to live in the shadow of the man who had gotten away with it, knowing he would again. My hands go to my neck.

"What do you know about the fire?" I ask now. I avoid Daniel's eyes as I do.

Sabrina looks me over before answering. "Not much."

"You never *heard* anything?"

"Oh, there was a lot of talk, if that's what you mean—*kids*. Boys being boys. What I do know is it happened late in the night when no one would notice until it was far too late. The question I kept asking was who would want to burn down an empty building. Some people just like playing with fire, I guess."

"Maybe someone who knew the truth," I suggest. I'm careful to keep my voice even, to give nothing away.

"Maybe," she says. "Maybe someone who wanted to make a point."

I'm not sure it matters, beyond ensuring the school never reopened. "You said there were four of you?"

"That I knew. But six who came out after Sister Margaret went to the police. Who knows how many more had already graduated like your mom?"

"Why the police? Why not have the church handle it?" Daniel asks.

"Oh, the church did handle it," she tells him. "The police did next to nothing. Our parents all received minor settlements without anything ever approaching a court of law. Father Terry was moved to another assignment. And Sister Margaret ended up dead."

"You think it's connected?" I ask her.

"Seems a little too convenient, doesn't it?"

"What happened to the others?" I ask now. "That you knew?"

"Nancy went away to college up north. Last I heard, she was living in Minnesota somewhere with a family and her own law firm. I didn't know her well, but it sounds like she overcame a lot.

"Carol stuck around town like I did, but she never married. She killed herself twelve years go. She was heavy into drugs. She might have burned the building down, but we can't ask her now."

I mumble an apology as though Carol's suicide is my fault.

"And then there is your mother. I always wondered what became of her. Worried, if I'm honest. At that time, she was reckless in a way the rest of us weren't."

I let this stir between us like dust motes in the air. And then I rise from my chair and thank Sabrina for her honesty. I take her number down and tell her I will have my mother call her when she can. And I apologize for taking time out of her day. Daniel and I head out the door.

Just as the screen slams, I turn to Sabrina one last time. "Real quick," I say. "You said my mom was troubled, and that's why Father Terry picked her. Did you know her before the rape, what she was like?"

Sabrina shakes her head. "Oh, honey, there is no *before*. There is just the rape and everything that comes after."

I look at Sabrina, breathe in sharply. I open my mouth to form a question, but she cuts me off before the first word.

"We were just in the wrong place at the wrong time," she says sadly.

XXXIII.

I SEE NEW ORLEANS WITH NEW EYES AS WE PULL INTO the city. A riot of artificial lighting holds the night at bay, yet every building purples in the growing shadows. Our little town, the one I've left behind, so quaint and predictable, is like a monster hiding its face behind papier-mâché. It's not a sanctuary from sin, as Moony thought. And the secrets it keeps are every bit as dark and visceral as any this city is built upon. Here, the demons don't lurk in grim corners but stalk the street openly. *At least New Orleans has the courage to be itself*, I think as we pick our way through the Quarter, *however broken, however misunderstood.* In this way, the city is like my mother. And I have wronged them both.

Our courtyard sits like a princess-cut jewel when I return, square and dazzling in the dying light, color bouncing off of every stone. It is the first time I look on it as *home.* Something in my chest swells like a balloon, like pride, like recognition. Daniel and I get out together at the curb. He wants to see me inside before he leaves, make sure I'm safe since we don't know if my mom has returned. We walk through the gate hand in hand.

"I wondered when you were coming back."

I look up to see Butcher stubbing out a cigarette on the edge of the fountain. "Sorry?"

His face is long, and his brows crinkle over his eyes like wiggling caterpillars. "Your mom was here," he says.

I look at Daniel, drop his hand, and step forward. "You spoke to her?"

"Nah," Butcher says. "I saw her go upstairs. Thought maybe she was turning in for the night." He digs his hands into his pockets. "I noticed she'd been away."

He says this last part gingerly, as if he is trying to spare my feelings with the truth. But his eyes tell me he understands much more than he is saying.

"She left maybe a half hour later," he adds. "I thought you should know." He inclines his head toward me with a look that indicates this is important information.

"When?" I ask now.

"About an hour ago," he tells me.

I give him a nod. "Thank you."

I rush upstairs, taking the steps two at a time with Daniel on my heels. When I open our apartment door, I don't know what to expect. But everything seems the same. I flip on the lights and set Moony's ashes down. I slide my hand under the pillow and drag out her watch for comfort, but the *tick tick tick* of its mechanical heart has stopped. The little hands are frozen in their places. I shake it and get no response. I can't ignore the feeling that I am too late.

Setting it back down, I begin to move slowly around the room, looking for anything that I might be missing. Did she leave something behind that might signal her whereabouts or state of mind?

"Cat?" Daniel asks. "Everything okay?"

I trace a finger over her card table, where she often sat to give readings, where I left the torn up pieces of my note for her. They lie right where I put them. I turn to face him. "Something feels off," I tell him. "I can't explain it. Don't ask me to try."

He holds his hands up. "I trust you. A needle, remember? Sounds like you're getting one now."

I move through the kitchen, peeking in cabinets, opening the fridge. Nothing has changed. There is the same amount of orange juice as there was when I left. The same amount of dirty dishes in the sink. The same amount of bread and sliced cheese. I turn to Daniel. "I don't get it. What did she come back here for?"

"Maybe she needed a change of clothes," he suggests.

"You're probably right," I say as I make a beeline for the bedroom, but the words feel sour on my tongue.

Her shopping bags still sit on the bedroom floor. Her closet doors are pulled together. Her dresser drawers all closed. Her bed made. But I can smell her in this room—her perfume or detergent, maybe her deodorant—like stale flowers and patchouli. And I can feel her like the shadow of a shadow. I quickly take inventory of the clothes hanging in her closet. I shuffle through drawers in her dresser. It's possible she grabbed a T-shirt or two, maybe some underwear. I can't really tell. But nothing obvious is missing, and certainly not much if anything at all.

Daniel is standing in the doorway. "Any ideas?"

I shake my head. The feeling of dread is growing like leavened dough in my stomach. "I know she was in this room. I can smell her."

"Okay. Let's just think. Take a breath and think. I'm sure it's not as bad as it feels." He's trying to be upbeat, and I'm grateful for it, but it doesn't help the fist tightening around my heart.

Why would Moony's watch just stop like that?

I look to her dresser one more time and notice the collection of pictures across the top. The order has been changed. The picture of her at Mardi Gras should be over to the left. And the one of me should be at the end. I pick it up, and the back flap of the frame falls open. It's been unlatched. The picture of my mother with the baby is gone.

I look at Daniel. "Something isn't right."

"What is it?"

"The picture of her and the baby, the one I showed you at the café...It's gone."

He recoils. "Why would she take that?"

I don't know, but I don't like it.

I go back into the living room and pick up Moony's watch, check the time. It stopped just over an hour ago—while Mom was here. Did she do something to it? Did she come all this way just to torment me?

"Maybe try calling her again. I mean, she responded to Gary. And she came here for something. So she's coming around. She might answer this time." Daniel looks hopeful.

"Yeah, okay." I pull my phone out and punch in her number, but it goes straight to voice mail. "She turned it off," I tell him, my heart sinking.

"Try texting," he suggests. "When she decides to turn it back on, your message will be waiting."

I nod and look at my screen, ready to open my messages, when I see the alert across the top of my phone that I have a voice mail. I'd forgotten I turned my ringer off at Sabrina's. Everything in me stops, like gears grinding to a halt. Time slows to a drip. With shaky hands, I press the screen to play the voice mail and lift the phone to my ear.

You have one new message. BEEP.

At first, I think she is laughing at me.

My mind whirls, connecting random dots—the late nights, the space-outs during readings, the belated and failed attempt at organizing, the shopping spree. She's manic, maybe even having a psychotic break.

It takes a heartbeat before I realize she is sobbing.

The blinking lights in my head all go out at once. I short-circuit. I don't know what to do with Sad Mary. My heart plummets. I want to reach through the phone and comfort her, but I can't. So I sit and listen to her cry, and then she finally speaks.

My baby girl, I'm so sorry.

There is a moment of hushed tears that follow. And then a *click*.

I drop my phone, barely registering the clatter as it hits the floor. My eyes meet Daniel's.

"Cat? What is it?"

But I can't answer him. I can't get the lights in my mind to come back on, can't get the stars to align. *There is a pattern to the dark...* Why can't I see it?

I shake in place, my mouth hanging open, before one blinding light finally switches on. *The medicine cabinet.*

I race to the bathroom and throw it open, but all the bottles are gone.

I haven't seen her in just two days. Could she have dropped that low that fast?

Rapid cycling is the term they give to bipolar patients who swing wildly between mania and depression many times in a year. In my hunt for answers, I wasn't just unearthing her past on the internet or in some boxes under her bed; I'd been excavating it in her own mind. She's not in a manic episode right now, but a depressive one.

"This cabinet was full," I whisper to Daniel. Slowly, the lights begin to wink back into being in my head, first one and then another and another until I can follow them like the bread crumbs through a storybook forest. But there is no candy house or daring escape at the end. Instead, there is a hanging tree, and a long red rope, and my mother's body twisting in the wind.

I turn to Daniel. "I think she's going to kill herself."

"Shit." Daniel's face is paler than I've ever seen it. "What do we do?"

I want to cry. I want to break like brittle bones, to smash like glass under stone and disappear. I want to disintegrate, to go to pieces and pour through Daniel's open hands like sand. I hear the *tick tick tick* of Moony's dead watch in my mind—Moony's dead heart beating a phantom rhythm in a dark room just for me. I see Madora Charles's smiling eyes and feel her legacy pressing in like a lead sky falling.

I don't want to be alone, I hear myself say in the hollows of my gut. It is a gong ringing in my heart and a cry ripping through my throat. It is a window on a moonless night and a red hibiscus bush and a car backing out of the drive. It is ten long years waiting and wanting and hurting and pretending I wasn't waiting or wanting or hurting. It is fear. And it is love. It is happening all over again. And it is now...and *forever*.

I clutch at Daniel's shirt. "Call the police," I squeeze out.

"Okay." His voice is shaking.

"Then call your grandmother." I start toward the front door.

"What are you going to do?" He calls. "I should come with you."

"No." I round on him. "I need you here in case she comes back. I'll text Gary," I tell him. "And then I'm going to find my mom."

XXXIV.

EVERYBODY DIES, CAT.

The courtyard is too quiet beneath me. The fountain has stopped running, and the water is silent in its dark bowl. A rare breeze sighs through the trees, skittering leaves across the ground. For a second, I think I smell her on the wind. Then I think I smell mint. But it's all gone as quickly as it blew in.

If I want to find my mother, I have to think like her. But Mary doesn't think in straight lines. Not when she is in the grip of her disorder. The dots I have to connect won't be obvious, not to anyone else. But the only choice I have is to look for them, one at a time, and hope they lead me to her before it's too late.

There is a pattern to the dark...

I send Gary a series of texts.

Mom's pills are gone.

She came and took all of them.

We called the police. I'm looking for her now.

Please help. I don't know how much time we have.

I rush past the staircase toward the gate and throw myself at the mercy of the Quarter. And then I am in a dream I've dreamt before, only in my dream the maze of the Quarter was silent and empty, and now it is pulsing with sound: raised voices and pumping music. And it is clogged with warm, flush, perspiring bodies—people milling and clotting and clumping in the streets, forming crowds and breaking away only to come together again on another block.

I take the first turn, remembering the turn I took first in the dream. But I don't know where to go from here. Sabrina's words keep sounding in my ears. *There is no* before. *There is just the rape and everything that comes after.*

How did I not see it? As I wound my way to the nucleus of my mother's story, I dragged her with me, right back to the heart of what broke her in the first place. And now, the whole thing is melting down. I was so desperate for answers, for something that would help me understand so I could put some of my own indignance behind me and forge a way forward with her, so I could feel something other than abandoned, that I didn't stop to think about whether her story should be told. I didn't stop to notice the triggers happening right now in my search for the ones from years ago.

What are you willing to pay for truth?

Were they trying to tell me all along? The strangers I have met? Were they protecting her or protecting me? Were they real or a shared delusion? A bubble birthed by Madora Charles's mind that expanded until it swallowed her daughter and Moony, my mother and even me?

The only lie that exists is the one you hold to be true. The only power is your own.

Where did I give myself away? In the hard, enduring denial that was my life behind the window with the red hibiscus, my life with Moony? Or in the weeks since? In the streets of this clash-and-clamor city and the movement of the low and mournful song that is my mother's life? Where did I lose sight of myself?

I hardly know.

I pick up speed. Pushing my frantic steps against the lively beats of the Quarter until I am running. My lungs begin to burn, and my sides begin to ache as if I've been stabbed, but I don't slow. All I know is that she is roosted in this tangle of streets like a flightless hen, and if I press on, I might find her before the fox does.

Ahead of me, I see a pop of white against the throng of color—a woman in a porcelain mask with red-black eye sockets and feathers in her hair. Her lips are white and painted like teeth, and her nose has been blacked out. A swirl of cobwebs dance around her cheeks and chin. She's draped in white lace, and her hair is a mane of black and white streaks. I let my steps slow until I can make her out clearly, until her face turns to mine and I see her wink at me, until she begins to dance away.

She is Death riding a pale horse through cobbled streets. She is my next dot.

Without giving my reason time to catch up, I dart after her. She blinks in and out of my vision, a swirl of winter and bone. I catch her in my sight just as she's rounding a corner or nearing another block, as though she is saying, with her whole form, *Turn here* or *This way*. Dauphine Street...Bourbon...Chartres—skeleton-white names on black street signs whir past me in a blur, and I lose track of where I am and where I've been. But I don't stop. Because I am riding the heels of Death on her way to my mother, and if I stop, I'll lose everything.

Without hope, what does anything else matter?

I see the steeple falling in my mind, see it crashing in a halo of fire and dust to the ground—the Tower come to life.

Some people just like playing with fire, I guess.

I see Sabrina's Coke-colored kitchen and the way her hands flutter around the glass of her bottle.

We were in the wrong place at the wrong time.

I see the Devil leaning on his tree in the square, one leg up, arms behind his back—a Hanged Man.

I don't have that kind of power.

I see the maze of the Quarter as it was in my dream, the woman with her cloak of stars wending her way to its center.

The only power is your own.

I see the empty baby cradle and the matchbook under my mother's bed.

The Pelican Room.

I see the Halloween card with the gypsy and her orange hair.

If you won't listen to me, maybe this.

Is Death leading me, or am I chasing Death? Is there a difference? It doesn't matter because I know where we are going.

I know your type, he said to me once. *Unable to see the grand design unfolding all around you.* He said it beside the confessional in the oldest cathedral in America. He said it, and it was true. It was all true. Every word.

I round a corner into Jackson Square and squint against the light. I try to get my bearings. The square is busy tonight. No less than three tour groups are all gathering in front of the garden, their guides decked out in goth wear—vampire tours or ghost tours. The tourists in each group flutter like swarms of flies, brimming with expectations. I don't see the woman with the skull for a face.

I walk briskly up to the steps of the cathedral toward the side gate. It must be nearing nine or ten o'clock. St. Louis Cathedral is normally closed now, the iron fencing reinforced with a lock and chain. But as I near the gate, I see a shadow shift in the alcove of the door beyond, detach itself from the wall, and emerge into the light. He is as I remember him from that first meeting—scruffy and unkempt, his clothes a hodgepodge of club wear, his face too young for his eyes. He wears a pileup of Mardi Gras beads in a rainbow of colors now, like the high collar of some derelict priest. A few dangle shot glasses and charms and other items—whistles and bottle openers and such—but they are in such a tangle it's hard to sort one from the next.

"I was starting to wonder if you would make it at all," he says with a sly smile. He reaches for the gate, giving the lock a deft tug, and the chain falls away. He holds it open for me.

"Is she here?" I don't know whether to be alarmed or relieved by his presence. "Why didn't you send her home, call someone?"

"I told you," he says dryly. "I don't have that kind of power."

I feel nearly invisible in the shadow of the cathedral's looming face. I lean against the wall just inside the doorframe and clutch my side, catching my breath, as he opens the door. I stare up at the arch above me and issue a silent prayer to whatever gods or devils may be listening, then I hear the click of the handle, and I slip inside behind him.

The cathedral is dark and quiet. With no light and no sound and no people, it feels like a shell with the ocean trapped inside, haunted by what it once was. At first, I think either the skull-faced woman or I have made a mistake. I move silently up the aisle past fat pillars of stone, looking for any movement I can find, when the sound of weeping reaches my ears.

"Mom?" I call, hearing my voice ricochet off the walls and domed ceiling.

The sound stops abruptly.

"Mom?" I question to the still flags hanging overhead and the altar that looms like the gates to heaven at the end of the massive room.

There's no reply, but in another few steps I see her on the dais, hunched and small like a child hiding in the corner. I run toward her just as the door behind me clicks closed, shutting out the damp night air.

"Mom!" I drop to my knees in front of her. "What are you doing here? Are you okay? Are you hurt? Did you take anything?"

She looks up at me and her face is a mess of mascara and tears, puffy and red and marked with anguish. She places a hand on my cheek. "My beautiful Catia. I will miss you most of all."

"What are you saying? What do you mean?" I run my hands and eyes over her, unsure of what I'm checking for exactly. Anything that will tell me if I'm too late.

"Isn't this fitting?" I hear him call from the back of the cathedral. His steps echo heavy on the checkered floor. He is moving slowly in our direction, like a cat with cornered mice.

"Mom, come on. You have to get up. We have to go."

She looks at me as if she is dreaming. "I'm so sorry, Cat. I wanted to tell you all of it."

"Shhh...I already know," I tell her. "You don't have to say anything. I know what happened to you. I know all of it."

We were in the wrong place at the wrong time.

She blinks, and her face contorts with fear. "It's too late."

"No, it's not. It's never too late, Mom."

Without hope, what does anything else matter?

Her words slur and jumble, until I can't make out what she's trying to say.

"Shhh..." I tell her. She is not making sense, and I don't know if that's because of her illness or the pills or both. I try to pick her up with one hand beneath each arm and get her to stand.

She points above and behind her to the altar, to the condemning expressions of the saints, to the angels glaring down at us. As she stands, two pill bottles tumble from her lap, along with the picture of her and the baby she lost. I snatch them up so I can let the paramedics know what she has taken. If I can just get her into the square, where there are people who can help us. She stands weakly, and I have to brace myself beneath her to keep her up.

"A perfect place for a perfect ending. Don't you think?" He starts laughing as if he's told a very funny joke.

"If you're not going to help, then leave us alone," I growl, still trying to get her to take a step, but she slumps against me and I fear she's losing consciousness.

He saunters toward us. There is menace in his eyes and booze on his breath, a cloud of peppermint around him. One person's devil is another's angel, and vice versa.

"I have to admit," he says, "there's a certain poetic justice to it."

Do you think people get what they deserve?

"This isn't justice," I snap. My mother slips from my hands and slumps against my legs. "Help me!"

He stands there staring, an unwanted audience in the worst moment of our lives.

I stoop over my mom, unsure how to help. Her eyes are rolling back in her head, and her mouth is flopping open. She's breathing at least. I can see her chest rise and fall. But the breaths are shallow...frighteningly so.

My phone is in my back pocket. I rip it out and dial 911. I can hear it ringing faintly and the operator's voice come on. I press the phone to my face. "Hello, hello? Can you hear me? I'm at St. Louis Cathedral on Jackson Square. Please send help. My mom has overdosed—"

Just then my mom groans and turns her head, vomiting to the side. I try to hold her head up so she won't choke and use my shirt to wipe at her mouth. I know I'm crying, and I see the tremble of my hands as I try to clean her up. *Please, please, please.*

"Hurry!" I shout into the phone, laying it down next to us as I sit and pull my mom into my lap, tilting her head up in case she vomits again.

He is standing over us now, his long shadow arching over our bodies. He cocks his head to one side and stares down, studying.

"What is it like?" he finally asks. "To love that powerfully?"

I look up at him, my face streaked with tears. "What?" I croak out. I think he means my mom and her lost baby.

He squats down and picks the polaroid up, holding it in front of his face. After a moment, he lets it fall to the floor. Gently, with a finger, he brushes a strand of wet hair from my mother's temple. I feel myself flinch reflexively as he does, but the motion is gentle... tender even. He looks up into my eyes. We are level now, face-to-face, with only the saints above us.

"What you feel—*for her*. What is that like?" he asks again.

I look down. Her face is so pale, like the underside of a fish. The color has even receded from her lips. A trail of flesh-colored drool is sliding down one corner of her mouth. I want to wipe it, but I don't want to jostle her. I am afraid that sudden movement will still the slow rise and fall of her chest, will end the *tick tick tick* of a dying pulse. Like Moony's watch.

"Help us," I manage to squeeze out. "Please," I whisper.

Why are the paramedics taking so long? How many minutes has it been? I try to shift her against me, to cradle her between my knees, but she's so heavy, as if she's sinking into the floor. I look at her face. Brush her neck. She is so still that, for a moment, I think she is already gone. My heart convulses inside my ribs. I choke out a garbled sob.

"Tell me what it's like," he insists.

I don't know what he means. "Can't you do something?"

But he just repeats his request. "Tell me what it's like, this love you feel. Right now. In this moment."

I look down at her face, and all the longing, all the anger and pain, all the hurt feelings and wrong words and lost time wash over me in a wave of agony that is nothing short of exquisite. I narrow my eyes. "Like fire under the skin."

"Yesss..." I hear him say, and then a flash lights up the sanctuary like lightning loosed from a bottle.

I cross an arm over my eyes and squint into the blinding specter. The woman in her blue veil made of starlight—the High Priestess—is standing where only moments ago was the man with the peppermint schnapps. When she lifts her veil this time, her face is painted white, with teeth marked over her lips and black-red eye sockets burning with cold flames.

"No," I beg as she leans down over us. "Please, just a little more time."

But she doesn't slow her descent. With benevolent grace, she places her lips to my mother's forehead, just between the eyes.

The light in the room goes out all at once, and the dark feels thick like smoke and closer than my own skin.

We are alone. There is no woman made of bones and stardust, no man with a collar of Mardi Gras beads. No devils or angels to intervene. There is my quaking breath in too much space. And the stillness on my mother's face. And the host of unseeing eyes overhead. And the feeling, once again, of being violently, horribly alive.

I look up to the tabernacle, to the figure in red perched above us who gazes down as I clutch my mother's body. Her face is as calm as the surface of an unbroken lake. For a second, I think I see Aimee's smile in hers, in the fair hair and pink-plaster skin. And then it's gone. Her arms wrap around a gigantic silver anchor. It is the last thing I see before the paramedics come crashing through the doors.

XXXV.

THE MISSISSIPPI RIPS A BROWN GASH RIGHT THROUGH the guts of the city. It smells of mud and crawfish, bottom-feeders and trash, and centuries of life thriving along its banks. We've found a rocky bank with a view of the bridge and picked a bright and clear afternoon. Daniel squeezes my hand for encouragement. To my left, Gary clears his throat.

"Did you want to say something?" he asks, trying hard to conceal how awkward he feels.

I take a deep breath and clutch her box to my chest. This is not how I pictured it happening. But then, nothing about the last several months has been how I pictured it. Isn't all of life that way? Somehow different than we imagine. Sometimes better. Sometimes worse. I feel the rightness of it under my breastbone and between my lungs.

I open the top and pull out the plastic bag, unknotting it. "I love you, Moony," I tell her, using both hands to hold the bag as I upturn it into the water. "You'll always be mine."

I hope she knows that I have chosen the Mississippi not because it is in the city, but because it will carry her away. I hope so, but I don't say it.

I hope she knows I decided against spreading her in her small town not because I couldn't bring myself to set foot there again, though I couldn't, but because I can't imagine her finding rest there with all that happened. I hope so, but I don't say it.

I don't say most of what I'm thinking because Moony doesn't need me to tell her story. She lived it. And this part—the part where I spread her ashes and finally let her go—is not the end of her story, but a piece of mine.

Who Moony was to me and who she was to my mother is a lot like this city. Some look at New Orleans and see life and art and joy and beauty. Others see crime and poverty and waste and corruption. One erodes the foundation even as the other builds anew on top of it. I am willing to see both versions of New Orleans. I am willing to hear its whole story.

I used to see myself like these muddy waters—all wavering lines and washed-out color, a flood of potential where nothing ever really takes full shape. But now, when I pass my reflection in the thick glass of an old window, I see a girl of flesh and bone, soft skin laid over hard lines, pink and gold and the rich brown of tree bark. I see the rough brick and cold iron of the city, forging itself to my form, building me up, making me strong.

My mother will be released from the hospital in four days, against the wishes of Dr. Angela, who thinks she should stay in for a month or more. But that's Mary, always in a rush. As long as she stays on her meds, I think we can handle it. This time, I will know when her appointments are and what she's taking. This time, I will be sure she stays on track.

The staff all agree that she is unbelievably lucky. If the paramedics had been even a minute or two later, they might not have been able to resuscitate her. But I know the truth. I am the lucky one. We've been given a third chance at a life together. What do they always say? Third time's the charm? Life with Mary may never feel charmed, but I am grateful all the same.

Gary is staying at our place in the meantime. He offered to take me out and finally buy me the real bed he'd been promising, but I decided I liked the sleeper sofa. Daniel is helping me register for school, which starts in a few weeks.

I hope Moony knows that my mom isn't here because I wanted it to just be us—as we were with no secrets and no sordid histories—as I remember us, one last time. I hope so, but I don't say it.

The strangers have stopped visiting me since the night in the cathedral. I half expected to meet one at the Mississippi when we arrived, but the water is free of ghosts today. I went back to Izora Jo three days after my mom's overdose. I took her the jar she gave me and told her I didn't need it anymore. I asked her to speak to the spirits, to thank them for me, and to tell my big sister that I was sending Moony to her. She crossed her arms, chuckled low and deep, and told me I could tell the spirits those things myself.

I brought the jar with me today, and now I pour it into the water after Moony's ashes. The Mississippi doesn't protest.

Dr. Angela doesn't know about the scandal at Our Lady. She doesn't know about the baby or Father Terry. I could tell her, but I won't. Some stories are meant to be told, and others are meant to be carried. My mother's story is part of mine now, and there are parts of each for the telling, and parts of each that belong to only us. I know Dr. Angela would disagree, that she believes getting to the root of my mother's trauma is important to treating her illness. But I realize now that I cannot follow the thread of my mother's pain to her past in an attempt to unravel the grip her illness has on her. I can't pull the bad threads out, the ones with knots and snags, without tearing apart the whole weave. Her history, her suffering, and her disorder are all a part of her. They live in her now, for better or for worse, just as mine live in me.

EPILOGUE

It's a warm day on Chartres Street, and my feet make a *tap tap tap* rhythm against the sidewalk. I watch the rounded toes of my flats pass green iron poles and dark wads of gum, white-washed walls and stacks of red brick on my way from meeting with Brittni for yet another round of retail therapy—her prescription for everything that ails you. I am part of the larger beat now, one of a million arrangements all laid down as a single track.

Which is why I almost step on it when it comes into view. But I manage to stop just in time.

Squatting down, I can't believe my eyes. I make a shield around it with my body, unsure if I am ready to pick it up. How small it looks against the pavement compared to how large it has loomed in my mind. I reach down with trembling fingers and catch the corner with my nail, lifting it from the street.

I hold the Moon card up to study it. There is a river of blue-brown water, and a wolf howling on each side of its bank—one black, one white. Above them hangs a disk and sickle moon, full and yellow on one side, wan and white on the other. She looks down on the river with a closed face, with downcast eyes and a curtain of star-bright hair. And her profile is like my mother's in the picture with my sister.

When I stand up, I look into a large, plate-glass window with a familiar moon decal. For a second, I don't trust what I am seeing. But then, the black-and-white awning fits so quaintly with the rows of historic buildings, the painted shutters, the old-fashioned streetlamps. There is a balcony this time, complete with a black-iron railing and hanging baskets of ferns.

It's been a while since I last saw the man with the peppermint schnapps or dreamt of the boy in the yellow waistcoat. So long, in fact, that I've started to doubt they were ever real at all. But when I see the letters over the doorway of Fortune's Gate—*Fortune Is a Strange Caller*—I can't resist the chance to step inside.

The bells signal my entry as before, and little else has changed. I see the same shelves lining the walls, full of unreadable books. I see the same tables spanning the floor, covered in wares with no prices or labels. The only difference is the curving spiral staircase that wasn't there back when it was only a single-story building. I finger a basket of dry, gnarled roots in a deep-purple color that smell a little like cat pee, when the clerk appears.

"There you are!" they exclaim. "Where did you go?"

I can't help but laugh. "You mean, where did *you* go?" I retort.

They grin at me. "I found your card," they say. "Now where..." They begin peeking under things on the nearest table.

I hold it up. "You mean this?"

"Ah, yes! There it is. The Moon."

I hand it to the clerk, and they give me a puzzled look. "Keep it," I tell them. "I don't need it now."

Then, reaching into a back pocket, I fish out the rest of the deck, which I was taking to one of the shops we'd visited before, to see if the woman who owned it wanted to buy it for her collection. "In fact," I tell the clerk, setting the deck on the nearest table. "Keep them all. They belong here."

They peer at me, then shrug as if to say, *Your loss.*

I emerge back onto the street, feeling about ten years lighter. At the corner, I can't resist turning around. Fortune's Gate, as I anticipated, has vanished, and the teahouse on one side and the bookshop on the other have pulled together as though it was never there.

And maybe it never was.

AUTHOR'S NOTE

On the left side of my fridge, hanging by a magnet for a local pizza delivery company, is a yellow sticky note with the numbers for the Crisis Hotline, the National Suicide Prevention Lifeline, and the instructions, "Go to the hospital or emergency room," written in my counselor's handwriting. Next to it hangs a picture of my daughter, Evelyn, in kindergarten or maybe preschool. It is framed by green construction paper she cut into the shape of a Christmas tree with a red yarn loop for hanging.

The sticky note used to hang on the front of my fridge. In three years, this is the farthest it has moved. My counselor wrote this note for me before the first Christmas we faced after my daughter died. I must have looked at it a hundred times a day that season, reminding myself that all I had to do if it got too hard was find this yellow piece of paper and follow her instructions, and someone, somewhere, would stand between me and my pain.

According to the National Institute of Mental Health, suicide is responsible for the deaths of more than 47,000 people in 2017 alone—more than twice the number of homicides. If you or anyone you know has ever thought about self-harm or suicide, please take this information and make your own sticky note. Keep it wherever feels right to you. Use it whenever you need someone, somewhere, to stand between you and your pain. Know that you are not alone.

While Cat's mother suffers from bipolar disorder, and I have the tragedy of child loss to contend with, it's important to remember that depression and suicidal ideation don't always have an obvious cause. You don't need a diagnosis or a trauma in order to own your pain. It is enough that you are hurting. There are people who want to help. It's important to reach out to them.

National Suicide Prevention Lifeline

1-800-273-TALK (8255)

http://suicidepreventionlifeline.org

ACKNOWLEDGMENTS

Writers don't exist without a backbone of support, a rigid column of cheerleaders, collaborators, and believers who make our work possible and, in many cases, better. I am forever indebted to each and every soul whose unyielding support nurtured this book into being.

I'm not sure how I managed to land such a stellar agent, but Thao Le's enthusiasm for my work, her drive to see it molded into the very best version of itself, and her passion for setting stories free in the world are gifts I never tire of unwrapping. To say that I know I am in good hands is a terrible and clichéd understatement and yet still true. Thao, I value our process more than I can express. You are not only a fantastic agent—you are an incredible human being. Thank you for being a guide, a listener, a friend. For always steering me right. For continuing to raise my work to a higher level. And for giving me the absolute best book recommendations.

Christina Pulles and the entire team at Albert Whitman & Co. have yet again taken my story and polished it to a high shine. I am so honored by their commitment and devotion to great storytelling, by their passion for beautiful books. Christina, thanks to your careful eye and continual encouragement, *The Salt in Our Blood* has so much more to offer. I love sharing my characters with you. I love how you get them.

I want to also give a quick shout-out to Lisa White at Albert Whitman & Co., who is forever fielding my questions about promotion and events and social media and more with total grace. Someday, we will get to have that conversation about books over that drink in that tiki bar we keep talking about. Hopefully, in New Orleans.

And finally, the biggest cheerleaders of all, my family. I am forever bouncing ideas off of you, lobbing questions your way without warning, hogging the dining table or the coffee table or that really warm spot in front of the fireplace, glazing over with developing plot ideas when you try to talk to me, and generally sidelining important tasks like cleaning and dinner in order to read, write, or simply dream. I don't know why or how you get me, but you do. I am so, so grateful.